TWO ROGUES
MAKE A RIGHT

A Seducing the Sedgwicks Novel

CAT SEBASTIAN

AVONIMPULSE

An Imprint of HarperCollinsPublishers

TWO ROGUES MAKE A RIGHT. Copyright © 2020 by Cat Sebastian. All rights reserved. Printed in the United States of America. No part of this book may be used or reproduced in any manner whatsoever without written permission except in the case of brief quotations embodied in critical articles and reviews. For information, address HarperCollins Publishers, 195 Broadway, New York, NY 10007.

Digital Edition JUNE 2020 ISBN: 978-0-06-282064-8
Print Edition ISBN: 978-0-06-282159-1

Cover design by Patricia Barrow
Cover illustration by Fredericka Ribes

Avon Impulse and the Avon Impulse logo are registered trademarks of HarperCollins Publishers in the United States of America.

Avon and HarperCollins are registered trademarks of HarperCollins Publishers in the United States of America and other countries.

FIRST EDITION

20 21 22 23 24   HDC   10 9 8 7 6 5 4 3 2 1

For my kids, who always want to know what I'm writing, even when they know the answer will be so unsatisfactory as to involve neither dragons nor magical cats.

Two Rogues
Make a Right

PROLOGUE

"A thousand thousand years ago—" Will said.

"Just say a million," Martin said. "Why do you need to make it sound so fussy?"

Will glared at him. It was high summer and his face was more freckle than not-freckle, his hair hadn't been trimmed since term ended, and Martin was frankly having a hard time taking him seriously.

"I'm telling you a story," Will said, with more sniffy impatience than any thirteen-year-old had a right to. "You can do your boring maths lesson later. A thousand thousand years ago," he said pointedly, "dragons swooped and dove through this very valley. The hills were sharper then, more like mountains, like teeth and claws sticking out of the earth. And where today we see lakes, back then were only the bones of the animals the dragons feasted upon."

"That seems exceedingly unlik—"

"Hush. In fact, it was getting to be a problem. There were very few small animals left for the dragons to eat. Those who could leave had long since fled, and those who could not had been eaten. The dragon council convened, and for five days and five nights they deliberated."

This, Martin suspected, was a metaphor, and not a subtle one at that. Will's parents and whatever other grown-ups were living (Living in Sin, according to Father) at the Grange had run out of money again. They certainly ought to be sitting up at night, figuring out what to do about things. Otherwise they weren't going to be able to afford Will's school fees. The last time this happened, Father paid a few of the Sedgwicks' bills and he had been none too pleased about it. Martin got the distinct feeling that most of the Sedgwicks weren't very pleased about it either, but he couldn't quite figure out why.

"For many years," Will went on, in his most pretentious storyteller voice, "these hills have been our home." Martin realized that now Will was voicing the verdict of the Dragon Tribunal or whatever he was on about. "But now we will need to seek a home elsewhere."

Martin didn't like the direction this story was heading, so he ignored it for a bit. If he lay back against the grass, he could drift a little. Climbing to the top of the tor had left him winded and sleepy, and maybe if he shut his eyes he could pretend he was just bored with Will's story rather than bone tired. Will worried too much. So did Father, in his way. He would be excessively cross when he discovered that Martin had once again slipped out past his tutor and the woman whose entire purpose in life was to chase him around with vials of revolting tinctures (he refused to call her his nurse—he was not a baby and he wasn't sick, even though his lungs didn't always work right and never would because he was Delicate).

"Then, from deep beneath the ground, so deep it was more a vibration than a noise, the dragons heard a shout."

Martin opened an eye. He had expected this story to end with the dragons finding a new home and the Old Ways being lost. Mysterious shouts were new. "What was the voice shouting?" he asked.

"They couldn't tell, that's how eerie and ominous the sound was. It was just—" He got to his feet and stomped his booted foot next to Martin's head. Now Martin opened both eyes and looked up at his friend. Will's face, usually distracted and slightly ridiculous, was—angry?

"Will?" Martin sat up too quickly, and was punished with a coughing fit. Will was on his knees beside him in an instant, a hand in the middle of Martin's back, just resting there.

"I'm fine. Hay fever," he lied. "What happens next?"

"I suppose we'll bring you home for a dose of—"

"In the story, you pillock." He had learned that word from Will and felt very worldly using it.

"Oh. Well, deep from within the ground, the sound came closer. Slowly, slowly, the vibrations began to shake the dragons, from the feet up. And the noise became louder and louder so the dragons let loose with their own fearsome shrieks just to drown it out. And then one of the dragons, one of the smaller dragons who wasn't supposed to be there, noticed that the ground was getting hotter. He tried to tell the elder dragons, but they were too busy throwing tantrums to hear him. It got so hot, the small dragon's feet began to hurt, so he perched on the branches of a nearby rowan tree. Still, the ground got hotter and hotter, so hot the adult dragons started to catch fire."

"I thought dragons breathed fire. Shouldn't they be fireproof?" Honestly, Martin expected better from Will's stories.

"This was eldritch flame. The dry grass caught fire, and the dragons caught fire, and all the hills, from peak to peak and along the valley of bones—it all went up in flame."

Martin stared, waiting for the next part, the happy ending that Will always finished up with. "Then what?" he asked, his voice a whisper.

"They all died. Even the little dragon, because he couldn't fly very far yet. That's why there aren't any dragons anymore."

"But—Will, that is not a good story, I'm sorry to say. What was the voice? What was it saying? Was it the devil, come from hell? It had better not be, because that's—that's—cheating."

"No, it wasn't any of those things. It was just the way the story ended."

CHAPTER ONE

It was hot—by God, it was hot—and the ground beneath him was rough and dry. In his head sounded a steady, rhythmic pounding. Martin felt that while it was unlikely that a sinister menace was about to spring up from the earth and consume the last of his race, he couldn't quite rule it out.

When he opened his eyes, there were neither unnatural flames nor shrieking dragons, but there was not much of anything else either. It was dim, but even that faint light was enough to make him squeeze his eyes shut. His head was—really very bad, no use mincing words. All of him was bad, but his chest and his head were unspeakable.

"Damnation," he rasped, those three syllables taking all the air from his lungs. "Will," he managed a moment later, because hadn't Will just been telling him that terrible story?

There was the sound of chair legs scraping across a stone floor, and then a cool hand on his forehead. "Sweetheart," said Will, because he was an idiot with no sense of self-preservation.

"Don't," Martin said, and batted Will's hand away. Or at least he tried to. He must not have been successful, because the end result was that now Will was holding his hand. Their fingers were intertwined and Martin lacked the strength, physical or mental, to disentangle himself. Besides, Will's hand was cool and familiar, and he was aware he was holding on to it like a lifeline.

"Do you know where you are?" Will asked.

No he bloody well did not know where he was. "Thousand thousand years ago," he mumbled.

Beyond the pounding in his head, he heard a vial being unstopped, then felt a cool hand on his cheek, followed by the unmistakable foulness of willow bark tincture in his mouth. He tried to spit it out—dignity was quite beyond him—but Will stroked his hand down Martin's throat and made a truly regrettable soothing sound, and Martin did not know whether to try to recoil or to purr like a cat. Before he could decide, he was asleep.

When he woke, the room was brighter, and that was unfortunate in every way, because it turned out that light was almost as ghastly as whatever was happening on the left side of his chest. For lack of anything better to do, he opened his eyes slowly, trying to make them adjust. Maybe the pain in his head would distract him from everything else. After he got one eye a third of the way open, he could make out the rough wood frame of the bed he lay upon. Beyond that were a pair of bare windows, clouded and cracked. Above his head was a ceiling crossed with dark wood beams. He was vaguely aware of a fire crackling somewhere behind him. When he breathed tentatively through his nose, careful not to strain his lungs, he could tell that it was a wood fire, not coal. On the one hand, he was more than a little alarmed to find himself in a totally unfamiliar place; on the other, this was certainly not his aunt's London townhouse, nor was it Lindley Priory. Relieved to have established that, he let his eyes drift shut again.

The next time he woke, it was once again dark. Somehow he had managed to roll onto his side. From this position, he could see a fire burning high and bright in a stone hearth. Before the fire was a plain, straight-backed wooden chair, and in that chair was Will Sedgwick, fast asleep, his mouth slightly open, his hair a disgrace, his jaw covered in highly lamentable stubble. He wore a coat of some rough brown substance that might once, much earlier in its lifetime, have been called wool. Martin was surprised to discover that he had been expecting a much younger version of Will. This was not the Will of long-ago summers, of hillside rambles and multiplying freckles. This Will was tired, haggard, and very pale. Martin strongly suspected that he was all of those things too. Good to know, he supposed. He certainly felt haggard and wrung out, but he also could not remember a time when he hadn't felt that way.

There were hands on his shoulders the next time he woke, and then another hand on the small of his back, lifting. Martin attempted an "unhand me" but it came out a sad mumble.

"Need to get you sitting, love," Will said, because he was the stupidest man to ever live and had never guarded his tongue, not once in his life.

"Shut up," Martin said.

Will didn't take his hands away, even after hauling Martin upright. "I'll shut up as much as you like after you have a swallow of this." He held up a vial.

Martin ignored this. "How long have I been here?"

"Just under a week."

"Not my aunt's house," Martin said, forgetting that he had already worked out the reasons for which this hovel could not have anything to do with Lady Bermondsey.

"No, not your aunt's house." Will was now smoothing hair off Martin's forehead. It felt good, which was not permitted. Martin shrank away from his touch.

"Promise me you won't send for her."

That made Will frown. That was appropriate, if slightly belated, because he ought to have been frowning minutes ago instead of petting Martin like a cat. "I can't do that."

Oh, Martin knew that face. It was the face of Will having a moral quandary. There was no use talking to him when he was in that sort of state, too profoundly in love with the idea of the moral high ground to actually get anything done. Something useless, like—fondness, maybe—swirled around in the vicinity of Martin's heart. "Fuck off," Martin said, for lack of any better ideas. He was almost positive he heard Will laugh. "And open the window, will you. It's sweltering in here."

When he woke the next time, blessedly cool air wafted across his body. The pounding in his head had diminished enough to let him think somewhat cogently. This was not London. The only sounds from outdoors were the hoots and shrieks of owls and the wind agitating bare wintry branches. He also knew that it wasn't Cumberland, although he would have been hard-pressed to say how he knew he wasn't home. Nor was it Will's house, because Will didn't have a house—he barely had a pair of trousers, judging by the looks of him. Will had taken him somewhere, and Martin didn't know whether to be grateful or to be outraged that Will had walked away from his life to sit in a—hut, or whatever this place was—playing nursemaid to his dying childhood friend.

Martin sighed. Good lord, he was tired of dying. He had been dying for over twenty years now and was slightly appalled that even consumption didn't seem to have finished the job. Whatever illness had prompted this little rural interlude had been worse than usual, however. He had the wrung-out and ragged feeling that only came after a long, brutal fever. But now he could fill his lungs partway and was aware of something resembling hunger, so he supposed he'd live to see this whole revolting cycle through from the beginning.

He closed his eyes and went back to sleep.

Two truths were dawning on Will Sedgwick.

The first was that he had, very possibly, almost certainly, kidnapped Sir Martin Easterbrook. He hadn't meant to—in his defense, he had had a lot on his mind—but he was aware that a magistrate, or, really, anybody with a functioning brain, would take one look at this situation and know precisely what to think. But Martin had been wavering between unconsciousness and delirium, and the doctor said he needed country air, so Will had done the only thing he could think of. He knew exactly what the papers would make of it: Invalid Baronet Kidnapped by Disgraced Sailor. Never mind that they had been friends for fifteen years. Never mind that they had grown up together. Never mind that Will, during his more maudlin moments, thought Martin might be his other half, the true north on his compass, the person his soul reached for like a plant to the sun—

The second was that Martin was going to die. That part really shouldn't have come as a shock. For six months, Will had assumed that Martin was already dead, foolishly reasoning that nothing short of death would stop Martin from answering Will's letters. He thought he had gotten used to the idea of Martin being dead. But it turned out that suspecting somebody was gone was quite different from the prospect of watching them slip away, cough by cough, under one's own care.

Martin was going to die in a one-room gamekeeper's cottage, under an assumed name, and with no company but Will. This, Will supposed, was no worse than his dying in a garret or an alley in London, which was likely what would have happened if Will hadn't intervened (he was resolutely thinking of it as intervention, not as assault followed by kidnapping) so in that sense he hadn't done Martin any harm. But they were already in Sussex, and Will had already deposited half the contents of his coin purse into the coachman's outstretched palm, when it occurred to him that he really should have brought Martin to his aunt. So what if his last coherent words had been a plea that Will not bring him to his aunt?

The fact was that he had a relation who could pay for doctors and seaside asylums and whatever else one was meant to do with a consumptive. Will had four shillings and a bottle of laudanum, and barely enough self-control not to drink it himself.

On a good day Will barely felt competent to manage his own life, and being responsible for another person's—the most precious person's—was daunting at best. He was not in the habit of eating regular meals or keeping predictable hours, but now he had to keep track of Martin's medicines and make sure he drank and ate a few times a day. And Martin fought him every step of the way, as if Will's ministrations were an annoyance, as if he wished Will had left him to rot in London.

They had a few things going for them, at least. The cottage was well stocked with oats, which was fine since a thin porridge was all he could get down Martin's throat. He'd need to go to the market soon, but he couldn't leave Martin alone yet, and he barely had enough coin to buy a round of cheese, but that was a problem for the future. There was enough firewood to last them through the winter, but if Martin's fever didn't break soon, they wouldn't be needing it that long. If the worst happened, he'd have to write to Martin's aunt to pay for the funeral expenses, but by then Martin would be in no position to complain about it.

At that thought, his eyes got prickly and hot. He stepped outside, hoping the cold air would clear his thoughts. It was almost dawn, the first rays of feeble winter sunlight just beginning to fade the night sky to the southeast. The cottage was nestled into the edge of the Ashdown Forest, with an open stretch of heath and meadow before it. In the spring it would probably be properly pretty, but now, only two weeks past the solstice, it numbered among the grimmer landscapes Will had ever seen. When he went back into the cottage, Martin was shivering again. Will could hear the sound of his chattering teeth all the way from the door. He hastened to the bed, grabbing the vial of willow bark tincture on the way.

"Time for a dose," he said, trying to keep the panic from his voice. He laid a hand on Martin's forehead and found that it was once again hot. His fever had been coming and going since they arrived, usually climbing as evening approached and abating during the night. But it was morning, and Martin's forehead was hotter than it had ever been.

Martin turned his head away with a petulant little noise. Will tried to convince himself it was a good sign that he was being fractious even now. "Sorry, love, but you need to."

"Let me die in peace," Martin rasped. It might have been comically theatrical if Will didn't believe Martin meant it. The effort of speaking brought on a coughing fit, so Will took out his handkerchief and wiped the blood from the corner of Martin's mouth.

"Some other time," Will said, and poured a spoonful of the tincture into Martin's mouth. Martin swallowed, then coughed and swore. Will soaked a flannel in vinegar and started bathing Martin's forehead. Maybe this was it. Maybe this was their last hour. Everybody had one, sooner or later. He tried to make peace with the idea of Martin dying here, in this cottage, of this being the end to a friendship that had lasted most of their lives. He had made peace with a lot of things lately, and was starting to suspect that his idea of making peace was other people's idea of expecting the worst, but that might merely be a semantic difference.

"If you're going to sit there," Martin said, his voice rusty with disuse and weak from lack of air, "at least tell me a story."

Will almost dropped the cloth. That was the first thing Martin had asked for in the last week, unless one counted "fuck off" and "let me die" as requests. "What, you're not going to ask nicely?" he murmured.

Martin opened his eyes long enough to raise an eyebrow and cast Will a baleful glance. "William," he sighed. "Really." And just the sight of Martin looking scornful and bored warmed Will's heart a little bit. Maybe everything would be fine.

Never in his entire life had Will been able to refuse anything Martin requested, so he launched into a tale of evil wizards and kindhearted ogres, of princesses who carried swords and merchants with enchanted ships. It was nonsense, and likely would only pass muster with a highly feverish audience. But as the sun crept higher in the sky, Martin dozed, and when he woke his fever was gone.

Chapter Two

Martin didn't know if it was the sound of Will's voice or the fact that it meant Will was nearby, but listening to him read aloud was soothing in a way no tinctures or balms had ever been. Even now, when Will was reading a thoroughly mad novel about villainous doctors hell-bent on grave robbing and vivisection, his voice acted like a snake charmer's flute.

As Martin listened, he looked out the window at this landscape that was neither strange nor quite familiar in its gentle near-flatness. Martin could, he supposed, ask Will where they were. But what mattered more was where they weren't: not near anyone who would try to browbeat or control Martin—for his own good, of course—nor anyone who thought Martin's illness was an excellent excuse to politely take away his choices and his freedom, to delicately turn the key in the lock.

And yet. He didn't think he had come willingly to—to wherever they were. He wanted to know where they were, but more importantly he wanted to know how they had gotten there, but he was afraid he wasn't ready for the answer to that quite yet.

He became aware that Will had left off reading. "Don't stop," he said. "At least not on my account."

"Your eyes were shut," Will said. He sat in the chair beside Martin's bed, his booted feet a heavy weight on the mattress. Martin could almost sense the heat pouring off Will's body. Will had always run hot. "I thought you might have fallen asleep."

"I'm paying perfect attention," Martin lied. His fever may have broken, but his mind was the hollowed-out husk it always was after a fever. It had been two years since he showed the first signs of consumption, which he had acquired in circumstances he strongly preferred not to think about, but before that he had a lifetime of frail health and weak lungs and ill humors and whatever else the physicians and apothecaries decided to call it. By now Martin knew the lay of the land. "I want to know what happens to the poor man." When Will didn't answer, Martin opened his eyes and found Will looking at him curiously, his hair tumbled across his forehead in a way that made Martin's fingers itch to brush it back.

"Which poor man?" Will asked carefully.

"The man who—he lives in the Alps and has an overbearing father."

Will closed the book. "I think we'll leave the rest of this novel for when you're more lucid," he said, his mouth twitching in a badly suppressed smile, "but I will always cherish the description of Victor Frankenstein as an overbearing parent."

"You're mocking an invalid. Shame on you." But just that short conversation had drained Martin and he already felt his eyelids drooping. "Later," he said.

"Wait," Will said. "Let me give you more medicine before you're asleep. Getting willow bark tincture down your throat while you're sleeping is a harrowing experience."

As Will brought the little bottle over, Martin noticed that it was nearly empty. He had the distinct sense that he ought to get better before that stuff ran out or Will would start committing highway robbery. And Will would be a terrible highwayman—all flustered apologies and not a bit of bloodlust—so he mustn't let that happen.

"What are you smiling about?" Will asked.

Martin shook his head and opened his mouth for the spoonful of tincture, his hands still too shaky to manage the job on his own. Almost as soon as he swallowed, he felt sleep overtake him. "That's it, love," Will said, kissing the top of his head.

This was going to be the death of him. He had survived this latest illness only to be murdered by casual affection. Will was the sort of person who could kiss your head and call you love and have it mean nothing other than friendship. Martin knew perfectly well that Will spoke that way to dogs and old ladies. The problem was that Martin was the sort of person who could go a twelvemonth without touching anyone besides the physicians who came to do his bloodlettings. The conversion rate was terribly unequal, like pounds to francs, which led to Martin cherishing all those touches, all that blasted sweetness, hoarding it all in his heart like a dragon jealously guarding its treasure. Which was fine, perfectly fine, God knew he had been doing that for years upon years, but he didn't want Will to actually notice. That was a degree of awkwardness that Martin didn't think he could face, and he didn't think Will could either.

Just before sunrise on their eighth day at the cottage, Will got up from the chair where he had been trying and failing to sleep, shrugged on his coat, and slipped out the door. His breath clouded the air and the ground beneath his boots was crisp with frost. The sliver of moon was barely visible beyond the clouds in the night sky, and Will thought nothing had ever been so still or so dark.

Purely for the sake of doing something, he split a few logs and gathered kindling, then paced a couple of times around the perimeter of the cottage. There was a flat piece of earth that looked like it had once been a potato patch, and where, if he allowed himself to think more than a few days into the future, he might think to plant carrots or turnips.

"And who might you be?" said a woman's voice. Will looked up to see a plump woman standing on the other side of the garden gate, her head covered in a scarf and a basket looped over her arm. On the way here, Will hadn't seen any houses between the London road and the cottage, and he hadn't been able to leave Martin long enough to explore. He was almost startled to discover that they were near human habitation, that they weren't on a desert isle, just him and Martin, marooned, alone.

"Will Sedgwick," he said. His voice was hoarse with fatigue. He couldn't be sure, but he didn't think he had slept since the previous morning.

"Are you the new gamekeeper?" she asked, more an accusation than a question. "The manor has been shut up for years. Can't say I know what the new owner wants with a gamekeeper, unless they mean to catch poachers, and that won't go over too well, let me tell you."

"No," said Will, startled. "Nothing like that. The cottage is being let by an invalid who needs the country air. As far as I know, the manor is still unoccupied," he added, which was true, if not precisely honest.

The woman gave him a long look, but something in her posture eased. "Hmph. And you're tending this invalid yourself?"

"Yes," Will said, with the sense that he was walking into a trap, although he couldn't guess what the trap might be.

"You look like you're ready to keel over. It's not men's work. Is he your brother or your gentleman?"

Will blinked. "Pardon?"

"Are you his manservant? I'm trying to figure out how a man your age finds himself looking after an invalid."

"He's a friend." When she continued to regard him levelly, he bristled. "I know what I'm doing, all right? I've done it before. I nursed my mother, and she had the same illness he has." It was true—he did know how to nurse a consumptive, and he also knew that there wasn't much to be done beyond getting food and water into them, keeping them warm, and hoping for the best.

"And what would that be?" the woman asked, stepping closer.

"Consumption, by the looks of it," Will said.

Now that the woman was nearer and the sun higher in the sky, Will could see she wasn't as old as he had previously thought. Certainly not forty, for all she was swathed in shawls and scarves like a village witch. "You've been nursing a consumptive on your own for how long?"

Will needed a moment to add up the days. "A bit over a week. But he's doing much better now," he protested.

"And what are you eating?"

"Tea and porridge," Will said, trying to keep up with the interrogation. "He can't really eat much more than that."

"But you can, you daft child. Daisy!" she called, cupping her hands to her mouth to make a funnel. "Get over here!"

A minute later a girl appeared from behind a hedgerow. In one hand she carried a brace of hares, and Will now understood why her mother had been worried about poachers being caught. "Mum?" she asked.

"This fellow here, Mister—"

"Sedgwick," Will supplied.

"Mr. Sedgwick is staying here, at the old gamekeeper's cottage, and he needs a maid of all work. You start tomorrow."

"But Mum!" she cried, imbuing the single syllable with all the outrage a girl of about fifteen is capable of.

"Off with you. Tomorrow morning. Be there before dawn. Now take those—" she gestured at the hares "—and dress them for supper."

The girl sulked off.

"I'm afraid I can't pay a maid's wages," Will admitted, his face flushing.

"Didn't think you could. The fact is that I need a man around the house, fixing the roof, splitting logs, helping Daisy catch the pig when it gets loose. Can you mend walls and fix barrels and that sort of thing?"

"Yes," Will said. After a childhood spent in a house that seemed always on the verge of collapse, followed by his years at sea, he could fix almost anything.

"Good. And," she said, lowering her voice to an ominous tone and leaning in, "the girl has too much time on her hands. The ostler's been making eyes."

"I see," Will said, unconsciously imitating her tone and her posture, so they were effectively whispering in one another's ears.

"Keep her busy a few hours a day, and she can come back in the afternoon with a loaf of bread and a pot of whatever I'm making for supper. You look like you could use feeding up," she said, casting a critical eye over Will's form. "You or your friend touch her, I *will* kill you."

"Yes, ma'am," Will said, startled.

"Good." She nodded and left in the direction her daughter had gone.

Will was very aware that he had just been manipulated, but he was also aware of something like relief. For a week, he had felt like the only person in the world who wanted to drag Martin back from the brink of death. Even Martin—especially Martin—seemed disinterested in his own fate. Having someone to help, even an obstreperous child, would be worth something.

CHAPTER THREE

"I swear to God I will not let another spoonful of that putrid nastiness pass my lips," Martin said, and, really, it was good to hear him sound like his old self. After two weeks in the cottage, Martin could shuffle around on unsteady feet and wasn't coughing half as much as he had been when they arrived. "I haven't had a fever in over a week and I'm hardly coughing up any blood at all. No more medicine."

That was just as well, because they had run out of the paregoric the day before. "How about some potato soup?" Will asked. He had already ladled some into the cup on the hopes that Martin would want it.

"Promise it's not gruel," Martin said, but Will saw him eying the mug greedily.

"On my honor." Will sat on the edge of the bed and held the cup to Martin's lips.

"I'm not a baby," Martin protested.

"Only acting like one," Will murmured, earning himself a glare. "Is your hand steady enough to hold the cup?"

With a roll of his eyes, Martin held up a mostly steady hand. Will helped him wrap it around the cup, keeping his own hand around Martin's just in case. It was slow going: Martin's grip was shaky, and Will needed to brace a hand at the back of Martin's neck in order to get the job done. Finally, though, Martin took a sip of the broth and swallowed, then groaned. "That was—well, if it's possible for potato soup to be ambrosial, it just was." He looked up at Will with a rusty, familiar smile and Will knew he ought to be glad to see it— Christ he *was* glad, he was so glad he could hardly believe it—but the sight of that grin on Martin's face suddenly made him want to take Martin by the collar and shake him. For the past two weeks, after finding Martin and dragging him off to the country, Will had tried not to be angry. But the healthier Martin became—healthiness being measured in relative terms—the harder it was for Will not to be furious with him. How dare Martin let himself get to death's door, how dare he let Will think he was dead? How dare he act like his life didn't matter, not to himself, not even to Will?

Martin, however, was utterly dependent on him; now wasn't the time for a fight. But Martin Easterbrook had been able to detect Will's less gentlemanly turns of mind for well over a decade, and when Will saw Martin's eyes narrow, he knew he was caught out.

"Out with it, William."

"No. I'm going to be a good friend," Will said virtuously.

Martin lifted the cup to his mouth again, this time by himself, and regarded Will over the brim. "You'll feel better if you get it out. Like lancing a boil."

"No, that's you. You're the one who feels better after saying every wicked thing that pops into your mind."

"Which is because it's an excellent practice," Martin said. "Come now. Either tell me why you're cross or we're going to spend the rest of the evening in terrible awkwardness."

The worst part of it was that he was right. "I was going to mention that you could have been gorging yourself on soup if you had come to me in the autumn, rather than camping in my brother's attic like a madman," Will said, the words out of his mouth before he could think better of it.

"So I *was* living in Hartley's attic," Martin said in tones of academic curiosity. "I half thought I dreamed the whole thing up."

Will had to concede that Hartley's attic wasn't the most bizarre place Martin could have chosen as a refuge. The house had once belonged to Martin's father, and Will could see how a feverish man might retreat to a place that had once been his home. But to choose an unheated attic over Will's rooms seemed like courting a death wish.

"A hair shirt would have been more to the point," Martin added thoughtfully, absently handing the cup to Will.

Will put the teacup down so he didn't accidentally crush it in his hand. "Imagine how he would have felt to find your body in his attic," he said.

"Imagine how you'd have felt to find my body in this bed one fine morning," Martin retorted. "We both know it's only by chance that you didn't. Kind of you to spare Hartley the drama, though."

Will drew in a sharp breath, because that's precisely what he had expected every time he turned his back that first week.

Every time he opened his eyes, every time he walked through the door, the first thing he did was check for the rise and fall of Martin's chest. He still did.

Perhaps sensing an advantage, Martin pressed on. "You can't stop me from dying, you know. I have consumption. I'm going to die."

"Some people are cured," Will protested. "And even those who aren't can live for decades. My mother—" As soon as he spoke, though, he knew it had been a mistake.

"Indeed, tell me more about how I can look forward to decades of increasingly severe illness. It's utterly unclear what you hope to accomplish here. As far as I know you're neither a necromancer nor a miracle worker. You could have let me die in peace."

"This again," Will said, throwing his hands up. "You really are a bastard."

"Well spotted." Martin picked up the cup and raised it in a mock toast.

"You're my friend," Will said. "If you think I was going to leave you to die alone, you—" He really meant to say something like *you're sadly mistaken* or *you never knew me* but what came out was, "You can go get fucked. Not everyone is as unrepentant an arsehole as you. You're my friend, even if you seem to be intent on getting rid of me."

"Seem? You haven't been paying attention at all. I've been trying to shake you loose for months. Why did you think I wouldn't answer your letters?"

Will knew from years of experience that Martin Easterbrook was a thoroughgoing lout when he didn't feel well (which was often enough to make loutishness his basic personality, Will sometimes thought) and was even more of a git when he suspected that he was being treated like an invalid. Will *knew* this. But that didn't stop it from hurting.

Will clenched his fists. He didn't want to fight—he hated it as much as Martin seemed to thrive on it. The middle of five sons, and raised in a house filled with quarrelsome adults, even a hint of disagreement made his skin crawl. Other people might like to linger on their differences, poking and prodding until they had aired all their grievances, but Will wanted nothing more than to smooth things over, bandage the wounds, and move on. He had to get out of the cottage before he said something regrettable. "I'm going for a walk," Will said, reaching for his coat. "I'll be back before dusk."

By the time he reached the village, his fury had subsided into a more familiar sorrow. He posted a letter for Hartley, drank a pint of ale at the pub, and then bought a loaf of bread and some cheese to take home as a weak effort at reconciliation.

Before stepping through the cottage door, he steeled himself for the chance of finding Martin in distress or worse, but only after putting his hand to the door latch did he realize that this time he fully expected his friend to be alive. Martin was still pale, but had lost the grayish pallor of illness. His coughs had diminished in quantity and severity. His fever showed no signs of returning. Whatever crisis had been brought on by the idiot's stay in a drafty attic had truly passed. Will had successfully nursed him through it. And while Martin might have preferred to have been left to meet his end alone, Will wasn't going to be sorry for having intervened.

He placed his parcels on the table and glanced up to find Martin looking at him with a faint blush and an expression that might have been sheepish on anyone else. Will raised his eyebrows.

"Can we take it as read?" Martin asked.

"Take what as read?" Will asked, shrugging out of his coat.

"That I'm sorry to have met your generosity with my ill manners."

"I accept your first three words. The rest is rubbish and you can shove it right up your arse. You know perfectly well you saved me—"

"We don't talk about that," Martin said, as he always did when reminded of those awful few months two years ago, when Will had returned from sea, shattered and broken.

"Fine," Will conceded. "But you realize you're not dying at the moment, right?"

"That possibility has occurred to me," Martin said about as primly as a man could while wearing a secondhand nightshirt.

"Yeah, well, it's occurred to me too. After I sat next to you for a fucking fortnight, trying to figure out what I'd have to do to afford a funeral."

"You needn't—"

"Needn't have paid for a funeral? What should I have done? Left you here? Flung you into the woods?" Will buried his face in his hands. "I'm sorry. I shouldn't be having this conversation with you."

Martin was silent for a long while. "I prefer it," he said. "I think about those things all the time, so it's just as well to hear them out in the open. But, as you say, you probably won't need to consider funeral expenses in the immediate future."

Will took out his knife and pared off a slice of cheese, then sat on the edge of the bed and handed the morsel to Martin.

"Really?" Martin asked, holding the sliver of cheese. "First soup and now cheese. We're living like kings in—where are we?"

"Sussex," Will said, and saw a glimmer of suspicion in Martin's eyes. Before Martin could ask any questions, Will said, "Now eat your damned cheese." For once, Martin did as he was told. Will smiled at the look of stunned pleasure on his friend's face. "I bet you're glad you didn't die now. No cheese in hell."

The look of barely suppressed laughter on Martin's face warmed Will's heart. "Fuck *off*, Will. That is—that is—just give me more cheese and shut up."

They ate half the wedge of cheese and the entire loaf of bread. At some point Will shifted so he sat beside Martin, his back to the headboard. His belly was full, his friend was alive, and that was really all Will had ever wanted. Happy and sated, he put his hand on Martin's leg. Just a companionable touch, nothing they hadn't done a thousand times before. There was nothing to it, so he was surprised when Martin batted his hand away.

"None of that," Martin snapped.

Will's cheeks heated. He hadn't meant anything pointed, anything particular. He hadn't even realized that Martin understood Will was the sort of man who *could* mean anything pointed or particular by a touch. "I'm sorry," Will said, and rose from the bed to sit in the straight-backed chair by the fire.

Martin woke to the sound of a broom swishing across the cottage's flagstone floor and furniture being dragged out of the way with more noise than he might have thought possible, given that the cottage contained about four pieces of furniture.

He rolled over to see what had possessed Will to start this clamor when the sun hadn't quite risen, but instead of Will, he saw a yellow-haired girl in a plain dress and apron, wielding the broom like it was a weapon.

"What on earth?" Martin said, propping himself on his elbows. "What do you think you're doing?"

"I'm your maid," she said. Spat, really. "He—" she pointed an accusing finger to where Will still slept on a pallet by the fire "—hired me."

"And I'll fire you," Martin said, "if you let that chair topple onto Mr. Sedgwick."

"Go ahead!"

"What on *earth*," he repeated. It occurred to him that perhaps his fever had returned, and that this entire scene was a febrile delusion.

Will, finally alerted to the battle progressing mere inches

away from his face, stirred. "Oh," he said, sitting up. "This is Daisy Tanner. She's been tidying up in the mornings and bringing us supper."

Which meant Martin must have slept through this uproar on previous mornings. He had wondered where the food had been coming from, and who brought clean linens, but he had been raised in a house staffed with an army of servants; he was used to things simply getting done. "She seems less than thrilled about it," he observed. "Did you win her in a card game? Buy her off a pirate ship?"

"My mother sent me here because she thinks the ostler is after me," the girl said.

"After—oh," Martin said. "Well, is he?"

The girl turned scarlet.

"Do you want him to be? Are you after him? Is the ostler some kind of rural Casanova? In any event, this cottage is hardly larger than a stable stall. I daresay you can finish your work in under an hour and you'll have the entire afternoon to get yourself seduced. Now, step outside for a moment while Mr. Sedgwick and I make ourselves decent. Neither of us are inclined to duel the ostler for your honor, I assure you." He made a shooing motion until the girl left. When the door slammed shut, he turned to Will and raised a single questioning eyebrow.

"I let myself get bullied," Will said. "Her mother told me nursing invalids is women's work."

"My God. And you listened to her?"

"Don't you feel healed by Daisy's tender ministrations? By her womanly gentleness?"

"Well, I suppose I ought to at least put on a pair of trousers and drag my weary bones from this bed so that child—Daisy, of all the foolishness—can clatter about." Miracle of miracles, he actually got his legs out of the bed on the first try, and stepped into a pair of trousers with minimal effort. He was weak, as anybody would be after being ill for so long, but he felt better than he had in months.

"You seem in fine fettle," Will said.

Martin could have told him it was always like this as his body slowly returned to itself. It was a base animal thrill at continued life, nothing more, and it would dissipate. He would have said as much, but Will was looking at him, his hair rumpled, his smile tense and fragile, and Martin didn't want to disappoint him. "I am," he said.

"I'm glad," Will said. He still hadn't attempted to get up from the pallet. One really would think that his years in the navy would have made him better at getting out of bed in the morning, but evidently one would be mistaken. Besides, Martin preferred not to think of Will's time in the navy. He had a list as long as his arm of things to feel guilty about, and the only reason he could get by from day to day was to resolutely refuse to think about any of them.

"I'm enchanted by the novelty of being able to fill my lungs." Martin demonstrated, and was stopped by a pang on his left side. "Or to partly fill them, at least."

"The doctor said you broke a rib coughing. He said not to try binding it up because then you'd risk injuring your lungs. So I'm afraid it may have healed badly. I'm sorry about that."

Martin was silent for a moment as he tried to organize

a suitable response to that nonsense. "Were you under the impression that I was about to complain about the care you took of me? Idiot." For whatever reason, that made Will smile daftly at him. When Will finally got to his feet, Martin looked away, becoming very interested in fluffing his pillow. "Get dressed so that young harridan can come back in. Speaking of which, have you been sleeping on the floor this whole time?" A kinder man than Martin might have noticed that already, but Martin was rather pleased with himself for noticing it at all.

"Uh. No. The first few days I just dozed in the chair."

"In that chair. The one that has a hard back and no arms."

"The very same."

"You do realize the bed is large enough to hold us both." He really shouldn't be asking Will to share a bed with him. It was a terrible idea by any standards, even Martin's, and Martin hadn't had a good idea in *years*. But he couldn't very well let Will sleep on the cold stone floor after quite literally saving Martin's life, such as it was.

Will shoved his hands in his pockets. "I'm a restless sleeper."

Martin gaped. "I wake coughing ten times a night. You can't possibly think that you'd disturb me."

"I mean." He scuffed the toe of his boot along the floor, as if he were ten years old and had been caught stealing plums. "Nightmares. You know."

Martin was seized with the usual urge to lay waste to His Majesty's Navy but contented himself with pressing his lips together. "Of course. Cold, hard floors are the preferred surface upon which to have nightmares. Well known fact."

"You needed rest and I didn't want to disturb you. I wasn't sleeping terribly well anyway, given that every time you stirred I thought—" He broke off.

"You thought I was having death throes. Good God we're a cheerful pair. When did you send for a doctor? I remember none of this."

Will looked shifty.

"William."

"I brought you to a doctor in London before bringing you here. He gave us some medicine and told me to get you away from the smoke as quickly as possible."

"And I went willingly?"

"Not exactly. The doctor dosed you and his assistant helped me carry you out to the carriage."

"You abducted me?" He was about to say something flip, like *I didn't know you had it in you,* but his voice caught on the words. He didn't like the idea that Will had made a decision for him, without his consent. It reminded him too much of his father, of all the doctors, of many years spent helpless. He knew that Will bringing his nearly lifeless body to a doctor and subsequently to the country wasn't the same as anything his father had done. But it still poked at a wound that was always a bit raw.

Chapter Four

Sharing close quarters with Will was an absolute nightmare in ways Martin had never before contemplated. The man was forever taking his shirt off and just walking around as if that were a perfectly normal and unremarkable thing to do. Perhaps it was; Martin had no experience with what other men did. Perhaps they all wandered around in various states of undress. Martin had made it his life's work never to find out; whatever moral failings he had inherited from his father, he wouldn't let debauchery be one of them.

For the first month at the cottage and a long while beforehand, Martin thought his interest in sex had been killed by the consumption. If anything, he had been relieved. It wasn't as if those urges had done him any good in the past. But now, it was like his prick was making up for lost time. He had gone months without thinking about the thing and now the bastard couldn't sit still.

It did not help that Will Sedgwick seemed to forever be missing half of his clothes, despite it being February, and Martin simply couldn't stop himself from looking. He had never been able to stop himself from looking at Will, damn it. That was the central problem of his life (other than the intermittent dying, at least). Despite his admittedly feeble best intentions, he caught his gaze lingering on Will's chest, its dusting of dark hair, its lean muscles. And his arms—wiry but strong, three birds inked high up, near the shoulder. Those goddamn birds, Martin could not stop looking at them. Surely officers in the navy did not get tattoos, which probably meant Will had gotten them done after being disrated and reduced to the status of a common sailor, but he couldn't ask without also asking about the rest of it. Martin felt vaguely perverse for the attention he paid to those birds, wanting to put his mouth on them, wanting to feel Will's biceps shift under his lips. The fact that they at best symbolized a youthful carefree innocence that Will could never regain, and at worst were the product of those last months of misery aboard ship, made shame spiral in Martin's belly. He really was no better than his father. He'd tell himself that, repeat it like the chorus to a hymn, but Will would flash a smile at him and Martin would find himself grinning back, unrepentant, and then he'd only look some more. At least Martin had put an end to the deliberate, affectionate touching. But even accidental contact, of the sort that was unavoidable in a cottage this small, sent waves of awareness throughout Martin's body. Every time their sleeves brushed or they bumped shoulders in the doorway, Martin wanted to lean into the touch and purr like a cat.

The worst part was that he couldn't get away from the temptation. He could walk outside, fill the kettle at the pump, and then put it on the fire. He could stroll twice around the outside of the cottage. Once, on a sunny day, he hung up some washing on the line. Martin needed to get better, and then needed to figure out where he would go, how he would live, because the sooner he left this cottage, the better. The longer he sat around pining after Will, the greater the odds that Will would notice.

The real problem was that he couldn't imagine what he'd do after leaving. He had been raised to be the owner of Lindley Priory, as had his father and his father's father and all the Easterbrooks before them. But the priory was gone, the coffers were empty, and there were no more Easterbrooks. There was no place in the world for Sir Martin Easterbrook, and he didn't know how to go about finding one. Until a year ago, Martin had never so much as combed his own hair or rinsed out his own teacup, partly because he was the pampered heir to the Easterbrook fortune, but also because he had always been told he was too frail to take care of himself. He was disgusted by his own helplessness, but didn't know how to go about learning otherwise.

With that in mind, Martin decided he could not live another hour without bathing. He knew he was hopelessly spoiled by a youth spent in the lap of luxury, but dabbing at himself with a sponge was simply not going to cut it. As there was no proper bath to be had, and no servant to draw one, he steeled himself, went out to the pump, stripped hastily down to his small clothes, and soaped himself up with the bar of tallow soap they kept by the wash basin. The water was freezing, but he dumped a bucket over his head and began working the soap across his scalp. He poured another bucket over his hair, shivering and shaking all the while, but the sense of weeks—months, even—of grime being rinsed clean away was nothing less than glorious.

"Are you mad?" Will sputtered, coming back from wherever he went when he left the cottage. "Are you trying to kill yourself? Don't answer that. I don't want to know." He stomped off into the cottage and emerged with a blanket, which he wrapped around Martin's shoulders.

"I just wanted to bathe," Martin said, his teeth chattering.

"You could have asked—"

"I could have asked you to bathe me? I think not, William," he said with as much asperity as he could muster. Will flushed.

"No, damn it. Just get indoors." He set Martin before the hearth, then climbed a ladder to a loft that Martin hadn't noticed before. A few minutes later a tin tub came clattering to the floor. Martin, his eyes occasionally drifting shut because of sleepiness and cold, watched Will fill pots and basins with water, then heat them over the fire. He couldn't have said how long it took before the tub was filled, but eventually Will wiped his hands on his trousers and said, "Come on, now. If you don't get in, then I'm using the water for my own bath."

The thought of having to watch Will strip and bathe was enough to make Martin spring into action. He was already naked except for the blanket, his small clothes having been discarded outside. He didn't drop the blanket until just before stepping into the tub. He was well aware that he wasn't much to look at these days—not that he wanted Will to be looking, not that he *cared*, but he knew that he was a sorry sight. He was naturally broad shouldered and large boned, and skinniness didn't sit well on him. As he stepped into the tub, he saw Will deliberate between turning his back out of decency or coming to his aid out of innate mother hennishness. Decency won, because it always did with Will, the bastard.

"Oh God," Martin groaned when he sank into the tub, his irritation draining away as soon as he touched the hot water. "This is lovely." He hadn't had a proper bath since he left his aunt's house in the autumn. The warmth and the sense of purification both seeped into his bones. Will had set a flannel, a cake of soap, and a cup next to the tub, and Martin set about scrubbing himself clean. "Thank you," he said, moved to goodwill by the soap bubbles.

"I should have thought of it sooner," Will said. He still had his back to the bath, and was busily arranging a stack of books. "I forgot what a finicky little shit you can be."

"Where did those books come from?" Martin asked. He was certain they hadn't been there earlier. For the past month they had been rereading the same books Will had read aloud when Martin had been too feverish to pay attention.

"Hartley brought them."

"Hartley was here?"

"He comes every week or two. I met him at the inn this afternoon."

"Does he know I'm here?"

Will turned around at that, a quizzical expression on his face. "Yes. He's the only one who does, though."

"But you didn't bring him here? To the cottage?"

"I didn't think you'd want that."

Indeed, Martin wouldn't have wanted to see Hartley, but he resented Will's assumption. He and Hartley and Will had once been the best of friends, in the way that boys of the same age who live in reasonable proximity will simply fall in among one another. They had traipsed about the hills and gone swimming during Martin's periods of good health. And during Martin's periods of poor health, the Sedgwick brothers had gone to great lengths to sneak into his rooms and pass him messages.

That had all gone to hell in the span of a summer. First, Martin's father had discovered Will in Martin's bed after one of those nights he had sneaked in. It had all been innocent, but Martin's father had the sort of mind that saw prurience everywhere, probably because Sir Humphrey was rather devoted to prurience himself, but Martin hadn't known that at the time.

Soon after this, Hartley started avoiding Martin. Martin assumed this was because Hartley, too, thought Martin was debauching Will, and Martin was too insulted to bother with olive branches. Soon after that, Martin's father arranged for Will to get a place in the royal navy as an officer's servant, which would put him on a path to becoming an officer. It was more than Will could have hoped for without Sir Humphrey's intervention, but at the time it had been blindingly obvious to Martin that this was an effort to separate Will from Martin. Martin supposed that Hartley came to the same conclusion, because once Will left, Hartley had never uttered another friendly word to Martin.

Around the same time, Martin's father began pouring money into the Sedgwick household. He paid the oldest brother's university fees and sent the younger boys to a proper school. He took Hartley about with him to house parties and hunts, to London for the season, to all the events Martin had been excluded from. At the time Martin thought his father regarded Hartley as the son he wished he had—healthy, clever, handsome. He thought his father was punishing him for his failures as a son by bankrupting the estate in favor of his own replacement.

It had taken years for Martin to understand that Sir Humphrey had never had fatherly feelings toward Hartley, and even longer to grasp how young Hartley had been when Sir Humphrey had first persuaded him to trade intimacies for his family's welfare. Martin had spent his entire life trying and failing to please his father, and it was only after Sir Humphrey died that Martin learned the extent of his father's evil. By then, he had spent years regarding Hartley as his enemy. Now he suspected that Hartley had first avoided Martin out of shame or embarrassment about the nature of his relationship with Martin's father. Martin had a long list of regrets, and toward the top of the list was that he had effectively abandoned Hartley at a time when all his brothers were away from home and he was being taken advantage of by a much older man.

Martin felt entirely justified in being leery of seeing Hartley again. He couldn't do it without a proper apology, but he didn't know how to even start. Some things couldn't be apologized for.

Gingerly, Martin got to his feet and reached for the sheet of toweling that Will had left nearby. Out of the corner of his eye he saw Will stepping near. "I'm not going to fall," he snapped.

"There are clean clothes in the trunk at the foot of the bed."

Martin dressed himself in a threadbare linen shirt and a pair of trousers that hung off him. God knew where they had come from. Perhaps Hartley had sent these too. Perhaps Hartley was paying for all of this, from the cottage to the soap to the round of cheese. Martin bristled at the thought, but found that he didn't care as much as he might have a year ago. If Hartley wanted to be stupid with the money Martin's father had left him, Martin wasn't going to object.

As he fastened the trousers, he heard a splash and turned in time to see Will lowering himself into the tub. He hastily looked away. Slowly, and with a great deal of shame, he looked back. Will was in profile, backlit by the fire, but even in silhouette Martin could tell that he was whipcord thin. He always had been; he was made of fine bones and a bare minimum of muscle, overlaid with freckled skin. It had been the sight of Will, casually stripping before plunging into the lake, that had been Martin's first clue that he might not be entirely like other men. And still, a single glimpse of him made Martin's heart twist around inside his rib cage in a way that the sight of nobody else ever had. The birds weren't visible from this angle, but the scars across Will's back were, and that was what finally propelled Martin to behave decently. He climbed into bed, pulled the covers up to his chin, rolled so he faced the wall, and pretended to sleep.

Will was aware of Martin's gaze on him as he shaved. "What?" he asked, angling the small hand mirror so he could get a look at his jaw. "Hartley's visiting again today and he'll act disgraced if I'm scruffy."

"I'm the one who's scruffy," Martin said. Out of the corner of his eye, Will saw him touch his face.

"Not as bad as when I found you in London. You had beard, and the doctor told me I had to shave it off and cut your hair."

Martin's hand flew to his head.

"No, I didn't cut your hair. But I did shave you, and you swore at me the whole time, so I didn't do it again."

"I rather wish you had."

Puzzled, Will turned to look at Martin. "You know you can use the razor anytime you want, right?"

"I'm afraid I don't know how," Martin said after a moment. Will wiped the blade on a wet cloth and regarded his friend. Martin's cheeks were pink and his gaze fixed on the floor. "I've always had a valet."

Will blew out a breath and tried not to dwell on Sir Humphrey's failings as a parent and a human. "Want me to teach you?"

"Would you?" Martin asked doubtfully, as if Will had offered him something highly valuable but also untoward.

Will didn't know what had put the uncertainty in Martin's voice. He already knew that Martin hated being helpless, but that usually just made him cranky and impossible. This was something else. His eyes were flickering between Will and the razor with something like longing.

"I offered, didn't I? Why didn't you ask earlier?"

At that, Martin's cheeks darkened even further. Will had never seen him so flustered. "It's just that it would feel so good to have a shave."

Will opened his mouth to argue that this was exactly why Martin ought to have asked for help weeks ago, but then he understood what Martin was saying. "You don't want things to feel good?" Martin's prompt glare was answer enough. Will sighed. "Come here," he said, wiping the last of the shaving soap off his face and getting to his feet.

Martin sat in the chair Will had vacated.

"So the first thing you want to do is use this brush to make lather from this wet cake of soap. Like so." Will twisted the brush on the top of the cake, then handed both to Martin. "Then dab it all over your face." He watched as Martin silently followed his instructions. "You're missing a spot on the left side, near your ear." He held out the hand mirror and also indicated the area on his own face. Still silent, Martin continued to spread the foam.

"Good, really good," Will said, handing him the razor. "Now start with your neck. Tilt your chin up a bit." He took Martin's hand and adjusted the angle of the razor, then did the first stroke with him. "Yes, just like that." Will pulled the second chair over and sat in it backward, so he could hold the mirror up for Martin. "No, here, you have to sort of pull your mouth to the side. There you go." It wasn't the first time he had taught someone to shave, although Martin at twenty-three was rather different from fifteen-year-old cabin boys, who were always comically proud of themselves for needing to shave in the first place. "There," he said, leaning in, "you've missed a spot." He spoke only as loud as he needed to be heard a scant foot away.

"Where?" Martin asked, equally quiet.

"The corner of your mouth." He tapped his own lip. "That's it." He liked watching Martin's face become revealed like this, liked watching Martin's long fingers at work. He also liked the closeness, and the occasional questioning glances Martin shot him, as if seeking approval. It was rare to see Martin so vulnerable; even at his sickest, he had been prickly and sardonic, but as he gingerly slid the blade across his skin, he seemed so uncertain. As Martin scraped off the layer of scruff that had concealed the bottom half of his face, Will saw the familiar contours of his friend's face materialize—sharp cheekbones, slightly pointy chin that echoed the widow's peak of his hairline, lips that were the only softness in the uncompromising landscape of his face. Will had known, in an abstract sort of way, that at some point Martin had grown up handsome. But there had always been so many other more pressing matters, and even at his stupidest Will knew better than to start thinking that way about his best friend.

Now, though, Will badly wanted to reach out and wipe

the extra shaving soap from Martin's cheekbone with his thumb. He wanted—well, he *wanted*. He shoved that realization firmly off to the side, more than a little dismayed with himself for having let it happen in the first place.

"There you go," Will said, when Martin finished. Martin touched his fingertips to his jaw. He had been nearly silent while shaving and now had an almost frantic, wild look in his eyes. "Doesn't that feel better?" Will asked, trying to break the tension, but achieving the opposite result—Martin now had one hand wrapped so tightly around the cloth that his fingertips had gone white. "You did really well," he added softly, trying to be soothing.

"Jesus Christ," Martin rasped, getting to his feet. The razor clattered to the floor, the cloth dropping after it. "I'm going for a walk."

Will stood alone in the cottage, not entirely certain what had just happened.

"You look less terrible," Hartley said, eying Will narrowly. As always, he looked more put together than anyone who had spent four hours on a stagecoach had any right to.

"Thanks ever so," Will replied, rolling his eyes. He watched as his brother slid onto the stool beside him, greeted the innkeeper by name, paid for both his and Will's pints, and then pulled a sheaf of paper from his coat pocket and placed it beside Will's tankard.

"Here's what I have." Will started to page through it.

"No," Hartley said, snatching it back. "Don't read it in front of me. Take it home, mark it up, and then next week I'll make a fair copy."

The first time Hartley visited, in an undisguised attempt to check up on his little brother, Will confessed to writing a play. He had started it in London and finished it while sitting up at night by Martin's bed. When Hartley asked to read it, Will was too tired to object—besides, it wasn't as if Hartley didn't know that Will was given to overwrought sentiment. But when he came back the following week, Hartley only remarked that it would make a better comedy than tragedy, and had all but begged to try his hand at altering it. They had been passing the manuscript back and forth ever since, Hartley adding dark humor and Will refining the language. If all went as planned, they would offer it to a theater manager Will knew.

"How's Martin?" Hartley asked carefully after their pints arrived.

"His fever hasn't come back," Will said, equally carefully.

"Good." Hartley patted him awkwardly on the arm. By Hartley's standards, this was a full embrace, almost mawkishly sentimental. Will didn't think Hartley cared much whether Martin lived or died except for how his death would distress Will, so he supposed he ought to be touched by the effort his brother was making.

"How's Sam?" Will asked, eager to change the subject. That set Hartley off on a lengthy monologue. It was almost unsettling to see Hartley this happy. He was actually smiling, an honest-to-god smile that showed teeth.

"I'm glad you're happy, Hart."

"Ugh." Hartley scowled. "Spare me."

Will hid a grin in his tankard.

"I wouldn't exactly hate it if you were happy, too, you know," Hartley went on. "And I can't help but feel that holing up in this godforsaken place with Martin Easterbrook—"

"Hush. We're not using that name."

"—is not exactly a path toward contentment."

Will took a long pull of his pint. "I couldn't be content knowing that he was alone. You know that."

"Hmm." Hartley regarded him appraisingly. "I wonder if I do."

"I'm trying to get him well. That's all. Then he can . . ." Will's voice trailed off.

"Mmm? What can he do then? Harass tenants? Run away from his aunt's house in order to haunt my attics? What grand plans will Martin return to?"

"A person doesn't need plans to make their life worthwhile."

Hartley's expression softened. "As much as it pains me to say this, it's probably for the best that he's with you. You seem to be the only friend he has. His aunt hasn't exactly been tearing up the country looking for him."

Will felt his face heat in anger and something else. "You talk about him like he's a stray dog in need of care. He's my friend and I hate that I'm all he has," he said, because that was the thing that saddened him the most.

"You might want to consider why that is," Hartley remarked, taking a sip of ale.

"Why I care for him?"

"Why nobody else does."

"His father cut him off from all society," Will said. "And now he's prickly and distrustful. He's so used to being alone that he deliberately alienates anybody who might be fond of him. He's been doing that all our lives." Will didn't add that Martin also seemed to be punishing himself—it seemed both too private and too confusing for Will to articulate.

"Believe me, I recall," Hartley said tartly. "Then maybe answer the other question. Why do you care for him when he manifestly does not want to be cared for?"

Sometimes it was a little heartbreaking that Hartley needed these things explained to him. "Because he's my friend," Will said. That was true, he supposed, for all it was a radical simplification. He didn't really think anybody could explain the whys and wherefores of friendship. Either you cared for somebody, or you didn't, and there wasn't much sense trying to make sense of it. Will and Martin had been friends since Will knew what the word meant, and it wasn't as if he could just undo that, nor did he want to. "And also," he added, sensing that Hartley needed this spelled out for him, "he's only in his current situation—poor, alone, etcetera—because of his arsehole father. He never had a chance. Sir Humphrey was—" Will's grip tightened around his pint "—ashamed of him. For being sick or maybe just because his father was a terrible person. But he never got to go to school and meet people of his own—" Will had nearly said *of his own station* but caught himself at the last moment. "He only had us. His aunt was hundreds of miles away. He has no connections and no money and it's not fair to him that I'm the best he has. He doesn't belong here in a drafty cottage with— with me, you know? He's—he's a baronet."

Hartley's eyes went as round as guinea pieces. "Which is . . . a good thing?"

"No, obviously." Will's face heated. "I mean, it's terrible." For God's sake, he had written a dozen screeds on the uselessness of the aristocracy and the evils of inherited wealth. But none of that had to do with Martin. "We were raised to think of him as the heir to Lindley Priory and I can't see him like this without thinking that he's been done out of his birthright."

"Birthright," Hartley repeated softly. "Listen to yourself. And anyway, he has been. Done out of his birthright, that is. There's nothing we can do about it."

"It's just—it's a fucking tragedy, Hart, that it's come to this. I spent the winter thinking he was going to die in a poky cottage on his own estate with nobody to look after him but me."

"But," Hartley said, with obvious effort, "if I heard someone say 'I fell ill and my friend took me to the country and looked after me' I'd think that person was lucky to have such a loyal friend. Why would I be wrong to think Martin is lucky to have you? Leaving class and his arsehole father out of it, thank you."

"Nobody should have to depend on me," Will said into his pint. Out of the corner of his eye he could see Hartley open his mouth and snap it shut again.

"How long has it been?" Hartley asked at length.

Will didn't need to ask what Hartley meant. "I bought my last bottle of laudanum in August. Haven't been to any opium dens or anyplace similar since even before that."

"That's good," Hartley said, not bothering to conceal his relief.

"It's hard, though," Will said, and drained the rest of his pint. "I don't want him to be around if I stop being able to resist temptation."

Hartley passed a hand over his mouth. "Jesus. I wish I had something useful to say."

"So do I," Will said, sliding his hand along the bar and squeezing his brother's arm. "At least being in the country means that much less temptation. Anyway, that's why I need him to get better and send him on his way, all right?"

Hartley looked like he very much wanted to protest, but knew better than to try.

CHAPTER FIVE

"Come for a walk with me," Martin said, casting aside the worn copy of *Bungay Castle* he had been reading. He could see the sun shining from the window nearest to his bed. It was March now, and they had been at the cottage for over two months.

Will put down his pen. "It's still cold."

"If I start hacking we'll come back. Come on. I want to stretch my legs. I haven't been further than the wood pile yet." He also wanted to confirm a suspicion that had been lurking at the back of his mind for some weeks. Martin got to his feet and grabbed a coat off the peg by the door. Outside, the landscape was mostly drab browns and grays with shoots of green signaling that winter might eventually end. Further from the cottage, the landscape opened up to a vista of rolling hills, a stand of spindly trees, a yew hedge in the distance. He walked on, past a few patches of bare dirt that might have once been a vegetable garden, past the well, past a rickety fence and straight to the top of the nearest hill. There, in the distance, he could see the barely remembered roofline of Friars' Gate.

The entire property was entailed, so Martin hadn't been able to sell it after his father's death. He had, however, ordered the manor stripped down nearly to the beams and most of the furnishings sold off. That had kept the creditors at bay for a little while, but it had been a drop in the ocean. It wasn't a large house, just a shooting box located halfway between London and Brighton. His father had used it to host house parties to which Martin had seldom been invited. At the time he thought it was because his father didn't want the world to know that he had a sickly son. Now he suspected it was because his father didn't want Martin to know what he got up to in his spare time.

"So you did bring me here," Martin said, not bothering to make it a question.

Will sighed. Martin didn't need to turn his head to know he looked guilty, and rightly so. "You needed country air. It was either here or Lindley Priory. Getting to Cumberland would have meant days in a carriage, and you weren't in any state for that. Besides, you own this place, so, well, I could afford it."

Martin let out a bitter laugh, but it turned into a cough. Walking so far had perhaps been unwise. Will looked at him with concern, and Martin waved his hand dismissively. "The people here, they don't know who I am. Daisy calls me Mister."

"I told Mrs. Tanner that you were a Mr. Smith."

Martin refrained from rolling his eyes. "Let me guess. John Smith."

"She didn't ask for a first name," Will said, a tiny smile playing at the edges of his mouth.

"Well. Friars' Gate. You could have told me. I was hardly in any condition to get up and leave."

"That's why I didn't tell you. I figured we could fight about it when you were well enough to fight back. So, do you want to?"

"Do I want to do what?"

"Leave."

Martin experienced the same ridiculous frisson of excitement that he did on each rare occasion that somebody gave him a choice. "No," he said after some thought. He was annoyed that Will brought him here—or anywhere—without his permission, but he hadn't been in any state to give permission, and he could grudgingly admit that Will had done what was necessary to save his life. "It was a good decision. I'm surprised you knew about the gamekeeper's cottage, though."

"I looked for you here," Will said. "In the autumn, after you left your aunt's house. That's how I knew there was a cottage standing empty."

"Thank you for not bringing me into the house itself," Martin said, and meant it sincerely. He leaned back against the trunk of a tree and crossed his arms in front of him. Will came to stand nearby, and Martin wondered if he were even aware that he had positioned himself between Martin and the wind. Happily, Will seemed blissfully unaware of a good number of things, or surely he would have said something after what Martin thought of as the Shaving Incident. Two weeks had passed, and Will still treated him as a reasonable adult rather than a person who had nearly been reduced to tears by Will's soft words and the feel of his own smooth jaw. Martin still couldn't shave without a pang of guilt that didn't even make sense to him, and he was ready to feel guilty at the drop of a hat.

"Since we're unburdening our souls," Martin said, trying to sound flippant and afraid he came off regrettably earnest, "I do suppose I owe you an apology for the unanswered letters." He swallowed. "I read them—at least all those I received before leaving my aunt's house—and I kept them." He nearly admitted that he had kept all Will's letters. For years, when Will was away at school and later at sea, they had written like paper was cheap and ink free and postage a trifling consideration; they had written pages upon pages, crossed and double crossed, and sometimes when Martin was feeling especially sorry for himself he'd read them all, right from the beginning.

"For a few months," Will said, his gaze fixed over Martin's shoulder, "I thought you must be dead, because surely if you were alive you would have written me back."

Martin felt like he had been slapped. He stepped to the side, placing himself in Will's line of sight. "You thought—it never once occurred to you that I didn't want you to disrupt your whole life to come fix mine? Which, mind you, is exactly what happened, so I think that we can agree I was quite right not to answer your letters."

"No we can't. We will never agree about that." Will

scraped a hand across the stubble on his jaw, then let it rest beside Martin's shoulder on the tree trunk. "I thought we were—" He shook his head, and Martin found himself holding his breath, wondering how Will planned to finish that sentence. "I thought we were—I thought we were important to one another. And then it turned out I was wrong."

"You think you aren't important to me," Martin said, his voice an embarrassing whisper. "You lackwit. You spent your childhood watching your mother die and I didn't want you to spend your adulthood watching me die. Idiot," he said fondly. Too fondly for someone standing so near. At this distance Will could look at him and see everything. "You know, I've had time to think about this," Martin went on. "I've never been well. The consumption is relatively new," he said, glossing over the details of precisely how new it was, "but the rest isn't. I've had a long time to think about how I don't want to be a burden."

Will, damn him, somehow stepped even closer. Martin could almost feel Will's breath against his cheek. "You aren't—"

"I see that now. But do you think that maybe, after twenty years of my father treating me as a burden and an embarrassment I might be justified in making assumptions?"

Will nodded. One strand of his hair tumbled across his forehead and Martin thought about how easy it would be to lift his hand and tuck that strand behind his ear. Instead he shoved his hands in his pockets. "That bastard," Will said.

"You'll get no argument from me. In any event, I promise I'll always answer your letters. It is—" he swallowed "—intolerable to me that you thought I didn't care." He was saying too much, but if faced with a decision between

Will knowing Martin cared too much and suspecting him of caring too little, Martin knew what choice he'd always make.

"Oh," Will said, and it was little more than a puff of air. Martin didn't dare meet his eyes.

"Regarding the letters. In my defense, I was not in the most reliable frame of mind last year."

Will let out a laugh and finally straightened up, putting some distance between them. "Christ, neither was I, for that matter. I don't think either of us have had two consecutive days of sound thought between us since 1814."

Martin snorted. It shouldn't be funny. There was nothing funny about what happened to Will, and only in his darker moods did Martin find much humor in his own predicament. But still he was laughing, and when he looked over, saw that Will was smiling, one hand over his mouth. It felt like—he couldn't think of anything less theatrical than *miracle*—that they were standing here, alive, relatively well in mind and body, and laughing about everything that had happened. Maybe that same thought struck Will, because for a moment it looked like he was going to embrace Martin. But then he stepped away awkwardly.

Feeling that far too much had been said and done between them for one afternoon, Martin turned and made his way back to the cottage, Will falling into step beside him.

"I saw your young gentleman up and about," Mrs. Tanner said when she shouldered her way into the cottage, Daisy trailing sullenly behind her. "That's a good sign, isn't it?"

"Yes," Will said, putting down his pen and sanding the topmost sheet of paper. "He's recovered about as well as could be expected." Since that first walk they had taken a few days earlier, Martin had made a habit of exploring the grounds every morning. Will didn't quite like it—it was cold, and Martin wasn't strong yet. But he also knew that arguing about it would only make Martin do something even more reckless, so he let it go, and tried not to look too anxious when Martin returned to the cottage, flushed and short of breath.

"Poor lad." The older woman hung a pot from the hook near the fire, and Will caught the scent of herbs and meat. "Now. Be gone with you. There's a jug of ale and some bread for your breakfast," she said, pressing both items into his hands. "Take them and go. The cottage hasn't been aired since old Jackson lived here and it could do with a thorough turning out. Daisy and I will do the wash and hang it to dry."

"Thank you."

"No need to thank me. Fair's fair."

In the past few months, Will had whitewashed the Tanners' cottage, inside and out; he had mended bucket handles and windowsills and everything that could be fixed; he had rounded up sundry geese and ducks and coaxed the milk goat down from the top of the chicken coop. More than once it had occurred to him that Mrs. Tanner had been getting by for quite a while without anyone's help but Daisy's, and he wondered why she hadn't years earlier come to an arrangement such as that she had with Will. But he remembered the way neighbors had steered clear of his mother—sickly,

French, and openly living with a married man—and reckoned that there was no shortage of reasons a woman might find herself shunned by her neighbors.

Will put the ale and bread into his satchel and took his coat off the peg. They had arrived at the cottage in January with little more than the clothes on their backs. In the loft, Will had found a couple of shirts and a coat that was only slightly moth-eaten, and Hartley brought even more. By Will's standards, they were pretty well set up, but whenever he saw Martin shrug into that tatty old coat he felt a pang of remorse that he couldn't have done better by the man.

It was cold, but not windy, so not a terrible day for a walk, Will supposed. The skies were a shade of grayish blue that made Will think of the ocean. He shoved that thought aside and wrapped the coat more tightly around himself. He was fairly certain that Martin typically walked to the top of the nearest hill and then returned to the cottage, so that was the direction he headed. Sure enough, he found Martin sitting against a fence post.

"Checking up on me?" Martin asked, but not impatiently so much as almost indulgently. Sometimes he looked at Will with naked fondness, as if the usual prickliness had slid off his face and he forgot to put it back on. Will was so used to seeing the fondness through the mask of surliness, that seeing it plain and unadorned on Martin's face took his breath away.

Will sat beside Martin on the cold, hard ground. "Got chucked out of the house by Mrs. Tanner and Daisy. Here." He took the bread and ale out of his bag.

Martin tore off a chunk of the bread and ate it in a few quick bites. "I passed Mrs. Tanner on her way to the cottage and I think she recognized me. Or, rather, I think she noted the resemblance to my father."

"You take after your mother," Will said. It was a poor lie, and the incredulous look Martin cast him told him so. There was certainly a superficial resemblance between father and son, but Will could never see much of the florid, ill-tempered old man in Martin. Well, apart from the ill temper, he supposed. Will had only ever seen a portrait of Martin's mother, but in that painting she had an expression he often saw on Martin's face—a wry twist of the mouth, a knowing glint in the eyes.

Will turned his head and regarded Martin. The sight of him was so familiar that sometimes he forgot its component parts. His hair, which had been wheat blond during childhood, was now the dark ash blond of driftwood, and his eyes were the dangerous gray of the North Sea but sometimes, rarely, flecked with the shifting blues of sea glass. It seemed so strange that Will had only learned these things after traveling thousands of miles away from Martin, but now he couldn't look at his friend without thinking of the ocean. It was as if his mind had taken the source of all his nightmares and mapped it onto the face of the person he loved best, as if to remind him that maybe the sea wasn't all bad.

"What?" Martin asked, turning to face him fully, one eyebrow hitched in question. He had a crumb at the corner of his mouth, which rather undercut the archness of his expression.

"Just looking at you," Will said, and when Martin flushed, he knew he had overstepped. He cleared his throat and looked away.

"In any event, I suppose I'm hardly the only person in this part of Sussex who bears a resemblance to my father," Martin said grimly.

"What? Oh, right. I suppose not." God only knew how many children Sir Humphrey had fathered over the years. He uncorked the jug of ale and took a long sip, then passed it to Martin. "Is it going to be a problem, do you think?"

"It's a problem every time I look in the mirror," Martin said. "Although I suppose I could do with the reminder that I have his blood in my veins."

"You're not him."

"Aren't I? You're unconscionably biased where I'm concerned."

Will stared. "You're nothing like him. He went to bed with—" He stopped, not liking the euphemism. "He took advantage of people who were too young and too poor to say no." That was what had happened to Hartley, and it stood to reason that Sir Humphrey hadn't stopped there. "You would never."

Martin drew his knees up to his chest and wrapped his arms around them, looking terribly small. "I took advantage of my tenants," he said. "Not in the way you mean. But I did it anyway."

"Your father ran his estate into the ground, leaving you with nothing but debts."

"And I handled that beautifully, did I not," Martin said, his lip curled in a sneer.

Martin spent a year raising rents, enclosing property, and in general trying to drain as much as he could from his Cumberland tenants to make the estate solvent. "No, you handled it like a horse's arse, but you were one and twenty. And, I might add, you made things right in the end. Furthermore, your father hadn't taught you how to manage an estate. He hadn't taught you a damned thing."

Martin bristled. "I'm not entirely ignorant."

"That's despite your father's efforts, you know." Martin spent his childhood with his nose in a book and learned as much as he could teach himself. But some things, like how to run a large and failing estate, couldn't be learned within the pages of a book.

"Hmph."

Will didn't know why Martin refused to listen to reason when it came to his father. It was almost as if he wanted to blame himself entirely for his own predicament. Will had no trouble acknowledging the role both their fathers played in their sons' present circumstances: poor, ill-equipped for any profession, and emotionally raw. He went to put his arm around Martin, then remembered that Martin didn't want to be touched, and pulled his hand back.

"I read that manuscript you left on the table," Martin said.

"You *what?*" Will sputtered.

"Was I not meant to? It was sitting right in the open. I wouldn't have read it if I thought it was a secret. It was very good."

"It wasn't a secret." Will's cheeks were burning hot. "The good lines are all Hartley's."

"And the parts where I actually—" he gestured to the vicinity of his chest "—*felt* things, that was you, damn you."

"Probably," Will said, grinning despite himself.

"What do you plan to do with it?"

"We offered it to a theater manager who is a friend of a friend. I suppose we'll hear back any day now."

Martin made an appreciative noise. "Perhaps I'll be well enough to return to London in time to see it staged."

"Are you eager to get back?" Will asked cautiously.

"Eager," Martin repeated. "William, you know better. I haven't been eager for anything in ages," he said, dry as dust. "I suppose I'm grimly resigned to returning to my aunt's house at some point. I can't very well stay here, living off your charity, can I?" Martin went on.

He sounded acutely miserable, and Will badly wanted to promise that Martin would never have to return to his aunt. But that was a promise Will couldn't make. "I'm literally living in your house for free, so that's a funny definition of charity," he said instead.

"What about you?" Martin asked. "Are you eager to get back to town?"

The truth was that he wasn't. He wanted to plant a few rows of carrots and be around when they were ready to harvest. He wanted to chop more firewood and know that he'd be the one to put it in the hearth next winter. He wanted—he wanted a lot of things, he was beginning to realize, and he wasn't going to have any of them. "I miss my friends," he said, because it was the truth, of a kind. "I'd say I miss Hartley but he hasn't given me a chance to miss him." For a moment he thought about telling Martin what he had already told Hartley, that being in the country made it easier to avoid temptation. After all, Martin already knew the worst. During those first months after Will had returned to England, Martin had been the one to drag Will out of opium dens and hells of every variety. But Martin looked fragile and young, and he was looking at Will with something like faith, and Will didn't want to shatter it, however misguided.

"It'll be grand when we go back to London," Will said brightly. "You'll see."

Chapter Six

A few times since they had been living in the gamekeeper's cottage, Will had what Martin privately thought of as a Gloomy Day. This was probably making light of a serious matter, but Day of Remembering Being Tortured by a Madman on a Boat seemed a trifle grim, however accurate, so Gloomy Day would have to do. On those days, Will would sleep even heavier and later than usual, then spend the rest of the day with a teacup clutched in his hands, his gaze apparently fixed on something like a whorl in the plaster or a crack in the windowpane. Sometimes he seemed not to hear when Martin spoke to him. Martin, for the most part, left him alone; he found that if he refilled Will's teacup or put a sandwich within arm's reach, Will would absently drink or eat. If Martin dropped a blanket over Will's shoulders, it would remain there hours later.

It reminded Martin of those months when Will only seemed to find the world bearable through the haze of laudanum, as if oblivion was the best he could hope for. That comparison was troubling, but it might have been even more so if Martin hadn't remembered that, when they were children, Will could spend an afternoon watching a spider weave a web. Sometimes, for good or for ill, Will's mind just went wandering. If Will needed to spend a day staring at the wall, so be it.

When, on a March morning, Will hadn't budged from his chair for over an hour, Martin realized that this was the first Gloomy Day during which he was capable of actually doing something useful for Will. He brewed a fresh pot of tea and topped off Will's cup, then dressed in a clean shirt and the better of the two pairs of trousers that sat in the trunk at the foot of the bed.

"Will," he said, his voice sounding loud in the stillness of the room. Will didn't answer, so Martin put his hand on the other man's shoulder. Will, as he did whenever Martin touched him, however incidentally, almost leaned into the touch, and Martin wanted to slap himself. Will was probably starved for touch, stuck here in a cottage with only Martin for company. All those weeks, Martin had only thought about how he couldn't bear to let Will touch him because every touch sent his mind reeling in forbidden directions, but he had neglected to remember that Will needed to be touched. Feeling like he was crossing a Rubicon, he squeezed the shoulder that was already under his hand, and then leaned in a bit in an awkward attempt at a sideways embrace.

Will turned his head to look up at Martin as if surprised to find him there, and then covered Martin's hand with his own. Martin could feel the calluses on Will's palm, the chill of his fingertips. It felt impossibly lovely, skin on skin, as if affection could be absorbed through flesh and bone. He could have stayed there for hours, awkward angle and all, soaking up the sweetness of it.

Instead he cleared his throat. "I'm going for a walk," Martin said. "I'll be back in a bit." He had leaned, so now their faces were close, close enough that he could see the individual hairs that made up the scruff on Will's jaw, the faint lines that had no business being around the eyes of a man who was barely twenty-three. It also meant he was close enough to see when something shifted in Will's expression, when his gaze flicked down to Martin's mouth and then back again.

He managed to give Will's shoulder another squeeze before standing upright and making his way to the door. Before crossing the threshold, he turned around, grabbed the blanket, tucked it around Will's shoulders, and then all but ran outside.

He walked until he was out of sight of the cottage, then braced himself against a tree. He was a fool, a prize idiot, stupid in ways he hadn't even considered.

Martin was quite aware, and had been for years, that all he had to do was crook his finger and Will would come running. The fact that Will had walked away from his home and his work in order to play nursemaid to Martin was proof enough. But until today, Martin hadn't considered that Will would oblige in more . . . carnal matters. He had tried very hard not to think of Will and carnal matters at the same time. He tried not to think of carnal matters, full stop, but that was another predicament entirely.

But now that he had the idea in his mind, it was hard to dislodge. He knew Will liked women, but that didn't mean he only liked women. Martin was fairly sure he himself liked women as much as he liked men, which was to say not particularly much. He supposed he was capable of being attracted to anybody, as long as they were Will Sedgwick. That was a problem he had long since become accustomed to: he knew how he felt about Will, and he knew there was nothing for it, and that was that.

But if there was a possibility—if Will might be interested in the same thing—

He nipped that line of thought in the bud. Will was interested in nothing of the sort. Will had looked at his mouth exactly one time, and Martin had no experience whatsoever with what men looked like when they wanted to be kissed, so it didn't matter what he thought he had seen.

And even if Will had been open to the idea of a kiss, that was probably because he had noticed Martin's attraction—and really, the spiders in the rafters had surely noticed by now—and responded out of whatever madness made him want to agree to anything Martin wanted.

Besides, if Martin acted on that sort of base impulse, he really would put paid to Will's future. Getting him sent to the navy had been bad enough. Being unable to help him after he returned had been even worse. To cut him off from the sort of proper loving partnership that he deserved would be the ultimate disaster. Because Martin knew Will, knew him down to the bone, and he knew that if they got together, however briefly, Will would stay by Martin's side forever. He was appallingly loyal and had no common sense whatsoever, especially where Martin was concerned.

During the years they had known one another, Martin had done nothing but take. It was the most unequal friendship ever known to man. And he was determined not to take another thing.

Once Martin collected himself, he went to Mrs. Tanner's house, which he knew was situated on the other side of a small wood, and which he recognized by virtue of seeing all the barnyard animals Will had described to him over the past months—a goat, a pig, various species of fowl. The cottage itself was ramshackle in a way that even the gamekeeper's cottage had not yet achieved. There seemed hardly to be a perpendicular pair of lines in the entire structure; everything bent and sagged in an alarming manner.

When he knocked on the door it was answered by Mrs. Tanner, her brow furrowed in consternation at the sight of Martin on her doorstep. "Something wrong?" she asked, not bothering to address him by a name she had surely guessed was false.

"No, no, but Mr. Sedgwick is a bit under the weather. I wanted to let you know that he won't be around until tomorrow, in case you were expecting him. But if you need an extra set of hands, I might be able to be of use." He couldn't quite imagine what he could do, but Mrs. Tanner brought them supper almost nightly in exchange for Will's help, and Martin felt that making the offer was the minimum required of him. And, if he were being honest with himself, he wanted Mrs. Tanner to stop looking at him with barely banked alarm, as if Martin were about to start ravishing young women and hosting orgies.

She gave him a long, skeptical look, almost a glare, as if she thought he were mocking her. Then she seemed to come to some kind of decision. "You can gather the eggs."

"Gladly," Martin said, trying to look like he gathered eggs every day of his life, like he was an expert in all matters egg-related. He turned in the direction of what appeared the area of the garden where a motley assortment of fowl congregated. They didn't seem to have any kind of system for where they laid their eggs, and he wasn't certain if this was typical of birds or merely of a piece with the disorder of the entire property. Soon enough, however, he spotted a small blue egg halfway beneath a rosemary bush. He bent down, picked it up, and held it gently in his hand. He found another egg, this one speckled and brown, being jealously guarded by a chicken, but he managed to spirit it away. A third egg, then a fourth, and Martin's hands weren't big enough to hold any more, so he returned to the house.

"Where would you like these?" he asked, rather proud of himself.

The house was dark and gloomy, but still he could see Mrs. Tanner lift her eyebrows as she relieved him of the eggs. "The next time you set about collecting eggs, you might want to use a basket." Indeed, he remembered seeing a basket by the door, but hadn't realized he was meant to use it. "And you might consider getting all the eggs. This time of year they lay two dozen a day. I sell them at market."

"I didn't realize," he said. "I can go back out and—"

"Don't bother." She sat at a small deal table, much worn and with one leg of a contrasting wood. Martin wondered if that were one of the items Will had mended for her. There was only one chair, although a three-legged stool stood nearby. He guessed that there had never been a second chair, and almost certainly never a Mr. Tanner.

"The next time Mr. Sedgwick is poorly, you don't need to trouble yourself in coming by." Her tone was not unkind, but Martin had the distinct sense that she was putting him in his place, showing him how little he knew and how meaningless his offer of help was. "Daisy's been bringing in the eggs since she was four," she added in a seemingly offhand way.

Yes, he was definitely being put down a peg. "I apologize for wasting your time," he said, and tried to sound sincere. He was sincere, damn it. But he already knew he was useless and didn't need this woman to drive home the point. Apart from the single trunk of possessions that he had left behind at his aunt's house, he owned nothing. Even the clothing he wore was Will's. Mortifying both of them in the process, Will had given him the coins that now jingled in his pocket, an audible reminder that he didn't have tuppence to his name nor did he have any prospects of ever having more unless he went to his aunt, and he was determinedly not thinking of that right now. He couldn't even gather eggs properly. He had, very literally, nothing to offer.

He walked the rest of the distance to the village and bought a pair of Bath buns at the bakery; Will had a sweet tooth and deserved something good after a hard day. He had a momentary thrill of accomplishment—he had successfully acquired buns!—that immediately dissipated when he realized that this was the single thing he had achieved in months: buying Bath buns with somebody else's money.

He needed to start figuring out what was going to come after this. Will had a life in London, a whole future waiting for him. It was already appalling—kind, but appalling—that he had walked away from all that in order to take care of Martin. And now Martin had to make sure that Will was able to return to his life as soon as possible.

Which, really, was now. Martin was as healthy as he was ever going to be. He couldn't in good conscience keep Will here any longer.

Will managed to thank Martin for the Bath bun, even though he mainly felt guilty that Martin needed to look after him when it was supposed to be the other way around.

"You don't need to eat it," Martin said when he saw Will staring gloomily at the bun. "It'll keep until tomorrow."

"No, I want to." Will took a bite and swallowed. It really was good, and the sugar momentarily cheered him up. "I just—you didn't need to go all the way to the village."

"Obviously not, William," Martin said dryly. "But I wanted to." He broke off a piece of his own bun and popped it into his mouth. "You were in one of your sorry moods and something had to be done."

Will found himself smiling. Martin could be relied on not to treat him with kid gloves even when he was at his most pitiable. It was one of the things he loved best about Martin—he never treated Will like the aftermath of a tragedy, even when Will was feeling especially tragic. From time to time he'd catch a trace of concern in Martin's eye, but never pity. Martin seemed to see Will as the same person he had always been, the person he had grown up with, but to whom bad things had happened. Will had learned that often when a person learned about his past—the debacle on board the *Fotheringay* having been the subject of countless newspaper pieces, as it wasn't every day a near mutiny occurred near enough to English shores for the actual court martial to take place in Portsmouth—they started to treat him as too broken to be taken seriously.

He took another bite of the bun, then washed it down with a mouthful of hot tea. He realized this meant Martin must have made tea at some point after coming home, although Will couldn't say he had noticed. What he did notice was that Martin looked better than he had in months. The walk had put color into his cheeks, and months of Mrs. Tanner's cooking had put some meat on his bones.

"You look well," Will said, before he could consider whether it was a good idea.

Martin paused a fraction of a second, his cup halfway to

his mouth, then raised an eyebrow. "Naturally," he said into his teacup.

"I mean that you look healthy." And he really did, but he also looked—some tiresome part of Will's mind would only supply the word *handsome*.

"Yes," Martin said, suddenly serious. "About that. I ought to go to my aunt."

"Oh." Will didn't bother to conceal his disappointment. He began breaking his bun into crumbs.

"I don't really have anywhere else to go," Martin went on. "You know Lindley Priory is being used as a charity school now," he said, casually eliding over the fact that he had all but given away his ancestral home for a nominal rent. "The terms of the lease don't include the dower house, though. I could live there, I suppose."

"You shouldn't go there," Will said. Martin had spent his childhood as all but a prisoner within the walls of Lindley Priory. It was in Cumberland, only a short walk from where Will and his brothers had grown up, but infinitely more stifling and dreary.

"And you shouldn't tear up that bun if you're not going to eat it. Look," Martin said after Will had dutifully stopped mauling the bun, "I'm thin on options. I can't stay here forever, and I—well, frankly, I'm going to have to beg my aunt for help."

Will wanted to argue, to say that Martin could always have a home with him, but that wasn't helpful or even true. Will didn't know if the play would sell or whether he'd have anything to live on in a few weeks. It was only because of his arrangement with Mrs. Tanner that he had been able to stretch his meager funds this far. On days like this, he didn't even know whether he'd be in his right mind for much longer. Besides, it was good that Martin was thinking to the future: only a few months ago he seemed content to waste away.

"This is your property, you know," Will pointed out instead.

Something odd flickered across Martin's face—embarrassment or maybe shame. "I can't stay here alone. I can't fend for myself the way you do."

"I could—"

Martin shook his head. "Let's not talk about this anymore. Not right now, at least. Now," he said, dusting the crumbs from his hands, "I think it's my turn to read aloud."

They settled into the rhythm they did most evenings, one of them reading while the other toasted bread at the fire or brewed tea. Sometimes they played a few hands of cards using a deck that Will found in the loft. Will realized he had taken that routine for granted, and that when it came to an end he would miss it. He didn't like to think of what might happen afterward. He didn't, if he were honest with himself, want to go back to London. He didn't want to go back to a shabby set of rooms, to shapeless days stretched out before him. Here, there was always something that needed to be done, if he felt like being busy, but he could sit idle if he had a day like today. And he liked seeing Martin every day. For years their friendship had been confined to letters and occasional meetings; seeing him daily, sharing a home with him, made something glad and grateful rise up inside Will.

"Will!" Martin called, and Will felt a chunk of Bath bun hit the side of his head. He grinned up to where Martin glared at him. "I've read the same paragraph three times. You aren't paying attention at all."

Will dragged his chair over to the bed where Martin sat, propped his feet on the bottom of the mattress, and shut his eyes as Martin resumed reading.

Chapter Seven

While Martin was cautiously pleased that he was able to go on ever longer walks, roaming about the Sussex countryside at ungodly hours every morning was not his idea of a good time. The alternative, however, was watching Will dress, sneaking looks out of the corner of his eye like a Peeping Tom. He was, frankly, disgusted with himself.

Later in the day Martin could control himself, but in the morning his guard was down. Fresh from a night of sleep and with the usual annoyance of an erection, he found himself regarding Will through a haze of want. Later on he could bury all that under the usual shame and guilt and maybe even some grief, but first thing in the morning his brain was in a shocking state of vulnerability. So every day after waking, Martin dragged himself out of bed and into his boots and through the front door.

By the end of March, when winter had slid into a bleak and soggy spring, Martin could easily make it all the way to the village and back without getting winded. Mrs. Tanner and her astounding brat of a daughter brought enough food for three men to eat, and since Will had always picked at his food as if he were afraid of being poisoned, that left the rest to Martin. His trousers were starting to fit snugly and he could no longer count all his ribs. When he chanced a glance in the tiny mirror they used for shaving, he saw that the circles under his eyes were all but gone. Of course, he also saw that the face looking back at him was more like his father's than ever, but that was no surprise. It was a timely reminder not to let his baser impulses get the better of him. It was a timely reminder to keep his thoughts away from Will.

In point of fact, he tried to keep those thoughts at bay, full stop. Better simply to pretend that none of that existed than to succumb and find himself reliving his father's sins. Sometimes when he got home from his walk and found the cottage empty and smelling of Will's soap, he let himself pause for a moment to want things that he couldn't have and didn't deserve. Just for that minute, he let himself want, and even that felt like an unearned indulgence.

One morning, he returned from his walk to find Daisy clearing the cobwebs from the rafters with a whisk broom. Her hair was up in a kerchief and her face was in its usual scowl. She was an accomplished scowler, managing to take the expression all the way from her pale, furrowed eyebrows to the tip of her sharp little chin, a masterful feat Martin had only seen achieved by his own father.

"You," she said, pointing the broom at him like a weapon, "need a haircut."

"You," he said, "need to mind your own business." He

resisted the urge to feel the ends of his hair, which were sweeping his jaw at a highly unfashionable length.

"You also need a shave."

That was tragically correct. He had shaved every few days ever since Will had taught him, but the looking glass was tiny and he kept missing spots. "Are you offering, or are you simply stating the obvious?"

"Offering."

He raised an eyebrow. "I can't wait to hear what you mean to extract from me in exchange." Daisy offered nothing for free, and he found that he grudgingly respected her for it.

"Nothing," she said. "I'm just tired of seeing you look like something the cat dragged in."

"Daisy, my child, I was raised by one of history's greatest liars and you are but a sad amateur. Tell me what you want from me, or leave me in peace." He pointedly sat at the table, a dog-eared copy of *Tom Jones* open before him.

"I need you to flirt with me. At the inn. In front of Jacob."

"Is Jacob the ostler? Our Casanova of the Southeast?"

"No," she said, scowling. "The ostler is a dirty old man. Jacob is one of the lads who works in the taproom."

"You'll want Will for that. He's an accomplished flirt." He remembered Will at seventeen, home on leave, rich in pocket change and tales of far-off lands, charming his way quite blatantly into the beds of more than one woman, and in such a way that years later they still asked Martin when Will was next due home. Martin had been struck dumb by jealousy, but also impressed and even proud that the friend of his childhood had turned into such a man. Will's next ship had been the *Fotheringay*, and now Martin thought that leave had probably been the last peaceful time in Will's life.

"You're better looking though," Daisy said, pulling him back to the present, "and that's what I need."

"You're blind and deluded. And I don't think I could hold up my end of a flirtation if my life depended on it. You cut my hair, I'll persuade Will to do your bidding. And I'll make sure he brushes his coat beforehand." He stuck out his hand. "Deal?"

She ignored his hand and proceeded to comb his hair with a ruthlessness he had not known possible.

"Good God, why are you like this?" he asked. "Do you mean to make my scalp bleed?"

She snorted. "No point in being sweet and gentle."

Martin, who had not once in his life considered being sweet or gentle, could not disagree. "Well, no, I quite—"

"Have you taken a look at me?"

He craned his head to get a good look. "You're . . . about sixteen. Yellow hair. Blue eyes. Clear skin. If you quit scowling, I'd say you were quite pretty."

"Nobody ever accused you of being much of a thinker, did they. If I quit scowling, and came over all sweet and gentle, I'd never have a minute to myself, now, would I?"

Much struck by this logic, Martin could only nod. "Quite."

Daisy muttered something that sounded like, "Look

what happened to my mum," but before Martin could inquire as to what she meant, she tugged his chin to the side. "Keep your head still," she snapped.

"You don't want every beau in Sussex chasing after you. Very wise. That sounds tiresome in the extreme. Perhaps that's been my secret strategy all along. I'm afraid that my good looks, combined with decent manners, would be very distracting."

He thought that he heard her laugh, but didn't dare turn his head to check. She began snipping at his hair with a pair of sewing shears, and he was half convinced she was deliberately marring his appearance until she stopped and shoved the looking glass into his hands. "How's that?" she asked.

"Huh." Martin twisted his head to various angles. "That's really not bad at all. Thank you."

She proceeded to attack his face with shaving soap and a razor, and it was only fear of having his throat slit that kept him from objecting.

"You could be a valet," he said, running his fingers over his newly smooth jaw. "Where did you learn to do that?"

"Seen my mum do it, haven't I?"

The cottage door swung open, letting in a blast of cold air. "Oh," said Will, arrested on the threshold.

"You might consider shutting the door," Martin suggested.

"Right. Yes," Will said, and proceeded to shut the door, fumbling with the latch no fewer than three times. Martin sighed. When Will was distracted, he was lucky not to walk off a cliff.

"Daisy was making me presentable."

"Right," Will said, staring. "Yes."

"You have an assignment. You're going to the Blue Boar tonight and flirting with Daisy in plain view of some young man of hers."

"She's a child!"

"Calm down. Nobody's asking you to touch her. Just bat your pretty eyes a couple of times and do whatever it was you used to do to make the blacksmith's daughter come over all sweet."

Will was now a very satisfactory shade of tomato. "I couldn't—"

"What time, Daisy?" Martin asked.

"Five. Be there for supper and then sort of loiter around afterward." With that, she swept out of the cottage.

"But I don't want to—" Will started.

"That was the price of my haircut. I'm selling your virtue. Deal with it. And put on the green coat and a clean shirt. Do our Daisy proud."

Will was still staring at him as if he had never seen a man with a proper haircut. He brought his hand up to his own thatch of shaggy brown hair. "Maybe I ought to ask Daisy to cut my hair as well."

"No!" Martin cleared his throat. "I mean, basic grooming would ruin the moody artistic effect."

Will tucked a strand of hair behind an ear. "I'm going to look like a vagrant compared to you."

"Yes, well, there's no helping that. This—" he gestured to his face "—such as it is, is the culmination of generations of Easterbrook breeding. In fact, it's all I have to show for all those generations."

Will smiled, the real smile that showed the dimple in his left cheek. "You're in a fine mood."

"It'll pass." But Martin was grinning too. How lowering that a simple haircut and a good shave could put him in such good spirits. A decent pair of trousers would probably send him into paroxysms of joy. He had forgotten how much he liked being neat and presentable. Lately he had started day-dreaming about getting his boots properly polished. He felt ungrateful, worse than ungrateful, for even wondering; he was living essentially on a friend's charity, and he didn't have the right to even think about wanting fine things. He had deliberately given all that up when he left his aunt's house, but he didn't know how to live without it.

"You all right?" Will asked, his head tipped a bit to the side as he regarded Martin.

Martin smiled tightly. "I told you it'd pass."

Will kept telling himself it was only a haircut and that there was no reason for him to be acting like such a fool about it. But every time he caught sight of Martin, freshly shaved and neatly trimmed and unarguably handsome, it was like a blow to the gut. When he noticed Martin pausing before the looking glass to preen a little, it only made things worse, for some perplexing reason—surely, vanity shouldn't make someone *more* attractive. Perhaps it was just that seeing Martin act confident and happy about anything was a bit of a thrill and a relief.

Will had known for a decade that he liked the looks of Martin, in a general aesthetic sense. He was Will's dearest friend; of course Will liked to look at him. And for the past few weeks he had been aware of an attraction, which he was doing his best not to dwell on. But now he was wondering if there was more to it than that, if maybe the combination of friendship and attraction created some third thing. Will suspected that if Martin had been anybody else, Will wouldn't have hesitated to give a name to what he was feeling.

"Off we go," Martin said after picking some invisible lint off Will's sleeve. "We don't want to keep Daisy waiting." He bustled Will out the door.

"If we're lucky, a parcel of books will be waiting for us."

"Excellent. From Hartley?"

"No, I bought them myself. The owner of the theater is going to stage the play, so I have a bit of money."

"What?" Martin elbowed him. "Were you ever going to tell me?"

"I can't quite believe it's happened. It's not much money, really. We'll get more if the play is a success, but it's only—"

"*Will.* This is excellent news." He turned to Will, flashing his most dazzling smile. Will had forgotten such a smile even existed, and was taken aback. "Congratulations."

Will stared hard at his friend, saw how his profile was caught in the setting sun, and was struck by how fleeting this

all could be. A chill, a cough, and Martin could be gone. He
was filled with a wave of—not sorrow, because the time for
that had come and gone—but the urge to make this count.
If their time was finite, then he ought to—he didn't know
what. He ought to take these tiny incandescent moments
and figure out a way to hold them in his heart. Instead he
shoved his hands in his pockets and scuffed the toe of his
boot. "Hartley is ecstatic," he said.

"But how are you?"

Will ought to have known that Martin would pick up on
his omission, but the truth was that he didn't know how he
felt. He was proud, not to mention relieved, to have earned
some money. He was nervous about having his work performed on stage in front of hundreds, if not thousands, of
people. And he was afraid that, somehow, this was going
to mean he needed to move back to London sooner than he
wanted. Hartley was already talking about how Will could
have one of the sets of rooms above the pub so they could
work together on another play. And Will did want to work
on another play, this time without Hartley having to make
weekly stagecoach trips. But—not yet. It was nearly April,
and they had been at the cottage for almost three months.
It felt like a fortnight, like a decade. And he didn't want it to
end. He knew he was being selfish and shortsighted, but for
a moment he didn't care. Hell, he couldn't even remember
the last time he had been selfish, and didn't he deserve—no,
he knew that it was lunacy to think people got what they deserved. But he might get what he wanted, and maybe the fact
that he wanted it was reason enough to ask.

"I don't want to go back to London," Will blurted out. He felt Martin's eyes on him, shrewd as ever.

"Neither do I," Martin said lightly.

"We're doing well here, right? You're healthy, I've written a play, and we're both doing better than we were a year ago."

"True," Martin said. "Although we could hardly be doing worse."

"So let's stay. We both know that we have to go back some time, but let's stay for now. For a little while longer." He swallowed. "It's just—I like being here. With you."

"I like being here with you as well," Martin said. His eyes were fixed on the lane straight ahead of him.

"I suppose I ought to ask your permission to keep using your house," Will said.

"Don't be stupid."

"So will you stay? For a bit?"

"I *said* don't be stupid. As if I would say no."

The idea of having more time together made Will almost sick with happiness. He didn't trust himself to say anything sane, and scrambled around for something that at least wasn't maudlin. "I'm thinking of getting some piglets or a couple of geese."

Now Martin turned to him and gave him a crooked smile. "Why?"

"They're easy to keep and easy to sell when we leave."

"Hmm," Martin said thoughtfully. He had obviously never considered animals in that light—of course he hadn't, he was a bloody baronet. But the empty garden around the cottage had been driving Will around the bend for months. It was a waste not to put it to good use.

"You can help me build a pen for the pigs," he said, trying to sound serious.

"I've never built a damned thing in my life," Martin said, putting on an especially fussy tone. "You can build the pen and I'll lounge around decoratively while I watch you."

God help him, but that image should not have made Will feel quite so heated. They arrived at the inn before Will could further investigate the issue. Daisy, who evidently spent her evenings pulling ale and clearing dishes at the Blue Boar, spotted them at once and beckoned them toward a table by the fire.

Will got to work straight away. He wouldn't ever describe himself as a flirt, but he supposed most flirts wouldn't. He knew how to make people feel that they were the center of the universe, that was all. There was something worth liking in nearly everybody, and it was no hardship to figure out what it was. The trick was to do so while also hinting, in the vaguest of ways, that it might be nice if they were able to continue this charming conversation in the nearest bed. That's all it was, a hint. Most of the time he didn't go to bed with anybody, or even intend to.

Well, sometimes he did go to bed with people—not so much more often than anybody else his age, and it wasn't his fault if not having much preference as to gender opened up the field quite a bit. Besides, it wasn't like he was seducing innocents or breaking up homes; he was only after a bit of companionship and comfort, just like anybody else, right?

As he flirted and teased, he knew Martin was watching him. That shouldn't have made it easier, but it did, and he decided not to think about why.

"Good lord," Martin murmured when Daisy took away their empty dishes, bending over the table in such a way as to ensure that Will got an eyeful of bosom.

"I feel like a lecherous old pervert," Will complained.

"It's for a good cause. Daisy's seemed happier this evening than she has in the past two months combined. She really is pretty. I hadn't quite noticed."

Perhaps the ale had gone to his head because this made Will choke out a laugh.

"Why are you laughing? I'm quite immune to the charms of women, as I think you know." Martin spoke the words with the hint of a challenge, his chin high.

"I do know," Will said immediately, even though he hadn't known, not really. But he had to say something affirmative before Martin got the wrong idea. He ransacked his ale-addled mind to come up with something else that might be suitable. "I'm not immune to anybody's charms," he blurted out.

Martin choked on his ale. "Good God, of all the ways to put it," he said when he recovered himself. "Your family. I mean, *really*."

That made Will laugh, and so the two of them were laughing like a pair of fools, warm and cozy by the fire. Will's heart was full with the hope that there could be more nights like this, more days in the sunshine, more time spent laughing and talking and doing all the things they hadn't been able to do before.

"I haven't seen you look so well in years," Will said as they left the inn. The night had grown cold, and he reached out to wrap Martin's muffler more securely around his neck. He let his hands linger a moment too long, let himself stand a bit too close. He told himself that he was glad to have Martin alive and near, that the drink had made him even more affectionate than usual, and that it didn't have to mean anything more than that.

"I could say the same to you," Martin said, not stepping away from Will's ministrations. And then whatever he saw in Will's eye must have given him pause because he frowned. "Let's get you home."

It was absolutely mad that after more than seven years in the navy and heaven knew how many hours spent in opium dens, all it took was three pints for Will Sedgwick to start petting at people like they were kittens.

"Your hair is soft," Will said, taking off Martin's hat and running his fingers through his hair. "Like a duckling. But all tidy, now that Daisy's cut it. Like a tidy duckling. A very well-bred duckling."

"This duckling's in *Debrett's*," Martin said, putting his chin in the air.

Will seemed in danger of wandering into a ditch, so

Martin took him firmly by the hand and returned him to the center of the lane.

"Did you know?" Will began. So they were at the Did You Know stage of inebriation, then. Martin knew it well, and suppressed a fond smile. "Did you know that your fingers are very long?" He held up their joined hands, pressing them palm to palm, as if to compare.

"Yes, well, that's generations of elegance and breeding at work." He was trying not to focus too much on the sensation of Will's skin against his own, Will's hand clasping his tightly, but something of his predicament must have shown on his face.

"Shit. I'm so sorry," Will said, dropping Martin's hand. "I forgot."

"You forgot what?" Martin asked.

"You don't like touching. It's all right, you know," Will said with the wide-eyed earnestness of the highly tipsy. "We can be friends without touching. Or with touching. There's no touching in letters."

"There is indeed no touching in letters," Martin had to agree.

"I lost all your letters on the ship."

Martin let the silence last while they walked a few paces, in case Will wanted to say anything else; as a rule, he didn't ask Will about anything that happened on board that ship, not wanting to poke at wounds that had only just healed. When the pause stretched out, Martin cleared his throat. "It's not that I don't like being touched. I like it very much. I just didn't want to give myself the wrong idea," he said, and then immediately regretted it. Well, in for a penny. "I don't mind if you touch me," he said. His face heated; he had meant only to convey that he was sufficiently in charge of his own emotions not to be led into perdition by a hand on his sleeve. But he made himself bite his tongue. Any clarification would be protesting too much. He was determined to be very normal about all of this: they were friends choosing to share a small cottage, and it would be bizarre and unnatural to insist on not being touched.

Besides, said a small and slightly drunk voice in his head, *You do like when he touches you. You like it and you could easily get him to touch you all the time.*

When they got home, they set about rebuilding the banked fire and putting their muddy boots outside the door. "If we're both to stay here for a while, then I can't let you sleep on the floor any longer," Martin said when Will dropped his pillow onto the floor before the fire. "It was one thing when I was—the patient, I suppose, and you were looking after me. But you have to let me have my pride."

"I'm really quite—"

"Oh, stuff it," Martin said. "I can't watch you sleep on the floor like a dog. Either we take turns or we share the bed." Martin knew that if he had a sliver of common sense he'd refuse to let Will into the bed with him. He wasn't even entirely certain why he was pressing the matter. Maybe he wanted to prove to himself that mere proximity to Will wouldn't transform him into a grotesquely rutting lecher—wouldn't transform him into his father. Or maybe he just liked the idea of opening his eyes and knowing Will was there. "The fact is that when I see you over there, I feel guilty and ashamed, and I don't need more of that in my life, thank you."

Martin couldn't quite make heads or tails of the look Will shot him, but it didn't matter, because a quarter of an hour later they were side by side in the bed. Martin, accustomed to having the entire mattress to himself, awkwardly tossed and turned, all the while conscious that his tossing and turning was likely keeping Will awake. Eventually Will let out a low laugh. "Do you need a bedtime story?"

"Oh, fuck off," Martin said, smiling into his pillow despite himself.

"It's worked in the past," Will reminded him, rolling onto his side so they were facing one another.

"I had half forgotten about that," Martin admitted. Sometimes, when Martin had been deemed too sick to go outdoors, Will would sneak into his room late at night. He had charted secret paths through sculleries and back staircases and once even arrived through an open window. At the time, Martin had been furious that nobody at the Grange seemed in the least bit interested in whether children were asleep in their beds or roaming about the countryside risking life and limb. Will would sit by his bed and tell Martin stories in a whisper so quiet that Martin's nurse wouldn't be wakened, and then slip out once Martin was asleep. They carried on like this for the entire summer of their fourteenth year, until one morning Martin's nurse found them both curled up together in bed. Will had fallen asleep in the middle of the story, that was all. But Martin's father was always on the lookout for vice, and within a week he announced that he had secured a place for Will in the navy. Martin had been horrified: anybody ought to have been able to see that Will had no business in the navy. He was absentminded, flighty, and sensitive. But Mr. Sedgwick was glad to have at least one of his sons' futures settled, and Will was dazzled by thoughts of adventure and faraway lands.

"You're not even listening," Will chided.

"I must be more tired than I thought," Martin said, and then faked a yawn. He remained very still, and Will was asleep in minutes.

Martin woke to discover an arm flung across his middle. He must have gasped or made some other stupid noise because the arm was immediately retracted. The next time Martin woke, Will's arm was once again around him. This time Will was pressed against Martin's back. And, oh God, this had been a terrible idea. All Martin could think of was how lovely it felt to have Will so close, as if warmth and safety were seeping into his skin. If they stayed like that, Martin would start to believe that he was the sort of person who deserved this sort of thing, that it had to mean something that their bodies fit together so well and so comfortably. He told himself that this was probably how everybody was; perhaps people just touched one another all the time and it always felt good and they let themselves like it.

He next woke to full sunlight and the sound of the door being flung open. "William Sedgwick," Mrs. Tanner bellowed. "I told you I would murder you myself if you so much as looked at Daisy."

Will, his face buried in the back of Martin's neck, hardly stirred at this intrusion. Martin extricated himself and rose to a sitting position, holding up a finger to his mouth. "Daisy asked Will to flirt with her to improve her standing with some lad who, you'll be pleased to know, is *not* the ostler," he hissed. "I assumed she had told you of her plans, and if she didn't, I apologize for not speaking to you first. I assure you that neither Will nor I have any interest in your daughter, and Will was fairly horrified by even pretending to flirt with a girl of her age."

Mrs. Tanner looked back and forth between them. Will, amazingly, was still asleep. "Oh," she said, as if recognition were dawning. "I see. Well. I hadn't figured either of you gentleman to be—well, I suppose it takes all kinds, and I do beg your pardon—"

"I beg *your* pardon, madam," Martin said. "I haven't the faintest idea what you're talking about. What I mean to say is that neither Mr. Sedgwick nor I have any interest in sixteen-year-old girls. Please curtail your wilder flights of conjecture. Be gone with you."

He had been harsh, he knew that. In that high-handed speech, he heard the echoes of his father's voice. And Mrs. Tanner hadn't even been insinuating any insult or threats of exposure. But his blood boiled at the idea of any harm coming to Will—not an insult, not a twisted bit of gossip, not a nasty rumor. The very idea made Martin want to salt the earth and burn the fields.

It was not, he realized, his best quality. It was a vindictiveness and ruthlessness that suggested he might have more in common with his father than a superficial resemblance. With a pang, he remembered the Cumberland tenants he had squeezed and used in order to raise money; that, too, had been for Will.

Mrs. Tanner was staring at him with wide eyes and Martin scrambled for something civil to say. "I apologize. I'm a bear when I wake up. Please tell Daisy she can have the morning to herself, thank you." Without replying, the woman backed out of the door.

"Back to sleep," Will mumbled, tugging Martin back to the mattress. Martin, idiot that he was, let himself be dragged down and tucked against Will's warm body, even though he knew he didn't deserve it.

CHAPTER EIGHT

Martin was simultaneously pleased and dismayed to discover that building a pig enclosure was the sort of work that required Will to take off his coat and roll up his sleeves. He had a lamentable weakness for Will's forearms, quite possibly a weakness for any part of Will's body that he chose to uncover.

"Can't put that rail up so high," Daisy said. She too had her sleeves rolled up, which explained why the two sons from a neighboring farm had come to help build the pen, and why Martin could therefore lounge on an overturned barrel rather than actually participate in any of the manual labor. "The piglets are still too little, and they'll scramble out underneath it."

Much discussion ensued, and Will proceeded to notch the wooden rail precisely where Daisy had indicated. Daisy was a font of wisdom when it came to rural living. Martin hadn't the faintest idea what she and her mother were talking about half the time, but it was clear that they managed to make do with a couple of animals and a talent for poaching. Daisy never mentioned any father, and Martin was now fully convinced that the late Mr. Tanner was an entirely fictive entity, designed to give Mrs. Tanner a scrap of respectability.

Will approached, wiping sweat off his forehead with the back of his hand. Martin got to his feet and handed him the flask of ale. Through the damp and threadbare fabric of Will's shirt, Martin could see the faint shadow of the birds that were inked on his arm. He let himself look for a moment before dragging his gaze away.

"I understand the general principle of penning pigs," Martin said. "But how does it apply to animals who can fly?"

"With chickens and ducks, there's a lot of optimism involved on all sides," Will said. "And also shoving them all into a henhouse at night. Did you know, they build hog pens differently here than they do in the north?"

Martin knew nothing of the sort and could think of few topics less fascinating, but listening to Will go on was a treat in itself. "Tell me more about your pigsties, William."

Will elbowed him. "The pig enclosure at the Grange was made of stone. There was even a little house at one end, where the pigs could get out of the sun."

"I don't remember you having pigs."

"I believe one of my father's guests let them out after reading too much Rousseau. But we did have pigs when I was very young, when my mother and Ben and Hartley's mother were around to make sure they got fed. To make sure all of us got fed, really."

Sometimes when Martin thought about conditions at the Grange during Will's childhood, he had to stop what he was doing and just seethe in anger for a little while. He pushed that thought aside for now. "So pigs in Cumberland live in stone-walled splendor. How will our Sussex pigs live?"

"In relative freedom. Rousseau might even approve. Except for the part where we'll eat them. In any event, they'll have three times the space as the Grange pigs, and Daisy and I—or Daisy and her beaux—will build a sort of portico at one end so they don't get sunburned."

"They're not the only ones in danger of getting sunburned," Martin said, and brushed his knuckles across Will's cheekbone. It was barely April, but Will had been living almost entirely out of doors these past few weeks, and his freckles were proliferating. Now, under Martin's touch, Will flushed, but he didn't move away. In fact, he looked like he wanted to move closer. Maybe sharing a bed had gotten them used to being near one another. During the fortnight since that evening at the Blue Boar, Martin noticed that Will's chair had inched closer to his own, and that Will had started doing things like adjusting Martin's lapels and clapping a hand on his shoulder in greeting. They had been waking up with arms or legs touching, and sometimes even had conversations like that without bothering to put some distance between their bodies. At first, whenever he and Will touched, the heady rush from that contact overthrew all Martin's other thoughts. Now, though, it felt almost normal. It felt safe.

Sometimes, they stood so close that Martin thought he

could lean forward and brush their lips together. It might be easy. It might not be a disaster. A kiss, and whatever a kiss might lead to, might be just another kind of touch.

"Oi! Will Sedgwick!" called a voice from the lane.

Martin dropped his hand and Will spun toward the new arrival.

"Is that—good God, Jonathan, what brings you here?"

"I'm on my way to Brighton," the stranger said. He was some years older than Will and Martin, and handsome in a bookish sort of way. Martin disliked him immediately.

"Daisy," Will called. "You can be done for the day. Martin, this is Jonathan York."

Before Martin could extend his hand, Will's friend grabbed it.

"Is this the Martin I've heard so much about? Let me see if I can remember. Sir Martin Easterbrook? Lord's sake, Will," York said, lowering his voice, "how did you rope a baronet into shacking up with you in a cottage? Not even much of a cottage either, by the looks of it."

"It's perfectly comfortable," Martin said stiffly.

"Oh, is it?" York said, somehow making the words sound like an insinuation. "Will talked about you constantly," he went on. "Drove himself half mad. Were you missing? In hiding? In prison?"

"Let him get a word in edgewise," Will said, but not unkindly. Martin rather wished it had been unkindly. He didn't like this York person, with his cheerful waistcoat and broad smile. He didn't like that Will had evidently talked about him to this man. He could only imagine what ghastly things

Will might have said about him. "Tried to starve his tenants, absolute git, probably evil." Even as he formed the thought, he knew Will would never breathe an ill word of him, but the presence of this Jonathan York made him unaccountably grumpy.

Now that Daisy and the others had cleared out, York leaned in and embraced Will, kissing both his cheeks and then holding him at arm's length as if to inspect him. "You look well, I suppose, but when can we expect you back in London? I'm afraid everything's dreadfully dull without you, and now with the news about your play, dare we hope that you'll return for opening night?"

Martin couldn't stand another minute of it. "I'll leave you be," he said to Will, then nodded coolly at York. He snatched his hat off the fence post where he had hung it, and made his way down the lane in a way he hoped didn't look too much like storming off.

He was jealous; that was no surprise. He had been jealous of all Will's friends since the earliest days of their acquaintance. When Will was at school, Martin silently seethed with jealousy of his schoolmates. He envied children from the village who played at bat and ball with Will when Martin was too sick to join them. Hell, he had even been jealous of Will's own brothers. During Will's years in the navy, Martin had found a way to envy his shipmates. He knew jealousy was pitiful, maybe even ugly, and he tried to keep it well hidden from Will. He certainly never acted on it. The jealousy was just always there, along with all of Martin's other less savory qualities. Logically, he knew that he couldn't keep Will to himself. He also knew that Will having other friends didn't make him like Martin less. But Martin was long accustomed to reason deserting him where Will was concerned.

His jealousy of this Jonathan York wasn't entirely unreasonable, though. The fellow seemed exactly like the sort of man with whom Will could have lasting companionship: affectionate and pleasant, clever and probably educated. His clothes looked respectable and clean, which likely meant he had a steady income. Martin could picture it, and he knew it was the sort of future he ought to wish for Will.

He got to a fork in the lane where Friars' Gate lay in one direction and the village in the other. With a sigh, he turned toward Friars' Gate—nothing like a cheerful reminder of one's failures to properly ruin a day. Thus far, he hadn't allowed his walks to take him further than the park that surrounded the house, but today he pushed open the creaky garden gate, made his way past overgrown hedges and the desiccated remains of the prior year's foliage. When he peered through the windows of the ground floor, he could see that the remaining furniture and fixtures were draped in holland covers. The floors were bare, the walls denuded of most art. Not having seen the house in years, and because no house looked the same through windows as it did from inside, he felt like he was peering into a stranger's home. He was surprised to find that he didn't hate the sight of the place. He didn't want to go indoors or linger a moment longer than necessary, but neither did he want to run screaming as if from the harbinger of an ancestral curse.

He could take a reasonable middle ground and figure out how to let the place. But he wasn't certain how that would work. He couldn't simply tack a notice to the front door or post an advertisement in the *Times*. Presumably, at some point there would need to be solicitors and leases involved. He could start by writing his solicitor in Cumberland, he supposed. It would be even simpler if he could swallow his pride and ask his aunt, but he knew that if he confided in her, he'd find himself living at Friars' Gate himself within a fortnight, very possibly married off to a coal heiress. His mother's younger sister and his only living relation, Lady Bermondsey was the sort of woman who couldn't see a problem without exerting herself to fix it. And Martin hated that the only solution anybody could come up with was restoring him to his place in the world—a place that was better consigned to the dust heap as far as he cared. Letting Friars' Gate would allow him to delay that inevitability, even though something within him recoiled at the necessity of being Sir Martin, even for the duration of a letter.

Before his courage deserted him, he went to the inn, got a sheet of paper from the landlord, and dashed off a letter to his solicitor.

Jonathan stayed for two hours, most of which he spent in a near unbroken monologue about theater, politics, and mutual acquaintances. Will was glad to see him, but he was also glad when the man left. The world Jonathan talked about felt as remote as a desert island, as unreal as a fairy story.

"Are you quite alone?" Martin asked stiffly, inching open the door to the cottage.

"Yes, and you could have stayed, you know."

"I didn't wish to intrude."

"You wouldn't have." Will got to his feet and crossed to the door. "It would have been a pleasure for me to have two friends together in the same place."

"Were you lovers?"

Will's eyebrows shot up. "Yes." Martin was silent for a long minute. "Does that bother you?"

"No, of course not," Martin said, plainly bothered. Martin already knew that Will sometimes went to bed with men, and implied that his own inclinations were not dissimilar, so Will doubted that was the problem. He supposed Martin might still find something wrong and shameful about it, but Will couldn't detect a trace of judgment or disgust on Martin's face. Which left—

Was Martin . . . jealous? Will had never caught Martin looking. When they woke in the morning, limbs tangled and sleep muddled, warm and snug under the quilt, Martin never let his hands stray. A few times Will wished he would, even thought about doing it himself, because it would be nice to have someone else's hands on him. The only thing that stopped him was the suspicion that for Martin there was no such thing as a friendly grope, no such thing as a cheerful shag between friends. Anything more than that seemed like it existed on the other side of a locked door, and if Will had ever had a key, he feared that it had gone missing at some point during the ordeals of the past few years.

"Let's go for a walk," Will suggested.

"I just got in from a walk," Martin responded, peeved.

"Let's go outside and sit on a rock and you can be cross with me in daylight, then."

Martin snorted, but followed Will out the door. Will gestured at the rock he had meant to sit on, but Martin waved a dismissive hand, and they kept walking into the woods.

The landscape of this part of Sussex consisted of both enclosed pasture and unenclosed heath and woodland, forming a peculiar patchwork more evident now in the spring than it had been when they arrived in winter. Raised in the country and possessing an adequate knowledge of what kind of living could be scraped from the land, Will doubted that the actual property belonging to Friars' Gate would support so much as a small farmstead, nor was it meant to. Will suspected that the previous occupant of the gamekeeper's cottage merely cleared the underbrush to make it easier for the gentlemen guests of Friars' Gate to shoot pheasants. As far as Will could tell, everyone in the village viewed the land and streams around Friars' Gate as fair game for poaching and fishing, just as much as if it had been unenclosed. And Will thought that was probably good for Martin—he saw the rabbit snares and heard the birdshot; this was a chance for him to be a good landowner, to see that he didn't need to be like his father.

They easily fell into stride as they walked along the footpath that traversed the woods. They always did, as if their bodies remembered all the rambling they had done as children, as if it didn't matter how much time had passed or where they were, or even what bad deeds they had done or had done to them.

"Oh," Will said, more an indrawn breath than an actual sound. He found himself standing before a proper bluebell wood. "I had no idea this was here." There was a bluebell wood near the Grange but he couldn't remember the last time he had happened upon it at the exact time the flowers were blooming.

"I stumbled across it a few days ago and the flowers weren't quite out yet," Martin said. "Thought you might like to see it."

"Thank you," Will said.

"You would have come across it eventually," Martin said. He was still doing his best to be prickly and fractious, but he stood so close to Will that their sleeves brushed. Lately, Martin was constantly placing himself within touching distance. Will wasn't sure he even knew he was doing it.

"I've had a lot of lovers," Will blurted out.

Martin turned toward him and blinked. "Congratulations," he said dryly, but with a smile playing at the corner of his mouth.

"Usually women, actually." Oh God, he was making this worse. His face was flaming and he didn't dare look at Martin. "In case that matters."

"Your father must rejoice that at least one of his sons might give him a grandchild," Martin said, casually examining his fingernails.

"You're impossible."

"Mmm," Martin hummed in agreement.

"My point," Will said, striving to remember what had possessed him to discuss his prior love life, "is that Jon is a friend. We've gone to bed together a couple of times but it isn't anything more than that."

"He looked at you like he might want it to be."

"Then surely I ought to run away with him immediately," Will said, throwing up his hands. "Because that's how these things work. Sit down, for heaven's sake." He gestured at a felled tree that formed a convenient bench. They sat side by side, shoulders touching.

They were dancing around the issue. He had always known that Martin was his dearest friend, but lately it had come to seem that *dearest* and *friend* didn't come close to explaining what they were to one another. And that was with the two of them as chaste as nuns; he didn't know what happened if anything sexual were added to a friendship like theirs. Martin wasn't Jonathan—a friend with whom he could blithely fall into bed. Will didn't know how to go to bed with somebody he was willing to lay down his life for. Worse than that, he didn't know how to go to bed with someone he knew he'd never walk away from. He felt like he had been dealt into a card game with stakes he didn't know and couldn't afford.

"He stopped by because he wanted to give me this," Will said, reaching into his coat pocket and bringing out a folded paper. He handed it to Martin and watched him open it.

"Is this—*The Bride of Malfi?*" Martin asked, staring at the playbill and then grinning at Will without a single trace of his earlier irritation. "And it's opening in two weeks? I'm going. I don't even care if the city is blanketed in smoke and awash in a foul miasma of disease. I need to see it. I'll sit in the pit and wear a disguise so my aunt won't recognize me. A false nose. A gray wig. A plague doctor's mask."

Will laughed and grabbed Martin's hand. Seized by mad impulse and pure affection he brought Martin's hand to his mouth and kissed his knuckles. He heard Martin's sharply indrawn breath, saw his eyes go wide, and nearly did it again. He could imagine letting his lips linger just a little, brushing across the back of Martin's hand. But he couldn't—he shouldn't.

Instead of trying to say anything, instead of doing anything that might make it worse, Will shifted his grip on Martin's hand so their fingers were laced together, then rested their joined hands on his thigh. It felt like a bridge, personal and intimate but not necessarily sexual; he wanted to show Martin that he was offering—maybe not more, but everything he had.

"Is that . . . all right?" Will asked, not even completely sure what he was asking about.

Martin didn't say anything, and he turned his attention back to the bluebells, but Will felt a brief squeeze on his hand.

"I think I'll always be jealous," Martin said several minutes later, but as if he were continuing their previous conversation. "I envied your shipmates, William, in case you wonder how perverse my jealousy can be."

Will let out a burst of shocked laughter. "That might be the first time anybody envied a single soul on the *Fotheringay*."

"I envied that they were near you, not anything else, obviously. Just that they were near you. I made Father hire a French tutor because I was jealous that your mother could speak to you in a special language."

That was so ridiculous that Will couldn't keep a straight face. "You must have been eight years old."

"Possibly seven. I started early on my path toward maniacal jealousy." Martin spoke lightly, but Will could hear the self-reproach beneath.

"But, Martin. That's—it's darling." He remembered Martin at that age—tiny and imperious—and could picture him furiously studying his conjugations.

"I feel certain you shouldn't think so." Will didn't need to turn his head to know Martin was blushing. "You're really a terrible judge of character." The air was heavy with the scent of bluebells and the weight of everything they were almost saying.

"I thought of you every day," Will said quietly. "Sometimes I thought you had to know, even from the other side of the world." He swallowed. "I had your letters all but memorized." He thought of that packet of letters, and how he had clung to it like a talisman to a dead God, like a latchkey to a home that had burned to the ground. Sometimes, if he stopped to wonder what had happened to that carefully folded and refolded stack of papers, tied and retied until the string broke, he thought his heart might break. "I don't mind you being jealous," he finally said.

"You ought to. It's the sort of thing my father would do."

"No, your father would take it out on the person he was

jealous about. You were properly civil to my friend, then sulked for two minutes and brought me to a lovely bluebell wood to make things better."

He heard Martin let out a soft breath and knew he had gotten it right.

Chapter Nine

Will had been gone all day, first running errands for Mrs. Tanner and then inspecting some piglets he wished to buy. He was tired, hungry, and more than a little dusty when he got home, and therefore not in the best possible frame of mind when the first thing he heard upon opening the door was a cough.

Will looked at his friend's pale cheeks, heard the hacking cough, and gritted his teeth. "I'm sending for the doctor."

"It's a cold." Martin sat at the table, a cup of tea before him and a book open on his lap.

"I'm serious. Have you been like this since I left this morning?"

"It's a cold, you silly man," Martin repeated, but he didn't sound like he believed it.

"That might have sounded more convincing if you hadn't been wheezing while you said it," Will observed. He turned back toward the door. "I'll be back in an hour with Mr. Booth."

"I wish you wouldn't. I mean, at least sit down with me for a minute and tell me how your day went before you turn me over to the not particularly tender mercies of the physician."

There was something in Martin's voice that was more than the usual sniping. He tried to remember how Martin had reacted during their visit to the doctor in London, but Martin had barely been conscious at the time. "You've never even met Mr. Booth. He might be perfectly nice."

"They're all the same," Martin grumbled. "Poking and prodding and bloodletting, followed by medicines that make me too weak to even sneeze properly, and all of it generally accompanied by ominous lectures and calls to prayer."

"I won't let him do anything you don't want," Will promised. "And if he tries to lecture you, I'll kick him out."

"You say that, but when he starts going on about how I'll die without some patent remedy that does nothing but make me vomit, you'll sing a different tune."

Will passed a hand over his mouth. "Look. You said you prefer when this sort of thing is out in the open, so I'm just going to tell you that if you die in the night, I'll feel better if I know that I did everything possible to help you."

Martin narrowed his eyes. "Do you know, that's almost exactly what my father used to say before locking me in my bedroom and drugging me stupid. To be fair, I'm not entirely sure whether he hoped to improve my lungs or my morals, but the principle stands."

Will stepped forward and put his hand to Martin's forehead. "You have a fever."

Martin ignored him. "He was such a hypocrite. To think

that he was carrying on with Hartley at the same exact time he was punishing me for even looking at you."

Will's heart stuttered in his chest. He held one of Martin's cold hands in between both of his and rubbed, as if bringing warmth to this one part of Martin could restore him to health. "Your father was a piece of shit and I wish he were alive just so I could kill him again."

"You'd have to wait your turn."

Will crouched before him, not letting go of Martin's hand. "All right. Can I send for the doctor tomorrow, if you aren't feeling better?"

"Do you know, that's why he sent you away. He found us in bed together and jumped to conclusions. So he found you a place in the navy."

"That's not what happened. Nobody sent me away." Will brushed the hair off Martin's forehead so he could get a better look at his eyes. Glassy, too bright. Will frowned. "We'll talk about this when you're well. For now, tell me if I can get the doctor tomorrow."

"Leave off, Will. I get to decide. Only me. I'm not delirious or unconscious, and you need to stop."

Will got to his feet and added a log to the fire, then hung the kettle over the flames. He stayed silent until the tea had steeped, then poured a fresh cupful for Martin.

"Should I apologize for having brought you to the doctor in London?" he asked softly. "I didn't know what else to do. I don't want to take your choices away. Ever. I just—my mother was very much the heroic martyr. She'd let things get to a desperate state before even agreeing to lie down. Once she fainted while hanging out the wash and we didn't even find her for hours. And then we all blamed ourselves for not noticing. I'm trying to do better by you than I was able to do by her."

Martin frowned into his teacup. "You cannot possibly know how badly I wish you didn't have to tend another invalid."

"You're not another invalid, you idiot."

"See," Martin said, his mouth curving in the beginnings of a smile, "now I know you don't really think I'm dying because you wouldn't have called me an idiot."

"That just goes to show how little you know. I'm sure I called you an idiot ten times a day that first week we were here, and I couldn't have been more positive that you were about to die."

"You're a terrible liar, Will, so don't even try. I remember you calling me sweetheart, and love, and all manner of soft things."

"I did." Will swallowed. "And you told me to stop."

Martin rolled his eyes and then slid his hand across the table so his fingertips brushed Will's.

"What's this?" Will raised an eyebrow. "Is this your way of telling me I can call you those things again?"

Martin was blushing and Will didn't think it was just because of the fever. "If you insist."

Will grinned and got to his feet. "Time for supper, love."

"Insufferable," Martin muttered.

Martin's fever crept throughout the evening, and Will

tried to tell himself he was overreacting. After all, Martin wasn't coughing blood, and he ate half a loaf of bread along with his stew for supper, so maybe it really was just a cold. But for a consumptive, mightn't a simple cold be truly dangerous? Will wished he knew what he was supposed to be doing. He was gripped with the fear that he was doing wrong by Martin, and that anybody else could have done better.

It was a rare cloudless night, and Martin could only catch the most futile of glimpses of the starry sky through the cottage's tiny windowpanes. When Will's breathing finally grew deep and steady, and the arm he had flung over Martin loosened its grip, Martin eased across the mattress and then gingerly set his feet on the floor. Carefully, he managed to stand without the bed frame squeaking. He cracked the door open just enough to slip outside.

It wasn't so very cold, and besides, he had a fever. Being in the cool night air was probably a good idea, even. Tentatively, he took a deep breath and found that he could almost fill his lungs. His head ached, but that was nothing new. Even his fever wasn't particularly troubling—it wasn't like he was actually seeing things or fainting. He was almost certain that this wasn't a worsening of his consumption. Probably this time, at least, he'd recover. He was less certain about the next time, and the time after that. Because there would be future illnesses, and eventually there would be one from which he couldn't recover. Even if it were forty years away, it still would come. It probably was the fever making the obvious seem profound, but Martin felt struck by how finite and precious his time was.

Behind him he heard the door open and the sound of Will's bare feet on the ground.

"What the hell," Will said. "It's the middle of the night and you don't even have on a dressing gown. Or shoes. Jesus Christ, are you trying to kill yourself?"

Martin forbore from pointing out that they didn't have a dressing gown. He crossed his arms and gave Will his best glare. "I thought I saw a shooting star."

"You thought—the sky will be teeming with shooting stars in the summer. And it'll be warmer. We'll make a regular picnic of it, I promise. Just get inside, all right?"

It wasn't often that Martin actually got angry with Will, but now he was. "No," he said, clenching his fists. "I want to look at the goddamn stars. They may still be here in the summer, but maybe I won't, and I don't want to wait." Will stood perfectly still, his eyes dark circles reflecting the moon. "I don't want to wait for anything anymore."

"Right," Will said after a moment. "Right." He went indoors and returned with the pillows and blankets from their bed, and arranged them on the ground against one wall of the house. "Mrs. Tanner will think we've taken leave of our senses," he muttered. "Come here," he said, sitting with his back to the wall. Martin lowered himself to sit beside Will, but Will stopped him. "No, it'll be warmer like this." He guided Martin to sit between his legs, and Martin leaned against Will's chest, no fewer than three quilts pulled up to his chin. It was lovely just being this close to Will, just knowing this was something he was allowed. He could feel Will's heartbeat against his shoulder blade, could feel him breathe. Even without the stars, this would have been enough.

"You can see Ursa Major," Will said, gesturing to a patch of sky near the plane tree. "And if you look for Polaris, which is right over the overhang on the pig pen, you'll find Ursa Minor."

Martin supposed that if he squinted he could detect a star that was brighter than the others, but as for the rest of them, he'd have to take Will's word for it. "Did you learn these at sea?"

"Not those. Everybody knows those. I remember showing them to you when we were boys."

"I always suspected you made half of those up, like you made up the stories you told me." Martin was wondering if perhaps he needed spectacles—if, somehow, in decades of being tended by various nurses and medical men, they had all missed something as obvious as that.

"I made some of it up, sure," Will said, and Martin laughed. Will kissed his temple and Martin found himself pressing into it, curling his body even closer against Will's. He let out a sigh, something between relief and anticipation, because he had wanted this for so long, just a sign that he wasn't the only one who wanted. He knew he was wrong to want this, knew that Will would be throwing away all his goodness and honor on someone as unworthy as Martin. Then, as if that sigh had given voice to everything Martin felt, Will kept kissing him—first his forehead, then his cheek, then the side of his neck, all while stroking his hands up and down Martin's sides.

"God," Martin said. Every nerve in his body felt alive with sensation. This—whatever it was, this heady combination of arousal and affection—didn't quite push away all the unpleasant illness-related sensations, but rather coexisted alongside them.

"Is this what you wanted?" Will murmured into Martin's shoulder, his voice raspy.

Something about that question brought Martin up short—he imagined Will doing all this to humor him, and it made him want to shy away.

"I mean," Will said, "are you all right with me holding you like this?"

"Yes," Martin said immediately.

"Good."

Martin suspected he was supposed to be doing something. With his hands, perhaps, or more likely his mouth. He doubted that most of Will's many lovers had just sat there in his lap. And yet, Will hardly seemed to be suffering. At that moment he was nuzzling into the place where Martin's neck met his shoulder, as if he wanted to get as near to Martin as he could. At the same time, Martin could very plainly feel Will's erection pressing against his back. There was no ignoring it—except Will did seem to be ignoring it. God, Martin wanted to touch him. He wanted to lie down and have Will's body cover him, press him into the ground, never ever stop kissing him.

"You know, I thought the consumption killed all that," Martin said, letting out a shaky breath.

"Killed what?" Will asked, moving so he could nuzzle into the other side of Martin's neck.

"My prick, William, pay attention. I thought it was broken." He heard Will wheeze and felt him shaking against Martin's back. "You had better not be laughing at me."

"I'm not. It's just funny. Especially since every morning I see for myself that it's working perfectly fine."

"Well, *now* it is, especially since I wake up with yours ramming me in the thigh half the time." Without even planning to, he pushed back, gently pressing against Will's length.

Will hissed and jerked his hips forward, then stayed there, not moving, just holding their bodies close together.

Then Martin sneezed and Will handed him a handkerchief so he could blow his nose, and the tension was broken. Or, rather, not broken, just eased enough that they could live with their arousal and not feel like they had to do anything about it.

When they went indoors, Will threw open the curtains and shoved the bed against the wall, announcing that this way Martin could see the stars without having to go outside if he didn't want to, then pulled Martin down into bed beside him. They fell asleep tangled up together, and the last thing Martin remembered before falling asleep was the feel of Will's fingers carding through his hair.

The next morning Martin was no better and grudgingly agreed to let Will send for Mr. Booth. As soon as the doctor walked through the door, Will almost sagged with relief to finally have an expert on hand.

His hopes were dashed almost immediately. "Not much to be done," the doctor said, clucking over Martin. "He needs brisk walks and fresh air. No need to keep the fire burning quite so high."

Brisk walks and fresh air? The physician in London had advised rest and warmth and spoken at length about the dangers of drafts. Will had no idea whose advice they were meant to follow.

The doctor took a vial out of his bag. "And a spoonful of this, whenever the coughing gets too bad for him to sleep."

"What's in it?" Martin asked.

"What's in it?" the doctor repeated, as if startled to hear his patient speak. "Things that will help you get better, young man."

"I believe he wants to know the ingredients," Will said, already regretting having sent for the doctor.

"I see," Mr. Booth said, as if Will had asked him something highly inappropriate. "Camphor, peppermint oil, tincture of opium, licorice, and honey. I mix it up myself, and can assure you—"

"I won't take it," Martin said. "Please remove it."

"I'll just put it here by your bed—"

"I said to remove it," Martin repeated, every inch the heir of Lindley Priory.

"Thank you, Mr. Booth, but that'll be all." Will paid the man his fee and sent him on his way. "I can afford medicine," he said quietly upon reentering the cottage.

"I'm well aware. But there's no sense in paying for a thing we already have."

Will looked at the assemblage of vials and bottles that stood on the chimneypiece. On the last market day, Will had stocked up on the remedies everybody seemed to recommend for a persistent cough. Peppermint oil, camphor, and licorice were all there, not to mention willow bark. The only ingredient they didn't have was—Will's face heated. "Tell me you didn't turn that medicine down because you don't trust me in the same room as opium."

From the look on Martin's face, Will knew he was right. Will shoved his hands in his pockets and stared up at the ceiling. "I'm going for a walk," he said, striving to keep his voice calm and failing utterly.

He walked to the hill overlooking Friars' Gate. That was where Martin ought to be, a house like that, with people who knew how to take care of him. He was sick with shame that Martin turned down a medication that might have brought him some relief only because he was worried about Will. That winter, Will had eyed that bottle of laudanum, had inhaled its peculiar odor and thought about what it would feel like to swallow just a little, but he hadn't done it. Partly because that laudanum belonged to Martin, partly because he didn't want to go down that path again, and, if he were honest, partly because he doubted the amount of opium in the tincture would have had much of an effect on him. But he had been able to resist.

When Will got back to the cottage, Martin was out of bed and in the chair by the fire, wrapped in a quilt. "Let me talk first," Martin said. "My refusing that medicine has nothing to do with not trusting you. I was with you those first few months after you got home."

"I know, and I'm grateful."

"I'm not looking for gratitude," Martin snapped. "I saw how the laudanum affected other people in those places. I saw how desperate people got when they were in the habit of taking it. And I also saw how much relief it brought you, at a time when nothing else seemed to help you at all. From all that, I can infer that it's taken an effort for you no longer to use the stuff, and I don't want you to be forced to look at it every day in your own home."

Will dug his fingernails into the meat of his thighs. "The first two weeks we were here, I gave you laudanum around the clock until the bottle ran·out. I was sorely tempted to help myself. But that's going to be the case for the rest of my life and—damn it, Martin, if you let my own bad choices ruin your health, I won't forgive you. I won't forgive myself."

"Your bad choices," Martin repeated, his voice suddenly gentle. "Will. When you came back to England with your mind half gone and your back still bleeding, I don't think a damned thing you did was much of a choice."

Will sucked in a breath. They didn't really talk about that. Will didn't talk about it with anybody. The events had been reported in the papers. The facts were there for anybody who wanted to know. No need for Will to have to think about it more than he already did.

"As far as this medicine," Martin went on. "Laudanum helps me sleep but it gives me nightmares. However, it does make me cough less and sometimes that's worth it. If I ever need it, you have my permission to do what it takes to get it. But perhaps give it to Mrs. Tanner to keep."

"I don't need to be babied."

"It's not about need, is it? It's about being comfortable in our home. I know you won't let the doctor do things I don't want, and you know you don't have to think about opium any more than you already do. That seems fair, doesn't it? It's just taking care of one another."

Will was aware that if it hadn't been for the fever, Martin wouldn't be speaking half so freely. He crossed the room and kissed the top of Martin's head. "You're right. I know you're right."

"If you can be stupid for me, then I can be stupid for you."

"You're stupid no matter what you do," Will said, trying very hard to sound like he wasn't about to cry.

CHAPTER TEN

"Mr. Sedgwick! You've been fiddling with that spar for five minutes!" Mrs. Tanner called from the ground. "Have you gone daft?"

Slightly, Will thought. His mind had been in a muddle all day. "Sorry, Mrs. Tanner." He gave the spar—the hazel sticks that held the bunches of straw in place—a final check and moved on to the next part of the roof that needed patching.

The Tanners' cottage was in a state of dilapidation that spoke to years of repairs that had been put off and parts that had been too pricey to purchase. It was a state Will knew well from his own childhood home: the Grange was always leaking from someplace or another, the fences always had a gap through which animals got in or out, and the chimneys smoked no matter the weather. The adults of the Grange hadn't been practically minded people; perhaps it was difficult to think about poetry and broken pump handles at the same time. Except—nobody would accuse Will of being a practical person. He was the coauthor of a play that he was fairly certain critics would dismiss as a trifling piece of nonsense. But he knew how to stop a leak, how to fix a creaky hinge, how to do all the other things that made a place safe and comfortable for the people who lived there. The difference was that Will gave a damn about the safety and comfort of the people in his care.

Will thought back to his rooms in London. There had been a fungus growing out of the windowsill and not a single uncracked windowpane. He had one decent shirt and forgot to eat more days than he remembered. He might know how to do a good many practical things, but he wasn't likely to bestir himself to do them on his own behalf. All the work he had done on the cottage and at Mrs. Tanner's had been for Martin. Broken fences and runaway pigs were solvable problems and gave him something to show for his labors. Left up to his own devices he dwelt on all the things that couldn't be fixed.

"God help you and save you, Mr. Sedgwick," Mrs. Tanner called. "Get down from there before you fall. You're off with the fairies. I ought to tie you to my apron strings."

"Woolgathering," Will said sheepishly. "I'm not going to fall, though." He was pretty sure that after his years at sea, he couldn't fall off anything even if he tried. "There's one more spot that needs work, so pass up that last bundle, if you please."

"If you say so," said Mrs. Tanner, hefting the bundle of straw and passing it to where Will stood at the top of the ladder. "But I'm giving myself gray hairs watching you, so I'll be in the vegetable garden if you need me."

Will secured the final patch and then climbed onto highest rung, checking with his hands for any places that might soon wear thin.

"Well," called a voice that was decidedly not Mrs. Tanner's. "This is a sight."

Will looked over his shoulder and saw Martin grinning up at him, bareheaded, his hands in his pockets. He lowered himself to the ground. "It's good to see you out and about."

"I told you it was a mere cold," Martin said. His voice was laden with a degree of smugness that would have been unbearable if Will hadn't been so fond of him.

"You seem to expect me to be quite put out to have been wrong," Will said, nudging him with an elbow as soon as he reached the ground. "I'm *glad* it was only a cold, you daft bastard."

"Daft bastard," Martin said, sighing dramatically. "I suppose I'll have to be at death's door if I want to be called sweetheart again."

Will paused halfway through brushing the straw from his trousers. He thought he had understood what Martin meant the other night when he said he didn't want to wait, and was pretty sure he hadn't only been referring to stargazing. But he thought they'd spend weeks edging closer, testing boundaries and limits. Will hadn't expected anything so blunt; Martin rarely came out and said what he wanted. Instead he hinted, suggested, slid meaning into the space between words that hadn't been spoken. By Martin's standards, this sideways remark would be an outright proposition from anyone else.

No—it was the equivalent of being pressed against the wall behind a molly house. Will was faintly shocked.

"Death's door? Two minutes ago it was a common cold," Will said blandly, "*sweetheart*. And here I was wondering whether I had to wait for you to jackass around in the middle of the night again to come up with an excuse to get you back in my lap." When he glanced over, Martin had flushed to the tips of his ears.

Really, Will just wanted to make Martin feel good, whatever that meant to Martin. If that meant soft words and gentle touches that never progressed to anything heated, that would be more than enough. Martin had spent a lifetime with too few good things. As far as what Will wanted—yes, he wanted to kiss Martin, to please him, to strip him bare and get his mouth on every inch of him. He had been thinking about that more and more, and now it was hard to be in the same room as Martin without noticing things—how his throat worked when he swallowed his tea, the way he sometimes blew a stray lock of hair off his forehead, the length of his legs, the smell of his skin.

"What else needs to be done before you leave?" Martin asked.

Will made his way across the garden to where Mrs. Tanner knelt in what appeared to be a potato patch. "Do you want me to fix that fence rail today or wait until we have Daisy around, ma'am?" he called. It was a two-person job, and the woman looked too knackered to hold up her end of a rail.

"It'll keep until—oh!" Mrs. Tanner broke off when she

saw Martin standing behind Will. "You gave me a fright," she said, clutching her heart with one hand.

"I'm afraid she definitely knew my father," Martin said grimly once they were on the path back to the cottage. "And odds are he was not particularly good to her."

"Where your father's concerned, those are always the winning odds," Will agreed. "That doesn't mean she knows who you are, though."

"I'm going to have to tell her, I think. She's poaching from under my nose and I ought to at least tell her that I don't mind."

Will considered this. "I don't know if that'll help or make things worse. If you tell her who you are, you're letting her know you could make trouble if you wanted."

"Then what do I do? I'm trying to do right by them. I like her, and I even like Daisy, despite her foul temper. Because of her foul temper, if I'm honest."

"Birds of a feather," Will murmured, then smiled when Martin elbowed him. "I wish I had an answer for you, but I don't. I think you have to earn their trust somehow."

When they reached the cottage, Will glanced down at his sweaty clothes. "I'm going to wash up," he announced.

For some time, Martin had been going to great pains to avoid seeing Will unclothed, but Will hadn't understood precisely why. Now he knew that Martin fleeing the cottage when Will began stripping was Martin trying to be decent. And God knew Martin had precious few models of what it looked like when a man decided to be decent, so Will was sort of touched by this bashfulness, and he tried to meet

Martin halfway by announcing well in advance when and where he planned to be naked. Will didn't much care about nakedness himself; he figured that was the natural result of four brothers and several years in close quarters at sea. He knew some people were troubled by the scars on his back, even more so if they knew their origin, but other than that he supposed his body was as unremarkable as anybody else's.

When he finished, shivering but clean and dressed in fresh clothes, he went indoors. Martin had set their little table with the plain earthenware dishes and tin spoons Will had unearthed in the loft, and when Will walked in he was fidgeting with one of the plates, turning it around so a chip wouldn't be visible from Will's seat. It was such a small and homely gesture, so totally pointless—Will didn't care about chipped crockery, but obviously Martin did, which was what made it sweet. And it was even sweeter because this was one of the days Mrs. Tanner didn't make their supper: all this effort was for bread and cheese.

"You're nothing like your father," Will said. "And I think I've known you longer than anybody else alive, so you should probably concede my expertise on the topic."

Martin gave him a tiny, crooked smile. "I'm glad you think so, at least."

"I know so," Will said, crossing the room to stand close enough to Martin that he was worried his wet hair would drip onto the other man.

"Will," Martin said. "I really don't know what I'm doing. I mean, not in any aspect of life, obviously, but especially not this." He gestured at the space between their bodies.

Will wanted to say that he didn't know either, that this, somehow, felt like uncharted waters. Instead he put his hand on Martin's hip. Martin shuddered. By now Will knew Martin wasn't flinching so much as bracing for something good, like a child about to get a spoonful of treacle or an extra bedtime story.

"Listen," Martin said, his eyes squeezed shut, "what I'm saying is that I haven't done this before, and I haven't wanted to. But I haven't wanted to want to, if you understand."

"I'm not sure I do, but I'd like to." With his thumb, he rubbed a circle into Martin's hip.

Martin let out a shaky laugh. "That makes two of us. With the people you've been with, it was good, right?"

Will raised his eyebrows. "I hope so?" Then he understood Martin's meaning. "When I've been with somebody, it's—it's a chance for two people to make one another feel good. And special, and cared for, and any number of pleasant things. Just because people like your father take something good and make it into something twisted and wrong doesn't mean that the act itself is the problem." He swallowed. "Anything we do, it's you and me. Whether it's going to bed together or playing cards or eating supper. I want you to like whatever we do together. That's the most important thing to me."

Martin nodded, and Will wondered if he had just needed to hear someone tell him that what he wanted wasn't inherently evil. Will hoped Martin had known it already and just needed reassurance. As Will watched, Martin brought his hand up slowly, as if giving Will time to stop him, then cupped Will's jaw in his hand. With the pad of his thumb, he traced Will's lower lip, all the while looking like he had been pole-axed. Then he leaned in and replaced his thumb with his lips, brushing over Will's mouth with his own. It was gentle, sweet, barely a kiss at all, but Will felt something unexpected and fierce coil up inside him.

Martin pulled away, his eyes wide and his fingertips covering his mouth, and Will knew he looked just as dazed.

Bemused, Martin watched Will pile pillows against the headboard before leaning back against them, still fully clothed, his arms stretched out to either side. Martin's mouth went dry with some unholy combination of nerves and lust. "Bring a book," Will said.

"What does a book have to do with anything?" Martin asked.

"We're going to read it," Will said, as if books were a very normal part of this sort of thing. Martin, despite his ignorance, was fairly certain they were not. "So pick something you like."

Martin turned toward the shelf that Will had put up over the chimneypiece. Over the last few months, the cottage had started to fill with books. It was, he supposed, only to be expected that Will would spend all his money on books rather than a decent coat, not that Martin minded the steady supply of reading material. He ran his finger over the spines. There was a well-worn copy of Blake, which he dismissed out of hand. He did not want poetry, especially not mad poetry. A novel, then. He did not want to read about unfortunate young ladies trapped in attics or cellars or fleeing from cursed ancestral homes, as that struck rather too close to the heart, and besides he had read all of them already. Nor did he fancy reading about genteel young people who saved their families through a combination of pluck and good character. He wanted misadventure and bad character. His hand alit on a well-read volume and he grinned. He crossed to the bed and handed it to Will.

"Really?" Will asked. "Seriously?"

"It's one of my favorites, and you don't have *Journal of a Plague Year.*"

"*Journal of a*— Do you need to have seduction explained to you?"

Squabbling was easy, familiar, safe ground. Martin already felt better. He pulled off his boots and settled onto the bed beside Will. "You can start reading to me whenever you want," he said primly, pulling the covers up to his chin.

"Oh no," Will said. "You're reading to me. I have other things to do with my mouth."

Martin made a noise that he hoped was a dismissive snort but was probably closer to a moan. But he opened the book and started reading at the frontispiece. "*The Fortunes and Misfortunes of the Famous Moll Flanders*, etcetera," he began. "'Who was born in Newgate, and during a life of continued variety for threescore years, besides her childhood, was twelve year a whore, five times a wife (whereof once to her own brother),'"—perhaps Will was correct, and this was not an inspired choice— "'twelve year a thief, eight year a transported felon in Virginia—'"

"Shove over," Will said, squeezing between Martin and the mountain of cushions behind them, one leg to either side of Martin's.

Martin continued reading, and Will did nothing more than wrap his arms around Martin's chest and rest his chin on Martin's shoulder.

"You're skipping bits," Will said. "You realize I can see the words."

"Of course I am." Martin flipped forward several pages. "I'm getting to the part where she—ah, there we are. 'Thus I gave up myself to a readiness of being ruined without the least concern.' See, it's thematically relevant."

"Am I meant to ruin you? I didn't know men ruined one another, but I suppose we could give it a go."

"No," Martin said, reaching behind him and swatting the top of Will's head with the book. "You'd be hard-pressed to find a happier heroine in all of literature."

"In literally the next clause," Will said, taking the book in his hands and jabbing a finger at the clause in question, his other hand coming to rest on Martin's stomach in a way that seemed accidental, "she says that other women ought to learn from her bad example."

"Yes, but she doesn't believe it. And we're not meant to believe it either, obviously. If we judge Moll, then we're judging ourselves for wanting to read about it."

Will made a skeptical sound but kissed Martin's temple and pulled him closer.

"Honestly, William, I can feel your erection. Don't tell me you judge Moll for going to bed with the wrong people when you could not have found a less suitable bedmate in the kingdom. In any kingdom."

Will pressed a kiss right underneath Martin's ear, and—oh, he hadn't expected that to feel so lovely. One of Will's hands was splayed on Martin's thigh, and Martin was not sure when it happened but it seemed that he had interlaced his fingers with Will's.

"The penniless and consumptive son of your brother's mortal enemy," Martin went on.

"You are so dramatic," Will muttered before again kissing that spot by Martin's ear.

"Your brother's enemy," Martin repeated with emphasis, "and who is, one might observe, a man."

"One might indeed," Will murmured into his neck. Martin was certain he could feel the man's smile.

"She's dealt such a bad hand," Martin went on. "Every human being in her life is useless or worse. And throughout it she's . . . delighted. Find me another character—a woman, no less—half as happy."

Will tugged his collar open and kissed his shoulder. "Keep talking."

Martin was not quite sure how much longer he could talk, though. Will's mouth was everywhere he could comfortably kiss, his hands equally busy. And Martin wanted more now, and he let himself want it. He turned his head to the side, hoping Will would know what to do, and then Will's mouth was on his, hot and soft. Just when Martin was getting used to the bizarre feeling of lips touching his own, Will pulled away.

"Bad angle," he murmured, and got out from behind Martin in order to kneel over him, gently taking the book from Martin's hands and placing it on the windowsill.

If that had been a bad angle, then this was a very good angle, because Will was above him, one hand threaded in Martin's hair, holding him close, but also sort of petting him. Martin put a tentative hand up to Will's head, letting his overlong waves slip silkily through his fingers. He let his other hand find Will's waist. The tip of Will's tongue sought out Martin's lower lip, and Martin heard himself gasp in response. When Will pulled away, just enough to put an inch or so of space between their mouths, Martin pushed up to close the gap. Will kissed him harder then, propping himself up on one elbow, his tongue slipping between Martin's lips. That made Martin arch his back, desperate for more contact. Will only stopped kissing him to whisper some utter nonsense. "So good," or "so sweet," or even, "you're lovely, just look at you." Martin was certain they were both going to be embarrassed about all of this, but he couldn't bring himself to care.

Will's shirt had come untucked, possibly because Martin was clutching it in one fist, and now Martin had an expanse of warm skin within his reach. He smoothed a palm down Will's side, then splayed his fingers over Will's lower back. Martin could feel the length of Will's erection against his belly, and knew Will could feel the same. Every time they shifted, Martin got a hint of friction, just a suggestion of what might happen if they let things progress.

"Can I take off my shirt?" Will asked. "I want your hands on me." Something about the way he asked—gentle but needy—made Martin's hands shake in his effort to help get the shirt over Will's head. He was so glad there was still enough light streaming through the clouded windows to see by. He had seen Will shirtless before, dozens of times this spring alone. But up close, and with permission to touch, Martin's mouth watered. He felt the coarse hair on Will's chest, then traced a finger around one pectoral muscle.

Will swore, then cleared his throat. Feeling especially daring, he kissed Will's collarbone, then pushed himself up on an elbow to press an open-mouthed kiss to Will's neck. Will rolled them over so now Martin was on top, and while he missed the feeling of Will's warm body pressing him into the mattress, he loved the sight of Will spread out beneath him. Martin bent his head and kissed the birds on Will's upper arm, then his shoulder, then pressed a line of kisses up his jaw.

"Please," Will said.

Anything, Martin wanted to say. But he needed some direction as to what that anything might be. "Please what?" he asked.

"Please . . . darling?" Will somehow managed to look mischievous and desperate at the same time.

"What do you want me to do, you idiot?" Martin asked, trying to sound arch but smiling fondly.

"Can I take your shirt off?"

Why the hell not, Martin figured. If Will didn't like pale, underfed men then he wouldn't be in bed with Martin, now, would he? Any shyness Martin may have possessed was quickly whisked away by Will's eager hands stroking his back and his lovely mouth kissing Martin's neck and chest. Will's eyes were wide now, the brown nearly turned to black. His lips were swollen with kissing and he was short of breath. Martin suspected he was in much the same state. Every time they moved, their hips rubbed against one another, and even through the layers of fabric, Martin felt out of his mind with want.

"We can take our trousers off, you know," Will said.

That shouldn't have come as a surprise. People took off their trousers when having sex. He was twenty-three years old. He knew that. He knew that taking off his godforsaken trousers was the logical culmination of all this kissing. He also knew that he wanted—well, whatever Will wanted.

"Or we can keep them on," Will said, in the same easy tone of voice. "We can keep kissing or we can stop. We can go for a walk. We can have supper. You can read to me."

"What do you want?"

"Any of those things. I want a chance for us to make one another feel good, and any of those options would do that, I think."

Martin raked his gaze down Will's body, from his untidy hair to his red mouth down to the extremely obvious erection in his trousers. "Go for a walk, indeed. I'd like to see you try in that condition."

"What would you suggest, then?" Will said, adjusting himself so casually Martin had to catch his breath.

"Trousers off," Martin whispered.

Will had his own off in about two seconds, and then lay a hand on Martin's waistband, his fingers curling suggestively under the fabric. "May I?"

Martin nodded, unable to take his eyes off Will, fully naked now, kneeling beside him, his cock jutting up toward his stomach. Then he felt his trousers sliding down his hips, cool air on his exposed skin.

"Oh fuck," Will whispered, looking down at him with something like reverence. Martin almost rolled his eyes, but then he felt Will's hand wrap around him. It was too much, the feeling of someone else handling him when he had tried so hard not to even handle himself.

"Wait," he choked out, and Will withdrew his hand immediately. "Let's go back to kissing." Kissing was good. Will seemed to agree. They were in perfect accord. As they kissed, he could feel Will's hard length against him. Martin wanted to touch him but didn't know if he was allowed—and he knew he was being incredibly stupid because Will had just touched him as if it were a perfectly normal and expected thing to do while naked and in bed with someone, which was compelling evidence that he would not mind his own cock being touched. And yet—

"You all right?" Will murmured.

"It's. Um." He waved a hand in the general direction of their pelvises. "You," he added eloquently. "My hand."

That was probably the moment Will realized he was in bed with a lunatic. Something crossed his expression like sudden understanding. But instead of scrambling to get dressed and beating a hasty retreat, he nodded. "Will you touch it for me?"

Fuck. Martin went utterly still. *Fuck, fuck, fuck.* How did he know? How could he possibly know that Martin needed to be asked? Martin himself hadn't known he needed that. He put his palm on Will's stomach, then slid it down until his littlest finger was near the head of Will's prick. He glanced up at Will, whose gaze was flickering between Martin's face and his hand.

"It'll feel good for me if you touch it. I'd really like it."

On the one hand, this should have been obvious. On the other, hearing it from Will in that gentle voice made all his thoughts turn into warm syrup. It was like the Shaving Incident all over again, Will's gentleness and praise working like witchcraft on Martin's warped mind. Or maybe it was just that Will was so good; if he was asking for something, praising something, then it must be good too. He wrapped his fingers around the silky skin, heard Will let out a breath.

"That's it," Will said as Martin stroked. "You're doing so well." And he pulled Martin in for a kiss. Kissing was good, already familiar, a reminder that this was Will he was touching, Will he was pleasing—and there his thoughts went dissolving into treacle again. Will was pushing tentatively into his fist and Martin realized he was rocking his own erection into Martin's hip.

"You could bring it alongside mine," Will whispered. "And hold us both together. That would feel good for me."

It was a testament to how far gone Martin was that he did it without hesitation. It took nothing at all after that—well, it took a steady stream of praise from Will, and the usual kissing and hair petting and general coddling, but very little in the way of actual touching—and Martin was spending onto Will's stomach, followed promptly by Will.

They lay there for a bit, still kissing, Martin feeling simultaneously very clever and like an absolute dolt, Will in some kind of post-orgasmic fugue state during which he could do nothing but pour utter nonsense into Martin's ear. Will eventually cleaned them up and drew the covers to their chins, and then they slept.

Chapter Eleven

Will was going to make Martin comfortable or he was going to die trying. In general he was happy go to along with whatever his lovers wanted. If they wanted to boss him around, he was game. If they wanted him to tie them up, he could do that too. Every now and then he encountered something he didn't care for, but even then if his partner enjoyed it he'd give it a try. Martin wasn't the first lover he had who needed to be fussed over and showered with praise.

But Will didn't even have words to describe how it felt to watch Martin figure it out, right in front of his eyes. He was already more fond of Martin than he was of anybody else he'd ever known; that fondness was not exactly increasing, but growing more tender—tender, but in the way a wound was tender. He wanted the best for Martin with a fierceness he could hardly understand.

He got out of bed before Martin, thinking that lingering in bed together would lead in the obvious direction, and wanting to give Martin a bit of space before he was confronted with more. As silently as he could, he built up the banked fire and slipped out to the pump to fill the kettle.

"What's this?" Martin asked blearily, sitting up in bed. "You've already made tea? Is this what I get for successfully fondling you?"

Will almost spit out his tea. He grinned over at Martin, glad beyond belief that there wasn't going to be any awkwardness. "It's the traditional gift," he said. He carried a cup over to the bed, having already stirred in a frankly silly quantity of sugar and milk, which was how Martin seemed to think tea ought to be prepared.

"Good to know." Martin took a sip of the tea, a strand of hair falling into his face as he did. Will brushed it away.

"I suppose you'll be getting another haircut when we go to London," Will observed.

"Is this your way of telling me I look too much like a stowaway to be seen with you?"

Will rolled his eyes. "Yes, I'm famous for cutting a dashing figure. I like your hair." It had grown out a bit since Daisy's haircut, and now the ends skimmed Martin's cheekbones when he didn't tuck them away. They had been spending so much time outside that the dark blond had lightened in places to a pale gold. "I suspect your aunt will feel otherwise, though."

Martin went still, both hands wrapped around the teacup. "I don't intend to come within shouting distance of my aunt while we're in town to see your play. I don't want to deal with any of that until after."

"After— Oh. After we leave here."

"Right," Martin said, avoiding Will's eyes.

Will found that after last night he didn't want to think about any future that lay outside the four walls of this cottage. "Is your aunt so bad, then?"

"Bad? No, she's rather determinedly decent. She doesn't mean ill, but she's used to getting her way. It's exhausting."

"And yet you left her house to live in an unheated attic. I assumed she was a villain." Will had never asked before why Martin ran away. At first he had been too furious that Martin had endangered himself in that way, and then Martin had been too sick to pepper with questions.

Martin settled back against the headboard. At some point during the night, he put on a shirt, and now it gaped open at the neck. Will wanted to kiss along his collarbone until he reached the hollow of his throat. He could hardly look away. "It's going to sound mad. I did it because I could. I realized I wasn't actually a prisoner in her home, and that I didn't need to hear her plan out the rest of my life. I know it sounds extreme, but I think that was only the second time in my life I got to make a real choice. I knew, even at the time, that it wasn't a good choice, but the idea of having a choice at all was exhilarating. I know it was mad."

Will sipped his tea. "Well, I'm an expert in making poor choices while more or less unhinged. But why don't you like your aunt? You act like visiting her is a trip to the gallows."

"She's a very . . . forceful personality. She views me as a problem in need of a solution, and in her world there's only one thing to do with a man who's both penniless and pedigreed."

Will furrowed his brow. "Which is?"

Martin cast him a glance that told him he was being very dim. "Marriage," he said bluntly. "She means to marry me off to the daughter of some wealthy industrialist who wants his grandson to inherit a title."

"And is this something you want?" Will asked carefully.

The glance Martin now gave him said he was being a monumental fool. "Do I want to marry an heiress? No. I don't want to marry anybody. But as she has said many times, marrying well is the only way I'll live as a gentleman. I've told her I have no wish to live as a gentleman, but the past few months have shown me I don't know how to live any other way."

Will knew he shouldn't be bothered by that—it was the simple truth that Martin had been raised to be a gentleman. Without Will around, he'd starve or freeze in a matter of weeks. And Will wanted Martin to have the luxuries, large and small, that he had been raised to expect. Will had never known a life in which supper dishes miraculously got washed by unseen hands, or buttons reattached themselves overnight, or the larder refilled itself at regular intervals. Will never thought about sewing buttons or washing dishes as unpleasant tasks: they were just what one did. But to Martin those acts would always be an effort, a reminder of something that had been lost. Will wanted better for him; he didn't want Martin to live out his life feeling resentful every time he needed to wear a shabby coat or eat off chipped china.

Still, it stung to hear Martin say that life in this cottage had been unsatisfactory in any way.

"I'm utterly dependent on you," Martin went on. "And I don't want to be."

Will knew it would be useless to protest that this was help freely given. He couldn't blame Martin for not wanting to be dependent on him; Will felt deeply uncomfortable and slightly ashamed about needing help on his worst days. He'd almost rather go without food or a fire in the hearth than let Martin see him at his worst. It was one thing to be looked after by servants, but another thing entirely to be looked after by a friend. With that in mind, Will tried to make peace with what Martin had said: Martin would eventually go to his aunt, who would find him a wealthy wife. Then not only would Martin have the kind of life he was accustomed to, but he could be looked after by servants and physicians who knew what they were doing. He would be safe and cared for.

Of course, that would also mean that this new physical aspect of their friendship would come to an end. At least, Will thought it would, because unless Martin married a very open-minded woman, being together would involve a degree of dishonesty that Will didn't think he could endure. But the rest of their friendship would remain intact. They wouldn't lose anything they hadn't had the previous day. That was fine, he told himself. The strange thing fluttering in his chest was probably just relief.

"Don't mind me," Martin said, nudging Will's knee. "I'm just being a sulky bastard."

"Yes, but you're my sulky bastard," Will said. He took the tea out of his hand and placed it on the windowsill, then climbed onto the bed so he was kneeling over Martin's lap.

"Thank you." He put a finger under Martin's chin and tilted his head up, then kissed him.

"What are you thanking me for?" Martin asked.

"For being my sulky bastard," Will said, then kissed him again, this time deeper.

It was all easier this time, maybe because Martin knew what to expect, or maybe because Will knew that his part involved a steady litany of praise and reassurance. Martin let his hands explore, roaming over the curve of Will's arse and the planes of his back. Will hadn't expected that—most people either avoided his scars, as if touching them would remind Will of their existence, or they made a great show of lavishing attention on them. Will didn't mind either way, but it felt right that Martin would treat his back just like any other part of his body.

"Why are you smiling like that?" Martin asked, breathless. "I'm not here to amuse you." The asperity of his voice was rather undercut by the fact that he was arching up beneath Will as their erections rubbed together in the space between their bodies.

"Yes, but you amuse me anyway," Will said, and Martin's only response was to pinch his arse and then move his fingers rather daringly close to Will's cleft. Jesus. Will knew Martin was a quick study, but this was— "God, yes, please keep doing that."

Martin laughed, the complete tosser.

Later, after they cleaned up and ate breakfast and then returned to the bed once again, Martin traced a path on Will's shoulder blade that Will knew was the tail end of one of his scars. "You know, you and Ben are the only people who never ask me about all that," Will murmured. Martin had simply shown up at the address Will had mentioned in his last letter and set about making sure Will had food to eat and someone to drag him home from whatever hellish places where he had sought relief. There had been no tears, no hand wringing, no well-intentioned offers for Will to unburden his soul. Martin just did his damnedest to get Will to go home to Cumberland with him, and when Will refused, stayed by his side until Sir Humphrey died and Martin had to go north to sort out the estate.

Martin raised his eyebrows, but didn't stop the path of his fingers. "Did you want me to ask?"

"No," Will said at once.

"I've always supposed that if you wanted to talk about it, you would. And," he added after a pause, "I thought you might have had your fill of talking at the court martial."

That was such a wild understatement that Will actually cracked a smile, which was not something he had ever anticipated doing when talking about the *Fotheringay*, but he knew this wasn't even the first time Martin had managed it. "My father wanted to write a poem about it." He coughed out a little laugh, expecting Martin to find his father's antics amusing, but Martin only narrowed his eyes and looked ready to commit murder. "Hartley bribed someone at the Admiralty to give him the transcript of the court martial. My younger brothers still don't know what to say to me. They remember me one way and see me like this and it makes them uncomfortable. But you and Ben treat me like I'm still me."

Martin looked away. "It's not every day I'm put in the same category as the saintly Benedict Sedgwick."

"Ben is good to everyone. You're good to me."

"You really shouldn't make that sound like a compliment."

There was no point in arguing with such arrant foolishness, so Will leaned in and kissed him.

Martin hadn't expected an epiphany to arrive in the form of an escaped pig. But piglets, it turned out, were very slippery and wished for nothing so much as anarchy. Whenever presented with a dull moment, they began devising new and horrible ways to get out of their pen. Martin, unwilling to let Will's new project escape into the wilderness, had spent the hours since the piglets' arrival alternately scolding them for ingratitude and chasing them around the perimeter of the cottage.

"I'm really not sure you can expect gratitude from an animal we intend to sell to the butcher," Will said, leaning against the plane tree and watching Martin's efforts with a badly concealed air of amusement.

"There you are," Martin said, cornering one of the escapees against the woodshed. "Finally. William, are you going to help me retrieve these creatures or are you— Ha!" he exclaimed, lunging as the piglet approached, and finally meeting with success as his fingers closed around its midsection. "Why are they so heavy? And so naughty? None of this can be normal."

Will took the animal from Martin's arms and shoved it

back into its pen. "You stand guard and shout if they try to make a break for it, and I'll wedge some stones beneath the bottom rail," he said. "When they're a bit bigger they'll just try to knock the entire fence down."

"Why do you sound impressed?" Martin called. "This is disorderly behavior. Reprehensible." He watched as Will took flat stones from an old, crumbled wall and began wedging them around the perimeter of the pen.

"Good work catching that pig," Will said. "I didn't think baronets could do that sort of thing."

"Oh, fuck off," Martin said happily, preening at Will's praise.

"In fact, you might be the first man with a title to ever have done something useful."

"I'll show you useful," Martin said, with what he hoped was a sufficient amount of innuendo.

"Promises, promises." Will had straw and feathers in his hair and a good deal of dirt everywhere else, which was pretty much how he looked every day when he came home from Mrs. Tanner's. His sleeves were rolled up and his collar was loose. He didn't look at all like a gentleman. Martin was aware that he was probably equally disreputable looking, which meant that he too looked nothing like a gentleman. Having been raised secure in the knowledge that his title and standing were his most important qualities, Martin felt some lingering shame at spending his days living in a way he would once have dismissed as squalor. He had just flung himself into the mud to catch a pig, for God's sake. Bigger and louder than the shame, however, was relief that he didn't have to be that past version of himself anymore. He could let all of it go—his father, Lindley Priory, his entry in *Debrett's*. None of it had ever done him any good; he had known from his earliest childhood that he was an insufficient heir, too thin and sickly to be trusted to survive to adulthood, too sallow and ill-mannered to bring into company. He could just . . . stop being that Martin Easterbrook. Instead he could catch pigs and share a bed with the only person who mattered to him.

This was, he knew, a pipe dream. He couldn't stay here forever. The day would arrive when he had to go to his aunt and face his future. But for now he could live like none of that mattered. For however long he and Will were to stay in Sussex—a few months, maybe a year, Martin assumed, although they had never discussed the particulars—he could try to live a useful life.

"Why do you look so daft?" Will asked.

"I could feed the pigs," Martin said.

"Is that something you want to do? Your dream can come true, young man. I can make it happen," Will said grandly.

Martin elbowed him. "I just mean that I can be useful. I don't think feeding pigs is my life's work, but it's . . . work."

"You know," Will said, his lips quivering with the effort of suppressing a smile, "if you really want to be useful, you could draw me a bath. Maybe that's your life's work."

"I can't imagine why I'd want to do such a thing," Martin said, leaning with feigned ease against one of the posts of the pig pen, idly examining his fingernails.

"I don't think you want me all sweaty and filthy in the bed," Will said, stepping near.

Really, it just figured that Will had no idea that sweat and filth looked so good on him. "Perhaps I'll draw a bath for myself," Martin said. Will was inches away now, blatantly crowding him. "And then sit in it until the water gets cold."

"There are better things you could do with your time," Will said, speaking the words into Martin's ear, his cheek almost against Martin's own. Martin could feel the stubble on Will's jaw, could smell clean sweat and fresh earth. He swallowed hard. Behind him, the pigs were making rude noises and never in Martin's wildest imagination did he imagine that the gentle harmonies of pig snorts would be the accompaniment to any seduction he was a part of.

"Prove it," he said, achieving something close enough to cool indifference.

Will's hand landed on Martin's hip as his teeth grazed Martin's throat. "I've got a shelf full of Defoe novels that you'll probably find weirdly titillating and a hard on with your name on it."

"Tell me something I don't know," Martin scoffed.

As if that were some kind of invitation—and maybe it was—Will leaned in closer, rocking his hips against Martin's. "I'm about two seconds from dropping to my knees and seeing what you'll let me do to you."

Martin jerked his hips forward involuntarily. "There's a real chance the answer to that is literally nothing." Will had been extremely patient these last few days, working around the edges of Martin's limits. But they both knew that Martin was most comfortable when they both pretended that everything they did was for Will's pleasure.

"Could be," Will said. He kissed Martin's throat, just a graze of lips over the place where his pulse beat. He really was filthy, and Martin was certain he ought to care. "Worth finding out, I'd say." Another kiss, this one harder. "But not until I have a damn bath." Will wrenched himself away. "Right. Yes. I'm going to take that bath, while you go find Daisy at the Blue Boar and tell her she doesn't need to tidy up for us tomorrow morning. While you're there, get a jug of ale and put it on our tab, will you?"

Martin hadn't even known they had a tab, but of course they did. In villages everybody ran tabs, otherwise every shopkeeper and barman would be perpetually counting out farthings.

"And maybe get a loaf of bread if the baker is still open. We still have some of Mrs. Tanner's jam. There won't be any milk for your tea, but—"

"It's all right," Martin said, slightly stunned, as he finally understood that Will was attempting to provision them for a day spent in bed. "I can take my tea black." He swallowed.

Will did something between a salute and a wave and sauntered off into the cottage. Martin was left staring after him, then shook himself into some semblance of intelligence and headed for the village. As always when he went to the village, he had the urge to pull his hat low over his forehead, but if anyone had recognized him as bearing a striking resemblance to the former owner of Friars' Gate, they didn't mention it.

Daisy was behind the bar at the Blue Boar, and her eyebrows shot all the way up to the ruffle on her cap when she saw him. "Out and about on your own?" she asked, pouring him a half pint of bitter without his asking. "Mr. Sedgwick must be worried sick, wondering what's happened to you."

"Very droll. I'm here for a jug of ale and to tell you not to bother coming tomorrow morning."

"Why?"

"Because the cottage is already in a state of impeccable cleanliness and you deserve a morning to yourself," Martin said, because it was the first thing he thought of. "Also, would you show me how to do the wash?"

"How to wash what?"

"Linens and shirts and that sort of thing." It had occurred to him that he did not want people examining any bedlinens he and Will had debauched. This was likely prudish and almost certainly eccentric, but he wasn't exposing Will to even the shadow of a rumor. At Lindley Priory, there had been a vast and steamy laundry where maids boiled and beat the household linens, then dried them in the sun. That was satisfactorily anonymous in a way that turning your underthings over to your neighbor was not. Besides, it seemed that laundry was something else he could do, like feeding the pigs. It wasn't, perhaps, an important task, but it had to be done, and somebody had to do it. Maybe, given time, the Martin Easterbrook who tended livestock and thought about laundry could also do other useful things. "If it wouldn't be too much trouble, that is. I'm not trying to do you out of work," he added, when she still hadn't replied.

"That," she said, an odd expression on her face, "is almost sweet."

"No it isn't," he said automatically.

"You're really harmless, aren't you?"

"Take it back." He was utterly confused about what was going on.

"You're stroppy, to be sure—"

"I beg your pardon, but are *you* calling *me* stroppy?"

"—but it's all on the surface."

"I assure you that I'm foul tempered down to my very soul."

She patted his forearm. "Drink up, lamb. One day next week I'll teach you how to do the wash." He had the uncomfortable sense that they had just taken part in two very different conversations.

On his way home, a loaf of bread under one arm and the jug of ale in the crook of his elbow, he picked a handful of primroses that were growing beneath the hedges that lined the lane. This was reprehensibly transparent of him even though he was fairly certain he had long passed the point where mysterious aloofness was an option. But he still felt like he ought to pretend that he hadn't passed that point, for Will's sake if not his own self-defense.

When he opened the door and thrust the flowers at Will with all the ceremony of a man trying to get rid of something nasty, he felt like he had crossed an irrevocable line. Judging by Will's expression—dazed and surprised but very far from displeased—he was pretty sure he was not the only one who thought so.

Chapter Twelve

Not in his wildest imaginings could Will have anticipated Martin bringing him a posy, but he supposed that if he had, he definitely would have expected it to be accompanied by the look of baffled mortification on his friend's face. Martin had never known what to do with an emotion other than be embarrassed it.

"Why are you looking at me like that?" Martin asked after depositing the bread and ale onto the table.

Will suspected that the look Martin referred to was best described as hopelessly fond. He dumped the contents of a teacup into the hearth, filled it with water from the ewer, then gently placed the posy inside. "Thank you," he said, hooking two fingers into the waistband of Martin's trousers and pulling him near.

"I don't know what you're talking about."

Will grinned and settled both his hands on Martin's hips, one chastely atop his hip bone, the other creeping lower. He kissed Martin's collarbone through the linen of his shirt.

"You know what?" he asked, steering Martin backward through the room.

"I daresay you aren't going to keep it to yourself," Martin sniped, because he was still prickly from having experienced a stray feeling. Will grinned into the skin of his neck, felt Martin's pulse pounding away under his lips. He guided Martin a few steps further until his back hit the door.

"I almost brought in a few stalks of larkspur." He kissed the underside of Martin's jaw. "I was going to act very casual about it, as if I had just thought they might brighten the cottage up a bit, but thought you still might actually throw up."

"Haven't ruled it out," Martin said, still peevish, but his hands were on Will's back, holding him close.

Will reached behind Martin and slid the bolt into place. "There," he said, satisfied that they'd be safe and undisturbed, and returned to kissing Martin's jaw. One of Martin's hands slid up to his hair, holding his head in place, and Will didn't quite know what was going on until he realized Martin was angling his lips over Will's. They kissed like that for a while, Will's body keeping Martin flush against the door, until Will was fully hard and could feel that Martin was much the same. Then he started sliding Martin's coat off, first one sleeve and then the next, never breaking the kiss. The waistcoat went next, and by the time he started untucking Martin's shirt, Martin was already tugging it over his head.

Will placed his palms on the other man's torso, spreading his fingers over his ribs, and kissed him some more. He had the notion that it would be worth anything, anything in the world, to regularly watch Martin melt from prickly irritation to soft capitulation like this. He could imagine weeks and months and years of easing Martin's irritability away with kisses and nonsense words and gentle pets.

"What would happen," Will said, barely lifting his mouth from Martin's, "if I got to my knees?"

"I'm not certain." Something in the tone of his voice suggested barely checked desperation.

Will kissed him again. "May I try? I like having my mouth on you." For emphasis, he pressed a wet kiss behind Martin's jaw. "And I'd like to do that, if you think you might like it too."

Martin swallowed. "All right."

Will cupped Martin's cheek with his palm. "If you change your mind, will you tell me to stop?" When Martin was silent, Will kissed him. "If you're not sure you can tell me to stop, then let's do something else. I need to know that you can tell me to stop. For me to enjoy this—to enjoy any of it—I need to be certain that you're comfortable. Otherwise it's—bad memories, all right?"

Martin looked at him sharply, but nodded his head. He didn't ask any questions, because he never did, thank God; he just treated Will like all the traps and snares in Will's mind were a normal part of the terrain. Will shucked his coat and threw it on the floor where Martin's clothes had landed, then began kissing down Martin's chest. He ran a thumb over one pink nipple, and when that earned him a curse and a shudder, he followed it up with his tongue. He took his time, because time was the one thing they had in any quantity. When he got to his knees, he didn't right away undo the falls of Martin's trousers, instead contenting himself with kissing and nuzzling the fabric on either side of a very obvious erection. All the while, Martin carded a hand through Will's hair, sometimes so bold as to tentatively hold him in place for a moment but never directing his movement.

"Will." Martin's voice sounded ragged. Will looked up and saw Martin gazing down at him, eyes wild. "I—just wanted to tell you I like this. I'm—comfortable."

Will felt something warm and dangerous slither around in his chest. When he finally mouthed along the hard line of Martin's erection, the hand in his hair went rigid. Will went motionless, waiting for a sign that this was all right. He raised his eyes and Martin nodded.

He unfastened the falls of Martin's trousers, waited for a nod, and then lowered them a few inches, watching the flushed length of him spring free. Martin made a choked noise that sounded like begging, and Will kissed the bare skin beneath his navel, the crease where his thigh met his torso, pretty much anywhere he could get his mouth other than the erection that was right in front of him. He remembered how Martin had reacted at first to Will's hand on his length, and supposed a mouth would not be any easier. Finally, he began mouthing around the base of the shaft, then slowly up, and by the time he had his lips wrapped around the head, Martin's hands were tight in his hair, his body taut with tension.

"Will," he ground out. "I need more—please."

Will pulled off. "You're doing so well. So good for me."

Martin made a broken gasping sound as Will drew him into his mouth. Will had been telling the truth when he said he liked this—the taste and the feel on his tongue, having to work to take it all in—but he also liked the sense that he was taking care of Martin in this way. He felt Martin's body go tense, climax approaching, and gentled him through it, feeling like he was giving himself over to something.

Martin's hands were on his collar, pulling him up. "Let me," he said, his knuckles brushing the front of Will's trousers.

Will swore and fumbled his way through opening his trousers, then groaned in relief at the pressure of Martin's hand.

"I don't know how you stand it," Will babbled. "You're incredible. I was kissing you for ages and touching you everywhere but your cock and you just waited. I'd have gone raving." He gasped as Martin did something with his thumb. "Do that two more times and I'll be gone." And so he was, shaking and swearing into Martin's shoulder.

This time it was Martin who got them cleaned up, Martin who led them into bed. Somehow the jug of ale even made it into the bed with them.

"It's not self-restraint," Martin said after taking a pull from the jug and passing it to Will.

"What isn't?"

"The . . ." He gestured in the vicinity of his trousers.

Will raised his eyebrows. "Then what is it?"

"I just . . . don't. I don't toss myself off." Martin spoke with a nervous tightness that made Will want to cover his face with kisses. "Is that unusual?"

Will was certain it was highly unusual, if his time living

among men his own age in the navy was any indication, but he wasn't going to say so. "Everybody's different," he said. "Why don't you? You don't seem to have any difficulty getting hard. Or coming, for that matter. Everything seems to be in, er, top form."

"I just . . . try to make it go away."

"Why, though?" Will remembered what Martin had told him about not wanting to want sex. He expected it had something to do with residual shame over wanting to shag men, but didn't want to assume.

"For one, I don't . . ." Martin snatched the jug away from Will and took a long drink. "This is enormously stupid." He swallowed. "When you touch me, my first thought is sometimes that I don't deserve it. No, shut up, I know you're going to tell me that I do deserve it, but you'd also tell me I deserved the crown jewels if I had just come back from robbing the royal vault, so your opinion on this matter is not required."

"Grumpy," Will said, and bit Martin's shoulder.

"The other reason, and this is even stupider, is that it doesn't seem right to think of someone like that without their permission."

Stunned, Will propped himself onto his elbow and looked down at Martin. "You think it might be . . . unethical . . . to toss yourself off while thinking about someone who hasn't given their permission to be used in your fantasy." That had never, not even once, occurred to Will, but it seemed like a not totally insane proposition; besides, Martin seemed pretty dedicated to overcorrecting for his father's sins—Sir Humphrey had certainly not been one to put much stock in concepts like permission, Will recollected grimly. "All right, fair, but why not just imagine some faceless bloke?"

"That's not how it works for me. I don't want to shag faceless blokes," Martin said, his face very red.

Will kissed his forehead. "Who do you want to shag, then? I mean, I'm assuming you want to shag me because here we are, and consider permission granted. Play with yourself until your hand goes numb."

"Oh, go to hell. Can we talk about something else? Tell me all your masturbatory oddities and I'll judge you for them."

Thinking that was a fine segue, Will pulled off his trousers and rolled on top of Martin, taking himself in hand. "I'll give you masturbatory oddities," he said, leering down at him. And that made Martin dissolve into laughter, which was rare enough that Will could only laugh in return.

Martin woke with a start. For a moment he didn't know what had interrupted his sleep, but then he felt Will twitching beside him. As Will usually slept like a stone, this wasn't a good sign. Martin nudged him. "Will. You're having a bad dream."

Will mumbled something garbled and unintelligible. The sharp edge of panic in his voice made Martin shake him more urgently. He remembered those first months after Will had come home—he hardly slept at all, and when he did it was broken up by nightmares.

"Will. William!"

Finally William sat up, gasping.

"You had a nightmare. You're safe in bed." Martin sat up beside him, stroking a tentative hand up and down Will's arm. "You're in England. It's 1819. You're safe."

Will stared straight ahead of him for long enough that Martin wondered if he had somehow fallen asleep sitting up, with his eyes open. But then he passed a hand over his mouth. "Fuck." He was shivering.

Martin put his arm around Will's shoulders and drew him back down to the bed, covering them both with blankets.

"A bad one?" Martin asked.

"Just the usual. I mean, they don't happen very often anymore, but when they do it's always the same."

"Do you want to tell me about it?" He kept his arms wrapped tightly around Will, leaving as small a gap as possible between their bodies.

For a moment there was no sound but their breathing. "It's the kids."

"The kids?" Martin repeated, baffled.

"I didn't care if he wanted to have me flogged, but some of the others were young enough to call for their mothers. Thirteen, fourteen years old."

"I hadn't realized." Martin knew that children of that age were in the navy, and he knew Will wasn't the only person aboard the *Fotheringay* who had been tortured—no use putting a fine point on it—by the captain. But he hadn't thought about what it must be like for Will to have to watch other people enduring the same treatment.

"I'm so sorry," Martin said. "I'm so sorry that happened to all of you." He was also sorry that it was his own fault that Will had been sent to the navy in the first place, but he didn't think this was the time for him to pour his heart out on that topic, not when Will's heart was just beginning to slow down.

"I really don't think about it much during the day. It's just a thing that happened. At night though . . . well, it helps to wake up next to someone. Especially you."

Martin stroked and caressed him, whispered soft foolishness in his ear, did whatever he could to help. He wanted to be there the next time, if that would mean Will had it easier. He wanted to be there anyway, beside Will in bed, always, forever.

Right when he thought Will might be about to fall asleep, he felt something press against his thigh. "That thing is relentless," Martin whispered admiringly. Will had managed no fewer than three orgasms last night. Martin hadn't known such a thing was even possible, and had been startled when he managed to come a second time. Will laughed, and Martin didn't think he had ever heard anything that gave him such relief. "What should we do about it?" Martin asked, nudging his own hips forward so Will would know he was interested.

"How's this?" Will murmured, rolling on top of him.

"I like it when you're on top of me." Martin wondered when saying things like that would stop feeling so bold.

"I know," Will said, with a roughness in his voice that made Martin wonder how many other things Will had guessed for himself. Did Martin have no secrets? He ought to have known that Will would see him exactly as he was. "I like when you're underneath me," Will went on, moving his hips. "So I suppose that works out well."

"Yes," Martin said. Will got a hand behind Martin's knee and hitched it up, and then Martin (again feeling idiotically bold) did the same with the other side, so his legs were wrapped around Will's middle as Will gently rocked against him. They were pressed together, safe and alone in the moonlight, neither of them particularly well but both were something like *happy* and it felt like a miracle.

Chapter Thirteen

"We're getting crumbs all over the bed," Martin said, tearing off a piece of bread and popping it into his mouth, then doing the same for Will.

"True," Will conceded after swallowing. "But I'm not moving." They were reading in bed at an hour they probably ought to be embarrassed to not yet be up. But Will's head was very comfortably cushioned on Martin's lap while Martin stroked his hair, and yesterday's bread had not yet gone stale, so as far as he cared there were very few incentives to go anywhere. If he turned his head just so he could see the cup of primroses on the table. From time to time he caught Martin looking down at him with a sort of dazed contentment that made Will feel smug in about a dozen different ways.

"We could shake the sheets out later," Martin said, as if puzzling the matter out. Watching Martin discover housework was a source of never-ending delight. "We could even put fresh sheets on the bed."

"That's right, love," Will said absently, and felt Martin's hand momentarily still in his hair. The word had come out absently, as it had dozens of times in the past. He hadn't meant anything by it. And of course he loved Martin—he had loved Martin for years, and assumed Martin loved him in return, in the way friends did love one another. This—hair petting and flowers—this was something different, though. This was something both tender and sharp that had been growing and growing in the pit of his belly. He had tried not to think too much about it, afraid that whatever this thing was, it would change his life irrevocably once he acknowledged it. But hearing the word *love* come out of his mouth had made it impossible to hide from the truth.

Martin's hand had long since stopped carding through Will's hair, and when Will sat up he found Martin glaring at him.

"What?" Will asked.

"Don't you dare," Martin said. "Don't you dare act like you're figuring it out now. Like you just realized there's a name for this. What did you *think* it was?"

"I didn't—"

"Did you think I just wanted to get off with someone and thought, oh, I'll vanquish all my bizarre sexual inhibitions with my best friend on a lark? That was all fucking *difficult*."

"You said you didn't want to wait anymore," Will protested, not entirely certain what they were fighting about.

"I wasn't talking about sex. I was talking about letting myself love you, you arsehole. Letting myself be loved *by* you. I thought you understood."

There it was, the thing he hadn't wanted to think about. This wasn't just love: it was being in love, and it made him greedily hungry for things he couldn't have. "You're going to get married!" Will said, seizing on the first and most obvious problem. "You told me so."

"Not tomorrow! Not even this year, if I can avoid it. And even when I do, it doesn't mean—"

"Yes it does," Will said, his teeth clenched. He had told himself that he could walk away from the physical part of their friendship when Martin ultimately got married, and so he could. He couldn't walk away from this, though—this feeling, grasping and needy, was going to follow him wherever he went. "It fucking does. How is it that you're allowed to be jealous but I'm not? What does it matter whether it's tomorrow or next year? It's worse if it's next year, or two years from now, or even further. Don't you see?"

"I see that you're not willing to compromise."

"You can't get married and then carry on an affair."

"You don't get to tell me what I can and can't do." Martin buried his face in his hands and groaned. "Fine," he said, throwing up his hands. "What do you suggest, then?"

Will twisted his hand in the sheet and took a deep breath. Martin was right. This fight was premature. Will had just been surprised to discover how angry he got at the idea of being separated from Martin. He didn't usually let himself feel anger or resentment, afraid that if he started down that road there'd be no coming back. "I'm not suggesting anything. I'm going to keep loving you and just occasionally be cross and dramatic about it, all right? Is that acceptable?"

Martin stared at him.

"What did you think I was going to do? Leave you?" Will asked. "Idiot." He passed a hand over his jaw. "It would probably be better if we could go back to the way things were, but we can't, so here we are."

"Here we are," Martin agreed, not meeting his eyes.

Martin knew he should never have told Will about his aunt's plans. Martin himself was able to forget them for days at a stretch, and instead believe in a fantasy where he lingered forever in the country, feeding pigs and doing the wash. The alternative seemed very distant, contingent on a future in which he stayed healthy enough to be a reasonable candidate as bridegroom. It was just the sort of arrangement Will would find distasteful—an exchange of money for looks and breeding. It had more than a whiff of the marketplace. He hadn't expected Will to actually object, though, at least not beyond a few minor aesthetic quibbles about marrying without love. If Martin thought about it at all, which he tried resolutely not to, he would have imagined that Will would be glad to see Martin set up in a household with ready access to things like money and food.

But Will *loved him* and would be *jealous*, two things that would make Martin almost ecstatic with delight if not for how miserable they seemed to make Will, and how very trying it was to watch Will stumble into a realization that had been the central fact of Martin's existence for more years than he cared to acknowledge. For Will, loving

Martin was fresh and new, probably easily undone; for Martin, loving Will was as basic a premise as gravity and just as easily reversed.

He hadn't expected Will to love him, not in that way. He had told himself that Will would be able to part with Martin as amicably as he had parted with the former lover who had visited him weeks ago—they would still be friends, but no longer lovers. He had told himself that all the fondness and care Will showed him was nothing more than what he'd give to anyone. Which, really, would have been the sensible thing for Will to have felt. It figured Will had to go making things as dramatic as possible. Martin ought to have known the minute he read that play that Will would need to indulge himself.

He was dimly aware that he wasn't being quite fair. But still. This could have gone on quite nicely, with Martin bearing the brunt of any emotional complications. But since that evidently was no longer possible, he had to decide what to do. He supposed they could carry on, which was what Will had suggested. "I'm going to keep loving you," he had said, as if it were a threat, and just the memory sent a warm thrill through Martin's body. They could carry on, and then at some point stop carrying on, and Martin would go to his aunt and proceed with her plan. If Will were half-way sensible, he wouldn't let Martin's marriage—and lord did that phrase sound impossible, like Martin's elephant, or Martin's summer house on the moon—change things between them. Will's parents hadn't even been married, for heaven's sake. Will's father had been married to another woman, and all three adults had been perfectly aware and content.

It was not, he feared, a good sign when he looked at the Sedgwick ménage as a model of common sense.

But Will was not going to be sensible. If they carried on, this spring would become the beginning of a tragedy. Will wouldn't quickly get over it. And the last thing Will needed was more tragedy in his life.

As soon as Will fell asleep, Martin dressed and walked to the inn, pausing only to kick rocks and then grumble when he hurt his foot. He was being a sulky child, but he fucking hated having to do what he was about to do. It was so unfair, just so bloody unfair, that Martin couldn't even have a good thing for a few weeks. He was no saint, and he had made bad choices, but now that he had determined to do the right thing it was just so annoying that the right thing always involved Martin doing things like giving away houses and giving up the man he loved.

No, he reassured himself, he wasn't walking away. There was nothing so simple as walking away where he and Will were concerned. He was just putting a period to this part of their friendship. It was a minor thing, really, and years from now they'd probably look back fondly on the short time they had spent in bed together. That was all.

At the inn, he dug in his pocket and realized he hadn't any money at all. But Daisy was behind the bar and gave him what he needed, waving away his protests. "I'll put it on Mr. Sedgwick's tab."

"Don't you dare put this on his tab. Not this."

She studied him with narrowed eyes while she trimmed the nib of the pen and handed it to him. "You look right—"

"Not in the mood," he said, not even able to muster up enough enthusiasm to insult her.

"That bad?"

To his horror, Martin realized his eyes were hot and prickly. He pressed his thumb and forefinger to the bridge of his nose to spare himself some modicum of dignity. "It is exhausting to be a decent person. I could be a villain with no effort whatsoever. It would be like rolling downhill."

"Why don't you, then?" she asked, and her tone held more challenge than it did curiosity.

"Because there's enough bad in the world. I'm trying to put my weight on the other side of the scale. Which I know is both futile and self-important but there you have it."

"You should talk to my mum," Daisy said as she handed him a sheet of slightly crumbled paper.

Martin pretended he didn't know what she was talking about, and set about writing his letter.

"I'm sorry," Will blurted out as soon as Martin walked in the door.

Martin shook his head. "You don't have anything to apologize for. You're a dramatic bastard and I should have guessed."

"Then we're all right?"

One corner of Martin's mouth hitched up in something resembling a smile, even though it didn't get anywhere near his eyes. "We'll always be all right."

Will felt a wash of relief sweep over him, and even more so when Martin put his arms around him. He didn't tell Martin that he loved him, not then, not when they were tangled together in bed, not in the morning when they drank tea or the evening when they read by the fire. It was always there, in his heart, on the tip of his tongue, but he was afraid that speaking those words aloud would only make them rehash that last argument. Saying those words would be the end of something.

Two days later, when the sound of hoofbeats woke them from an afternoon nap, he had occasion to realize that "We'll always be all right" didn't mean much of anything.

"What the hell is that?" Will asked, sitting up in bed. The lane was wide enough for a pony cart but he had never seen any conveyance come within a hundred yards of the cottage. And now he could hear that this was no pony cart—he could make out at least two separate sets of hoofbeats. He got out of bed and stepped into the first pair of trousers he laid his hands on, then scrambled into a shirt and waistcoat. He collected the clothes he had removed from Martin a few hours earlier and tossed them onto the bed. Martin's hair was rumpled and his lips were still swollen with kisses. Will hoped whoever this was would promptly go away.

Will waited until Martin was decent, then unbolted the door. In front of the cottage was a chaise and four. Two liveried servants rode on the chaise, one in front of the body of the carriage and one behind. One of them hopped down and swung open the carriage door, which Will could now see was emblazoned with a coat of arms. As he watched, the servant helped a woman step down from the carriage.

"What the hell," Will muttered. The woman was swathed in about an acre of dark green fabric, and on her head was a hat the approximate size and shape of a punch bowl, apparently consisting of feathers dyed the same unlikely shade of green as her gown, or cloak, or whatever that sort of getup was called.

Will's first thought was that Martin had found some rich woman to hire Friars' Gate and neglected to tell Will about it. He knew Martin had written to his solicitor some weeks ago. But in that case, surely the new tenant would confine herself to correspondence with the solicitor, rather than squeezing her elaborate chaise down a cramped country lane and calling at a tiny cottage. Whoever and whatever she was, she didn't belong here. As if to prove him wrong, Martin came up beside him, and Will was forced to remember the fact he had been trying to shove from his mind all these months—Martin didn't belong here any more than this stranger with her elaborate hat did.

"Oh no," Martin muttered.

"Martin?" the woman said. "Well, you aren't dead. That's something, I daresay."

"Aunt Bermondsey," Martin said faintly.

"This is your aunt?" Will said. "*This* is your aunt?" The way Martin talked about her, Will had imagined a dragon of a grand dame, at least sixty, with gray hair and a certain amount of gravitas. This lady was not much older than they were, although it was difficult to tell with her face shadowed by the brim of that hat. She was willowy and unmistakably fashionable. When she tilted her chin up to get a look at her nephew, he could see that her mouth was set in a familiar wry twist.

"Lady Bermondsey," Martin said, "this is William Sedgwick."

Will managed a small bow, and she flicked a glance at him as if surprised to have been introduced to a servant.

"How did you manage to find me?" Martin went on. "In my letter I only told you that I was well."

"And that you were in need of stagecoach fare," she said, dropping her voice as if loath to be overheard speaking of such common things.

"Stagecoach fare?" Will repeated. Both Martin and his aunt ignored him.

"Some weeks ago, your solicitor kindly informed me that you had requested his aid in finding someone to let Friars' Gate. He mentioned that you were staying in one of the out-buildings." She spoke as if Martin had been living in a root cellar or milking shed, and Will had the mad urge to defend their cottage against her insults.

"I specifically requested that he not divulge my whereabouts," Martin said. His face was a mask of bored passivity that Will realized he hadn't seen in a while.

"Well, then, I suppose you can number your lawyer among those who don't wish to see you die in poverty. Not a bad quality in a solicitor," Lady Bermondsey observed. "In any event, I didn't seek you out immediately. I waited to hear from you. You may congratulate me on my restraint when we're back in town. You didn't think I'd actually let you take the stagecoach, darling. If we leave now we can be back in London before dusk."

"'Thank you for your solicitude, ma'am, but I'm not prepared to leave quite yet." Martin's hands were clenched into fists by his sides. "As I said in my letter, I have business in town at the end of April."

Will's mind reeled. That business in town was Will's play. "I thought we were traveling up together. If you had wanted to go earlier, I would have given you the money for the fare."

Martin didn't look at him. Lady Bermondsey, however, lifted a lorgnette to her eyes and peered at him closely. "Nephew, have you been living entirely on the charity of this man?"

"No!" Will said. Martin said nothing. "It's his house," Will added feebly.

"Mr. Sedgwick and I grew up together and he kindly looked after me during my last illness. I hesitated to trouble him for any further expense. That is all."

"To *trouble* me—" Will shook his head. "The money from the play is sitting there on the chimneypiece and I've told you to help yourself." And Martin had even done so a few times to do the marketing. Perhaps he hadn't wanted to take a sum as large as the stagecoach fare. Or perhaps he hadn't wanted Will to pay for Martin to leave. That latter explanation sent a chill down Will's spine. Had Martin not thought he was permitted to leave? Did he think he was as much a prisoner here as he had been in his father's house? Will steadied himself with a hand to the door frame, trying to make sense of what was happening.

"How long do you need to pack your things?" Lady Bermondsey asked.

"Martin, may I speak to you indoors, please?" Will cut in, and stepped through the still-open cottage door, Martin directly on his heels. "You do know I wouldn't have stopped you from leaving, don't you?" he asked as soon as the door shut behind them. "If you want to go, then by all means go. I would never try to stop you."

Will expected Martin to be relieved, but instead his jaw tightened and he refused to meet Will's eye. "Of course you wouldn't," he said.

"Why didn't you tell me, though?"

"I didn't know she was going to come and get me," Martin said, his gazed fixed somewhere over Will's shoulder. "I thought she'd give me a draft on her bank for the coach faire, and then I'd go up to town a day or two ahead of you."

Will furrowed his brow. "Why wouldn't you have just gone up with me?"

"I wanted to part here, rather than at Charing Cross."

"Part?" Will repeated.

"It's time for me to stay with my aunt. What we talked about the other day, we both know it's going to only get worse if we keep doing this. Let's cut our losses."

Will pressed his lips together so he didn't say anything he'd want to take back. He knew that by *our* losses, Martin meant Will's losses. It had been Will's inane crisis the other day that prompted Martin to write to his aunt. He was trying to spare Will future pain. He was trying to make a sacrifice for Will, not to hurt Will. "Were you going to tell me beforehand?" he asked, as gently as he could.

"Honestly, I was hoping that after we got to London you'd be distracted."

Will tipped his head back on the closed door. This was all so typical of Martin. Evasive, passive, intent on stepping sideways around his meaning. He was used to his desires being treated with scorn at best and punishment at worse, so he had learned to appease. And now he was treating Will as a person who needed to be appeased, someone who might turn on him. That, more than anything, came close to breaking his heart.

Will took Martin's hands in his own. "I'm not going to be distracted from how I feel about you, you know. But if you want to end things now, if you want to go with your aunt, then I'm not going to stop you." He wanted to try to persuade Martin that he was wrong, that they didn't need to do this, but he was afraid that Martin would see that as Will trying to pressure or manipulate him. He told himself that this was what Martin needed, and tried to ignore the sensation that felt suspiciously like his heart splitting in two.

Now Martin looked at Will almost as if he expected Will to say more. "You're telling me to go," Martin said when Will remained silent.

"I'll be in town next week and we can see one another then," Will said, trying to sound happy about it.

"Will," Martin said, and it sounded like a protest, but Will couldn't understand what Martin was protesting.

"It'll be fine," Will said. "We'll still be friends. Just like before. It'll be easy, you'll see. We've been through worse than this, right?" And then, because he had to, he had to do it one last time, he took Martin's face in his hands and kissed him. "I'll see you in a week," Will said, pushing aside the jealousy and sorrow and reminding himself he was doing the right thing.

Chapter Fourteen

Martin supposed he shouldn't have been surprised when his aunt refused to have the carriage stop at Bermondsey House until Martin had visited the tailor. "All your things are still in your room," she said. "Including your clothes. But I daresay nothing will fit you anymore, so we may as well buy new."

Martin, having been cast out of the cottage and sent packing to London, found that he didn't much care where he was, and let his aunt and the tailor hold lengths of fabric in front of his person as if he were a sofa in need of reupholstering.

"Six pairs of pantaloons, I should think, and another six pairs of trousers," Aunt Bermondsey said. "Mostly pale gray. Waistcoats in gray, black, and various blues. Coats in black, gray, and blue. All the usual shirts, cravats, underthings, and so forth." The tailor's assistant took furious notes, while another assistant pulled bolts of fabric from the shelves that lined the room. "If you have an ensemble he could wear immediately with minimal tailoring, that would be even better."

Martin allowed himself to be led behind a folding screen, then went through the motions of removing his clothes with a sort of mechanical detachment that he suspected was just his mind's way of holding off a tantrum. He was breaking his heart only a week before he meant to; surely that shouldn't matter so much. He had always thought that doing the right thing would offer some sort of moral reward but it turned out it felt like complete shit. No wonder people resorted to villainy.

One of the assistants dropped a clean shirt over Martin's head and a pair of dove gray pantaloons of the softest wool were placed in his hands. The feel of crisp linen and expensive fabric offered some distraction from his dark mood. There really was something to be said for decent clothing, and it probably was only further proof of his bad character that he thought so. The threadbare shirts and loose trousers he had been wearing in the country were perfectly fine, of course. But this felt the way clothing was meant to feel. He slid the pantaloons over his hips and buttoned up a subtly striped gray waistcoat with no small degree of enthusiasm, then stepped out for his aunt's approval.

"I knew I was right about the gray," she said, regarding him through a lorgnette that she could not possibly require. "But those pantaloons need to be taken in. So does the waistcoat, for that matter."

"The pantaloons fit perfectly," Martin argued. He pinched the scant inch of fabric at his hip.

"On a man twice your age or twice your size loose pantaloons would be forgivable, even advisable. But on you, they need to be snug."

"I can't imagine how you expect me to sit in anything more snug than these," Martin protested.

"Who said anything about sitting? Just lounge and lean, darling. You'll thank me."

A mere half an hour later—he did not dare contemplate what this service was costing his aunt, because if she wanted to be idiotic with her money, he wasn't going to stop her— he tried on the altered pantaloons. Regarding himself in the cheval glass, he had to concede that, yes, his aunt had been correct about the grays. She was probably also correct about the pantaloons. He had never wasted time in considering his looks beyond an awareness that he was attractive in the way all the Easterbrooks in the portrait gallery at Lindley Priory were attractive; he had always had graver matters to occupy his mind, things like bad lungs and despotic fathers and empty bank accounts. Besides, even if he had once been handsome when he was at the peak of his health, he was now underweight and pale. But his reflection looked . . . elegant. Perhaps a trifle delicate—there would be no concealing his thinness or the pallor of his cheeks—but he looked rather like the drawings of men in fashion plates.

He spared a small, stupid thought for all the things he'd never do in these clothes—all the pigs he wouldn't catch and laundry he wouldn't learn to wash. It was a fistful of dirt on the grave of a life he hadn't ever quite believed he'd have, and which he knew he didn't deserve. His attempts to be useful now seemed laughably inadequate. The fact was that he had no idea how to even keep himself fed without someone else's aid. And if he couldn't keep himself fed, then he couldn't hope to look after Will, if Will needed him.

He remembered those frantic months after his father died, trying to scrape together the funds to get Will out of London. He had failed miserably, succeeding in nothing more than harming his tenants and providing himself with enough shame to last a lifetime. He still received rents from those farms, but had directed that it all be deposited in the parish poor box or put toward the running of the charity school that now occupied Lindley Priory. He couldn't bring himself to touch the money, and didn't think he could live with himself if he tried. No, the only hope he had to be useful to Will was by making the sort of marriage his aunt wished for him.

His aunt caught the attention of a passing tailor's assistant. "Please also furnish Sir Martin with all the usual country attire," she said, not bothering to look up from the stack of fabric samples on her lap. He nearly gagged at the sound of his title, but his aunt was using it relentlessly.

"I know you don't like it," she said when they were back in the carriage. "But it's both your name and your greatest asset. No, don't look at me like that, I'm not in the mood for the universal rights of man and I never will be. Practically speaking, your title is your greatest asset, and that's all there is to it."

"Be that as it may, it's still worth precisely nothing. It hasn't done me any good at all, as you well know." He was being peevish and difficult and he couldn't bring himself to stop.

"I shouldn't think it would, not when you're holed up in a hut in West Sussex. You're hardly likely to find an heiress at a pig farm. But your timing couldn't be better. It's the very beginning of the season so we have three full months to get things settled."

"I already feel sorry for the girl."

"It wouldn't have to be a proper marriage," his aunt said, without missing a beat, as if she had already given the matter some consideration. "There are plenty of young ladies who wouldn't expect you to have anything to do with them. You wouldn't need to share a house, let alone a bed. You confer a title on them, they confer some money on you, everybody lives happily ever after."

He narrowed his eyes and turned sideways on the seat to face his aunt. "You seem to be making a number of assumptions."

She sighed. "Darling, I'm making exactly one assumption, and it's that you don't want to go to bed with women, and frankly I don't care. Why are you looking at me like that? I found you keeping house with a young man, both of you in a frightful state of dishabille and covered in various bite marks and so forth. You ought to be grateful I got you out of there before you got yourselves arrested. Love in a cottage is all very romantic, and I'm certain I've read many tiresome poems on the topic, but a little bit of discretion would not go amiss in the future, nephew."

Martin tamped down a swell of horror that she had seen

all that. "And yet you still want me to marry some poor unsuspecting woman."

"Oh, be quiet. Not every woman wants a man in her bed. You could come to a very peaceable arrangement."

For one horrifying moment Martin thought he might cry. It had been a long day. His aunt's hand covered his own. "New clothes do go a long way toward mending a broken heart, I always find," she went on, and he didn't have it in him to protest that she had the wrong end of the stick. He was almost grateful that she seemed to understand.

"No clothing is that good," he sniffled.

"We'll visit the bootmaker tomorrow, then," she mused.

When the carriage stopped in front of Bermondsey House, Martin excused himself from dinner and followed a maid to the bedroom that was to be his. Peeling off his new clothes, he tried not to remember where he had been not twelve hours earlier. When he glanced in the looking glass, he tried not to take stock of the faded bite and bruises on his neck. If he thought of those things, he'd miss Will too much.

As that thought settled over his heart like a lead weight, he felt more than a mere thirty miles from the cottage. Maybe this distance would give him the strength to move past these months with Will. After all, Will had been able to part from Martin without any sign of distress. Martin had always suspected that his own feelings ran deeper than Will's and now he had evidence. It was just as well that they ended this before Will's feelings became more entrenched, because Martin felt truly miserable, and the only bright spot was that at least by parting now he had spared Will from that pain.

Will leaned against the closed door, his eyes squeezed shut, his heart pounding against his ribs, until he could no longer convince himself that he still heard the sound of hoofbeats and carriage wheels retreating down the lane. He could hardly stand to look around the cottage, knowing Martin wasn't there.

It was better this way, better to end their—his mind stumbled over the word *affair*—at the beginning. Their hearts would mend easier that way. Martin had been right. Besides, this separation was only temporary. In a few days—tomorrow night, even, if Will hurried—they'd both be in London. And, no, it wouldn't be the same, but they could be together. As friends, which had been enough for most of their lives, and which would still be enough tomorrow. If something angry and demanding lurked in the pit of his belly, he could just ignore it.

Will wrenched open his eyes and took in the unmade bed, the book Martin had been reading still facedown on the table, the cup of flowers. He wanted to shut his eyes again. Instead he threw on his coat, grabbed his coin purse, and left the cottage. He found Mrs. Tanner plucking a goose while Daisy collected the feathers.

"Didn't expect to see you today," Daisy said.

"I have a favor to ask. I'm going to London tomorrow,

rather than next week, and I'm hoping you can look after the cottage and feed the pigs for the extra time that I'll be away. I'll pay you, of course." He took the coin purse out of his coat pocket. "If I'm not back in two weeks, the pigs are yours." He tried not to dwell on that *if*, because then he'd have to admit that he wasn't coming back—he couldn't, not without Martin.

"What about your young man?" Mrs. Tanner asked.

"He already left."

"He can't have," Daisy said, her brows furrowed. "He asked me to show him how to do the wash one day next week."

"The wash?" Mrs. Tanner squawked, regarding her daughter with wide, scandalized eyes. "The *laundry*? A *gentleman*? I've never."

"That's what I said," Daisy agreed. "I've never seen a man do the wash in my entire life. But he insisted."

"I'd like to know how you suppose laundry gets done aboard ship if not by men," Will said absently, distracted by the idea of Martin setting out to learn how to perform such a humble task.

"Probably very badly," Mrs. Tanner said. "Probably not particularly often either. And I'd bet no *gentlemen* do laundry on any ship."

Will had to concede that she was correct on all points.

"Why did your Mr. Smith go to London without you?" Daisy asked. "He hardly even goes as far as the village by himself."

"His aunt arrived unexpectedly and he returned to town with her," Will said.

Mrs. Tanner and Daisy exchanged a glance Will could not interpret. "Was that the carriage we saw turn up the lane a few hours ago? Shiny, green, and with a picture of a lion on the door?"

"Yes," Will said.

"That's your friend's *aunt*?" Daisy's eyes were wide. "In a carriage like that?" Mother and daughter exchanged another impenetrable glance. "No wonder he went with her rather than learn to do the wash."

"It wasn't like that," Will said. "I think he'd rather have stayed to do the wash." The truth of his words sunk in as he spoke them. Martin would have stayed if he could have; in a world where they had their druthers, they both would have stayed. That something so humble as a one-room cottage and a couple of pigs was to be denied them seemed wretchedly unfair. Will dragged his mind away from that line of thought—if he started dwelling on things that were unfair, he might never stop.

He spent the rest of the day settling his bills at the village shops. In the morning he made sure the cottage was as safe and secure as he could make it: no imminent leaks, no bits of food left out for mice to get at, the pig pen as sturdy as it could be. He double-checked that the windows were shut tight and the teapot properly rinsed. He knew they weren't returning but the idea of the cottage becoming damp or infested with mice made him want to cry.

Only when he was finished did he begin to pack. He had arrived with little more than the shirt on his back, but since then the cottage had filled with books and jars of ink and all the detritus of life, all the little things that made a home, and far more than he could fit in his satchel.

On the shelf he had built with his own hands was the final manuscript of the play. He picked it up, considering making room in his satchel for it, as if Hartley didn't have half a dozen bound copies of the printed copy. But as he looked at the manuscript, he saw that in between each of the lines of dialogue were words written in a different handwriting. He stepped into the light to get a better look.

It took him a minute to understand what he was seeing, because while the handwriting was unmistakably Martin's—he'd recognize it even in the dark, he thought— the language was not English. He sounded out the words, and after stumbling over a few lines he realized he was reading French.

He didn't know when Martin had done this, although it must have been during the time Will spent helping Mrs. Tanner. Will could speak French—his mother had been a native—but he could read it only haltingly and couldn't write it at all. He recalled what Martin had told him, and imagined an eight-year-old Martin, alone in his sickroom, insisting on learning French because he missed his friend. Martin had called it jealousy, but maybe that was because he had the idea that wanting things—specifically closeness and affection—was wrong. To Will, it seemed only natural that a lonely child would do what he could to feel close to what few friends he had.

He read the first few pages aloud, remembering his mother's lessons on how to pronounce the language. A few pages later, he felt almost confident in his reading, and could hear the words as if it were his mother speaking them. It was an odd sensation—his words, Martin's pen, his mother's language—and even odder to know that Martin had sat at this table and translated his play. It was a good translation, too, preserving both the sense and the humor of the original. He took a few books out of his satchel to make room for the manuscript.

Before closing the flap on his satchel, he took the primroses from the cup and carefully pressed them between the pages of the book he was reading, then slid the book into his bag.

CHAPTER FIFTEEN

Martin stood in the doorway of the elegantly appointed bedchamber that his aunt had kept clean and ready for him. In one corner sat a trunk that contained everything he had brought from Lindley Priory the previous year. Almost afraid to peer inside, he tried to remember what he had thrown into his trunk in that hurried flight to town: a few changes of clothes, a shaving kit, a miniature portrait of his mother, Will's letters.

When he opened the lid, the first thing he took out was the clothing. It all looked enormous compared to the clothes he currently wore. But it was good quality, and he could sell it. He refolded the garments and stacked them on the dressing table. Then he looked at his mother's portrait. She had died before he was old enough to remember her, and when he thought of her it was mainly as the idea of someone who might have loved him, who might have prevented things from going the way they did with his father. But that was a heavy burden to put on a person he didn't know, a person who, at the time this portrait was painted, had been some years younger than himself. He really looked nothing like her, despite what Will might say, but he could see his aunt in the wry turn of his mother's mouth and the sharpness of her gaze.

He reached into the depths of the trunk for Will's letters, which was what he had come for in the first place, but was distracted by a gleam of gold. He bent and picked it up without thinking. He knew, even before his fingers closed around the cold metal, that it was his father's signet ring. Martin had worn it every day between his father's death and the day, a year later, when he finally left Lindley Priory, and not once since then had he thought about it. He didn't even remember tossing it into the trunk. Absently, he slid it onto his third finger, but it was precariously loose. On his middle finger it was a better fit but still wobbly. The band, made of intricate swirls of gold, was in need of polishing. In the center was the Easterbrook coat of arms, which was supposed to be a dragon and a unicorn holding up a shield, but those creatures looked so belligerent that Martin always thought they appeared to be quarreling over it.

He remembered the ring forever glinting from his father's finger, glinting when Martin was ordered back to his room for another bloodletting, glinting when his father hared off to London for a round of debauchery. But the ring was tarnished now, a vaguely embarrassing reminder of faded glory, a sad relic of misused power. Put it next to his mother's portrait and you got a pretty little picture of landed aristocracy—old power, a compliant bride, a tale that spun itself out again and again.

And here he stood, in his soft wool coat and his newly cut hair, getting ready to play his part in the latest telling of the tale. Except now the Easterbrook baronetcy wouldn't be purchasing compliance, but solvency. He, Martin realized with a shudder, would be the compliant one. He'd be forever beholden to his new wife and her family. The first time he got sick they'd realize how bad a bargain they had struck. Christ, they might realize it before then, if he couldn't manage to get his wife with child. And while he didn't think his wife's family would be able to lock him away, he also knew he'd be too guilty to protest if they insisted on putting him in a sea-side asylum for invalids with weak lungs—for his own good, of course.

It would likely be fine, he told himself. People entered into these sorts of marriages every day, if his aunt were to be believed. He slid the ring over his finger and it gleamed back up at him like a warning.

"I'm sorry, but I can't let you go like that," Hartley said, looking about as formidable as a man could with a drooling baby on his hip. "It's eight o'clock in the morning, which I assure you is a thoroughly bizarre time for social calls, but more importantly you haven't eaten since you got here last night. I need hardly mention that you look like you were dragged behind the stagecoach all the way from Sussex. You simply cannot saunter up to Bermondsey House looking like that and expect to be let in."

"But—"

"He'll still be there later, Will," Hartley said severely. "Now sit down." Will sat in one of the straight-backed wooden chairs in the Fox's still empty taproom. "I saw that you arrived with a satchel. Dare I hope it contains presentable clothing or will you be borrowing something of mine?"

"Er. Probably the latter," said Will.

"Let the man eat his food," Sam said, approaching the table with a plate, and then leaving with the baby. Will dutifully ate his breakfast as Hartley stared balefully at him from across the table.

"I knew it was a bad idea," Hartley said. "The two of you in one another's pockets for so many months."

"You're an oracle, Hart. Who knew?"

Hartley ignored this. "And now, because you're you, you'll assume that whatever happened is actually a grand passion that requires you to make an enormous mess of your life rather than two people doing exactly what people do when they're cooped up together."

"I don't know what you're talking about," Will grumbled.

"Dare I hope it's only physical?"

"Hartley!" Will knew he was blushing.

"How bad is it? Does he feel the same way?"

Will thought of the flowers pressed between the pages of his book and mumbled something that might be interpreted as assent. "In any event, it's over," he said, pushing food around on his plate.

Hartley sighed, whether with relief or sympathy Will could not tell. "You did the right thing by handing him over to his aunt. Well done. Heroic self-sacrifice, accomplished."

"It was his idea," Will said.

"Never thought sacrifice was much in Martin's line," Hartley mused. "But I suppose he yearned for the comforts of civilization—"

"It wasn't like that," Will protested, but even as he spoke he realized that Martin probably was very much enjoying having three hot meals a day and servants to draw his baths. And Will wanted Martin to have those things. He tried to remind himself that Martin was where he belonged.

"Regardless, now what you ought to do is give him some time to learn how to be Sir Martin again. You'll call on him later, but first please finish your breakfast, shave as if you care about the results, and make some kind of effort with your hair. I'll put some clothes that might fit you on your bed."

When Will went upstairs, he half expected to find one of Hartley's elaborate waistcoats and gold-buttoned coats sitting out for him. But instead there was a suit of clothes in brown wool, perfectly ordinary, and showing signs of wear. In fact, the last several times he had seen his brother, Hartley had been wearing unremarkable clothing—the sort of clothes one might expect to find on a man who lived above a pub, the sort of man you wouldn't look at twice. With something of a start, he realized Hartley had done this to protect Sam, to keep anyone from reading anything specific into the nature of their friendship.

"You gave up your waistcoats," Will said, pointing an accusing finger at Hartley when he walked into the room with a ewer of hot water. "And you dare accuse me of grand passions."

"Fashions change, darling," Hartley said. And then, busying himself in laying out a razor and a comb, "I'd go about in sackcloth for him if he required it, as much as it pains me to admit it." He looked up sharply. "Don't you dare throw it in my face."

"I didn't mean to!" Will held up his hands in surrender. "I think it's . . . nice, that's all."

"You would," Hartley sniffed.

An hour later Will was deemed sufficiently presentable to visit Bermondsey House. He knew where it was, because he had spent countless futile hours lurking around the place when he was looking for Martin the previous autumn. He lifted the brass knocker and let it fall. "I'm here to call on Sir Martin Easterbrook," he told the servant who answered the door.

Will's borrowed clothing felt scratchy and too tight as he waited for the footman to return, but eventually the man did, and led him up a flight of stairs. Will found himself in an empty sitting room filled with furniture that he felt certain he shouldn't be allowed to sit on. Everything was dainty, edged with gilt, and likely worth more than Will could ever hope to earn. He'd count himself lucky if he got out with nothing crashing in pieces to the polished parquet floor. On the chimneypiece stood a clock that seemed to be made of solid gold and comprised of intertwined cherubs who were up to no good. He stepped closer and squinted.

"I didn't expect to see you so soon."

Will whipped around to see Martin in the doorway. The clock wobbled precariously and Will lifted a steadying hand, but was seized by the notion that he didn't want to look like he was trying to steal it. Which was patently absurd—of course Martin knew he wasn't in the business of stealing clocks or anything else. He tried to collect himself.

"I came as soon as I could," Will said. "I told you I would."

"You told me a good number of things," Martin remarked flatly. He was wearing a pair of gray pantaloons that looked like they were sewn onto his body and a dark blue coat that threw the paleness of his skin and hair into relief. Will didn't think he had ever seen Martin look so beautiful or so refined, but it was a reminder that Martin belonged to the same world as this sitting room, a world of thick carpets and impossibly delicate teacups. Will had known this all along, had known it when they were children and he had needed to tiptoe through the servants' entrance at Lindley Priory if he wanted to see Martin. He had never not been aware of this fundamental inequality. Never before, though, had he felt like this gap between their stations could actually keep them apart. That gap was filled with gilt clocks and liveried servants and finely tailored clothes. In the country they had lived in a fantasy land where none of this mattered, but in the real world it did; even if it didn't matter to Martin, it mattered to Will. Will hadn't thought he had any pride left. He thought it had quite literally been flogged out of him, stripped away alongside his rank. But sitting here he felt like being among all this finery humbled him in some way that he didn't want any part of.

They still had half the length of the room between them. Will took a tentative step to close the gap, aware that this should not have felt as difficult as it did. "You look good," he said, aware that he was making an understatement. "All of that—" he gestured to Martin's attire "—suits you." It did more than suit him. It looked like a second skin and was just this side of obscene. Then Will remembered that he no longer had any right to look at Martin that way, and dragged his gaze to Martin's face.

"You didn't come here to congratulate me on my tailoring," Martin said. He still leaned against the door frame, as if deciding whether to step into the room.

"I came because I missed you."

"It's only been a few days." Martin's expression was closed off, his eyes flinty and hard. It was nothing Will hadn't seen before; this was fairly typical of Martin, in fact. But over the past months Will had started to take for granted Martin's moments of openness and vulnerability. He had gotten used to being looked upon as something rare and loved and now he felt the lack of it.

"And I've seen you every day for months. Christ, Martin, this shouldn't be so awkward." As soon as the words left his mouth, he regretted it—admitting to the stiffness between them would only compound their problems.

But Martin huffed out a laugh—not a pleasant laugh, but a laugh nonetheless. "I've reverted to form. I'm hardly known for my warm and inviting nature."

"You can be warm and inviting," Will said. "And you can be prickly and difficult. I like you this way and every way."

Martin stared at him for a long moment, cool and considering. "You're making a poor fist of returning to our usual friendship."

"Bollocks. You're my friend and I'm allowed to tell you

that I like you." He stepped closer, now within touching distance.

Martin shrugged. Will stuck his hands in his pockets and scuffed his toe against the pile of a carpet that he could only assume was priceless.

"So," Martin said, "this is the friendly rapport we have to look forward to."

"No," Will said, gruffer than he intended. "It'll just take some time to adjust."

Martin gave skeptical little hum. "Has it ever occurred to you," he said, a dangerous note in his voice, "that things could have been different?"

"Different in what way?" Will asked, not sure he wanted to hear the answer.

"We were both doing marvelously in the country. If we wished to feed pigs and live in near poverty, we could have spared ourselves this detour into trauma and illness. We could have simply stayed in Cumberland. There are cottages by the dozen and any quantity of livestock."

It took Will a moment to understand. "You're talking about what would have happened if I hadn't joined the navy, if instead I had tried to scratch out some kind of living up north. You're imagining that we could have stayed there and somehow wound up feeling as we did in Sussex. Feeling as we do," he amended.

"Precisely," Martin said tightly.

"No, Martin, I don't think about that. I don't let myself. I don't know who I'd be if I hadn't—if none of that had happened. And neither do you." Will clenched his fists. He had thought Martin cared for him the way he was, not as a second-rate version of the person he would have been, and he tried not to be too disappointed to learn the truth. "There's no what if. This is not something I can while away a morning hypothesizing about. That universe doesn't even exist in my imagination, all right? It can't. I won't let it."

Martin looked like he had been slapped. He looked like he wanted to go to Will, to take him in his arms, and Will didn't know why he wouldn't. Martin might be in a mood that was foul even for him, but he was never anything other than kind about the things that had happened to Will at sea. Will braced himself, waiting for Martin to say something—to either make it worse or to make it better. But they were interrupted by the arrival of a servant carrying a silver tea service, and the tension in the room dissipated. They sat, Will on the edge of a strange backless sofa and Martin in a chair made of wood carved to look fine as gossamer. Will had the distinct sense that if either of them moved wrong, all the furniture in the room would crumble to toothpicks, and he almost wished it would, just to give him an excuse to walk out the door. He watched silently as Martin poured the tea.

"Any luck finding a bride?" Will blurted out. He had been aiming for jocular friendly banter, a remark that would show Martin he supported his plan and didn't intend to let his own feelings get in the way of their friendship. Instead it came out bitter and hostile.

"I've been here three days." Only the faintest lift of an eyebrow disturbed the impassivity of Martin's expression.

"I'm trying to be supportive."

Martin blinked. "Why? It's a bit of a blow to my pride that you're so complacent about this, that you're so ready to walk away from me."

"I'm not walking away from you," Will protested. "That's my point."

"Ah, yes. Silly me. Nobody walked away from anybody else. This is just a cessation of fucking, followed by a return to how things used to be. It was your idea, even. My idea was to spend the rest of our lives going to bed together. No. Bugger that. My plan was to spend the rest of our lives loving one another."

That was the first time Martin had said the word *love* and it just figured he had to do it during a fight. Will was equal parts fond and devastated. "While you're married to someone else."

"Correct." The syllables were crisp and uncompromising. "Did it occur to you," Martin hissed, "that I don't want to be passed around from pillar to post like an embarrassing burden, and that I don't like this any more than you do? Considerably less, in fact. Did it occur to you that I might, just possibly, be humiliated not to able to earn my keep in some way? That I don't enjoy being entirely helpless? That maybe, just maybe, after being told my whole life that I'm a useless waste of space, I might want to prove that I'm something more?"

Will felt a wash of shame pass over him, because the fact was that he had not considered any of that. All he had thought of was how miserably, hideously jealous he was at the idea of Martin belonging to anyone else. "I'm sorry," he said.

Then, as Will watched, some of the surliness slid off Martin's face. "I know I'm being a bastard. But I'd go back to Sussex with you now, right this minute." His jaw was set, but he didn't meet Will's eyes, instead gazing at the small, perfect teacup he cradled in his hand. "If I thought that was a good idea for either of us. But if this needs to end—which it does, if you can't accept that at some point I'll marry—then it's better to end it sooner rather than later." He blew out a breath. "This awkwardness will be temporary. God, Will, we've been through worse. We need to remember what it's like to be friends in the usual way."

"Right." Will got to his feet. "I know you're right. I just—" He clenched and unclenched his fists, trying to will away the anger and jealousy that threatened to well up within him. "I just can't do this right now. I'm staying with Hartley. You can ask for me at the Fox on Shoe Lane." He didn't suggest coming back to Bermondsey House.

CHAPTER SIXTEEN

W<small>ILL'S</small> visit at Bermondsey House had been about as disastrous as possible, and Martin knew it had been mostly his fault. They were going to need some time—time for Will to move on, and time for Martin to learn to act like he had. That was all. Maybe it would help if they didn't see one another for a while. After all, there had been years during which they hadn't seen one another, and they had still been friends.

That gave Martin an idea. He swept into the morning room and found his aunt's writing desk unoccupied. As soon as he dipped the pen into the inkwell and scribbled the date at the top of the page, he felt like he was on sure ground for the first time in days. There was something about the familiarity of writing to Will that soothed Martin far more than Will's presence had. Letters had been the medium of their friendship long before their bodies were. The neat stack of letters sitting in Martin's trunk stood as proof that they could do this, that they could exist as something other than lovers, that the past few weeks hadn't ruined anything.

"Dear Will," he wrote, and then the rest of the words flowed out, with none of the awkwardness they had in the Bermondsey House drawing room. It was as easy and natural as talking to Will when they shared a pillow. He wrote about a friend of his aunt who lost an ear bob in the punch bowl the other night. He wrote about visiting his mother's grave in the parish churchyard. It was one page, front and back, filled with mostly trifling concerns, and containing not even the faintest suggestion of anything that could get either of them into trouble, but when he signed his name he knew he had written a love letter.

And when Will wrote back—a letter filled with slightly less trifling material than Martin's, but with words underscored and scratched out and ink blotted in a manner befitting a twelve-year-old—that was a love letter too. He had closed with a simple "Yours, W.S.," but the *yours* was underscored by the tail of the *Y*, and the postscript simply read "Soon."

There was no undoing the fact that they loved one another. Even if they never touched one another again, even if they never saw one another again, even if they never spoke or wrote the words—the truth was still there. At some point, the fundamental material of their friendship had undergone a sea change and it couldn't be reversed. Martin had already known that he would go through the rest of his days in love with Will, but now he had to face the possibility that Will might do the same. When Martin reread Will's letter, the stubbornness was there in every pen stroke, in every turn of phrase, and Martin feared Will was going to hold on to this. It was a stupid thing to do, and Will was going to do it anyway, and Martin was an idiot for not having seen it earlier. What was worst of all was that this knowledge made Martin love him even more.

Well, Will was a stubborn fool. That was hardly news. What mattered now was what Martin did about it. Clearly Martin was going to have to do the thinking for both of them.

"You haven't seen Martin in days," Hartley said.

Will looked up from under the table where he was tightening screws. "I didn't realize you were keeping an eye on me."

Hartley shrugged, not bothering to deny it. "I'm trying not to act completely insane about it, but I'm worried you're going to get your heart broken and repair to the nearest opium den."

Will sighed and got to his feet. "That's not going to happen."

"Which one? Getting your heart broken or going to an opium den."

"The opium den." Every time Will left the Fox, some old and unsettled part of his brain reminded him how close he was to his old haunts, but he wasn't going to visit one, even though not doing so required more of an effort than he might have preferred.

"Just—tell me if you're going to, though. That way I'm not imagining you dead."

Will was ready to protest that he was fine and Hartley's concerns were unnecessary, but Hartley had every right to be worried, he supposed. The thing about losing one's mind once was that everybody expected it to happen again. He sighed. "All right. I promise."

Hartley ran a finger along the glossy wood of the bar top, then took a rag out of his pocket to polish away a probably imaginary blot. It was early, and the Fox was still empty. "I thought for certain Martin would be loitering around here all hours of the night and day."

"I had hoped he would," Will admitted, turning his attention to fixing a wobbly chair leg. "We parted under less than ideal terms in Sussex, and even worse the other day."

"I gathered as much."

"He means to marry. He says it's the only way he can be sure to have a roof over his head and food in his belly. His other option, I suppose, would be to rely on me, and while I'd be more than happy to let him, it's not like I have much to offer."

"It sounds like you support his decision to marry," Hartley said. He spoke in the measured tones of a man trying his best to bite his tongue.

"I don't like it. But I want the best for him. I can't be with him if he's married, though."

"Why not?" Hartley looked up from the tap he was polishing.

"It's dishonest."

Hartley tapped his finger. "It's not ideal. But I'm not certain it's dishonest either. He wouldn't be making a love match. It wouldn't be unusual for both parties to have liaisons. Unless you were tremendously indiscreet, his wife would have no cause to be jealous. You'd be her husband's friend, not a rival."

"I doubt you'd be advising me the same if I were a woman."

"I'm not certain either, but that may be because a husband's spending time with a woman is more obviously an affair, while a man's spending time with another man is unremarkable. The lady's feelings wouldn't have to be hurt. She'd probably consider herself fortunate to have so faithful a husband."

Will got to his feet and sat on the edge of the table. "You've thought about this."

"Martin Easterbrook isn't my favorite person, but I want you to be happy. But, Will, surely you knew going into things with Martin that he'd eventually have to marry."

Will didn't know how to explain to his brother that he hadn't thought that far ahead. "I just wanted to be with him, and he wanted to be with me, and we're already—God, Hartley, I don't need to explain to you how he and I are, because you already know. We're important to one another."

Hartley frowned at him. "I know. That's why I said what I said. There was a time when Sam and I were being stupid about things. Mostly me, if I'm honest. And sometimes I think about how easy it would have been to let things go wrong." He gave Will a faint smile. "If you and Martin can figure out a way to be happy together, I think you ought to do it. I think that his getting married is a small consideration."

"How would you feel if Sam got married?"

"Horrible, obviously. But Sam doesn't have consumption. And he has a trade. He doesn't need to marry. But if he came to me tomorrow and said he needed to, I know we'd see our way through, because the alternative is too grim to think about."

"My plan was to go back to how things were with him. We were only lovers for a short time, but we were friends for so long before that." He refused to think about how even friendship would be strained with a man who was ensconced in a world of silver tea pots and velvet draperies.

Hartley gave him a look that plainly said he thought Will was full of shit, and went back to polishing the bar.

Chapter Seventeen

When a letter arrived from Will that was unprecedentedly riddled with words that had been crossed out, and perilously close to the sort of declaration that could land one or both of them in the pillory, Martin decided enough was enough. For the first time ever, he threw one of Will's letters onto the fire instead of placing it with the rest of his collection. His plan to let time and distance restore their friendship to its earlier state had clearly been a failure. He needed to see Will in person.

He couldn't quite work up the nerve to call on Will at the Fox, partly because he knew Hartley wouldn't particularly want him there, and partly because he thought they ought to meet somewhere very public. So he wrote Will a short letter requesting that they meet the following day at a particular bench in Hyde Park.

"I'm going to see a friend this afternoon," he announced to his aunt at the breakfast table.

"You say that as if you expect me to bar the doors," she

said, looking up from her newspaper. "Go call on your friend. Call on ten friends."

He had rather thought she would insist that he accompany her on her usual round of morning visits. "Nothing of the sort," he said, feigning confidence.

"In fact," Aunt Bermondsey said, her attention firmly fixed on her newspaper, "if you think you might not return until tomorrow, dress in a way that passes as morning clothes. Don't give me that look. I acquired my wealth of information the hard way, and now I'm passing it on to the next generation, which is very auntly of me, I should think." She winked at him and he felt his face heat.

"It's not—I don't—"

"I shouldn't make you squirm. I'm sorry, darling. My point is just that I really don't care what you get up to. You're only young once. And you needn't worry what Lord Bermondsey thinks," she added. "I'm not entirely certain he even knows you're staying here." Indeed, Martin had seen his aunt's husband at the dinner table a mere handful of times, and was aware of him only as a vague, moustached presence. "He asked me only yesterday why there was a tall, spectacled man in our library, and it gave me quite a fright before I realized he meant you."

Martin laughed despite himself. Aunt Bermondsey, noticing his squint, had dragged Martin to her oculist the previous day, and now Martin had a pair of silver-framed spectacles in his coat pocket, through which he could see an astonishing array of previously invisible objects. And his aunt had seemed happy for him, as if she were glad to do this service and had no intention to hold it over his head. He found that the more time he spent with her, the more willing he was to put his aunt in the same category as Will and Daisy, rather than his father and his father's servants. He suspected he was being overly trusting, too willing to see an ally because he had nobody else.

It somehow took nearly an hour to get to the park, because every conveyance in London had apparently decided to take to the streets that afternoon. An hour spent in a carriage with nothing to do and nothing to look at was just the thing to ratchet his nerves up to an unbearable level, and he would have regretted not going on foot except for how walking in town made him short of breath. But finally the carriage stopped and he all but flung himself onto the street.

He found Will waiting for him at the bench Martin had specified. Will opened his mouth to greet him but Martin made a silencing gesture, then sat beside him.

"There can't be any letters like that last one," Martin said.

"I know. I meant to be careful, but it didn't last."

"If we can't write without exposing ourselves and we can't meet without quarreling, then we'll need to stop meeting and writing."

"No," Will said at once.

"Do you have a better plan?" Martin didn't turn his head. He kept his attention on the brightly dressed women, the tiny dogs pulling at their leads, the horses and carriages in the distance. He didn't want to see Will's face as he conceded defeat.

"We'll have it your way," Will said.

"Meaning that we part ways for a while," Martin said calmly. It was nothing he hadn't expected, and he was certain it was for the best, however miserable he felt about it presently.

"No. I don't want to do that. God forgive me, I don't want to stop loving you," Will said, his voice low and heated. "It's felt like a gift, and I don't want to give it up. What I mean is that I think we should ignore the fact that you plan to marry. The future isn't guaranteed. A lot of things can happen."

Martin still didn't turn his head, afraid to see what he might read on Will's face. "After all, I might die before I get around to marrying," he said, aware that some of the calm had slipped from his voice.

"You're so dramatic. Sometimes I can't believe that I'm the one who wrote a play." Martin could hear the fondness in Will's voice and felt something in his chest expand. "No, Martin, I mean that it's intensely stupid to whistle happiness down the wind, and I am—was—happy with you. If I have to make compromises to be with you, I can do that."

Martin's heart beat hard in his chest. "Compromises?"

He felt Will shift on the bench beside him. "Being with a married man seems . . ."

"What does it seem?"

On the wooden slats of the bench between them, Will's hand opened and closed. "I want to apologize," he said. "From the first minute you told me you needed to marry, I've been difficult about it. I want you to be happy and safe. I ought to just accept it."

"Why?"

"Because my jealousy is a small thing compared to how much you need to be secure—how much we both want you to be secure. God, if I could offer you a home—not a cottage, not a make-do sort of existence—then we'd be having a different conversation. But things are the way they are."

"Are you so very jealous, then?" Martin asked, trying to sound as if he didn't care about the answer.

"I know jealousy isn't fair to you and I ought to be ashamed—" Will began. He was wringing his hands.

"Get up." Martin regretted ever thinking that meeting in a public place was a good idea. "Come this way." He began down a path away from the more populated parts of the park. And—to hell with everything—he looped his arm through Will's. Men walked arm in arm; he had seen it himself. So what if the feel of Will's body next to his made him want to get pressed against the nearest tree.

"What's happening?" Will asked as they proceeded off the path and into a copse of trees.

"Shut up," Martin hissed, and all but dragged Will further into the wooded area. "You think you're the only jealous one?" he asked, finally rounding on Will. "Tell me again," he demanded.

Will's eyes were wide, and Martin saw the moment he understood what Martin wanted. "I'd be so jealous," he admitted.

"More."

"I don't want anyone else to touch you."

"Is that so?" Martin said, low and demanding.

"In that get-up, I don't want anyone to so much as look at

you." Will cast an appraising glance from the top of Martin's head to the tips of his boots.

"Oh yes?" He put a hand on Will's hip.

"I want to haul you into the nearest carriage and take you to Sussex and throw you on the bed and never let you leave, and these are all barbaric sentiments and I feel properly ashamed of myself—"

"To hell with that. I like you selfish." He walked Will backward toward a tree. "I like to know that I'm not the only one. I've always been jealous over you. You know this." He cupped Will's jaw, running a thumb along his lower lip. Then he leaned in and brushed their mouths together.

Will supposed that at some point he'd understand why confessing what he considered his most regrettable personal failing had gotten him kissed to within an inch of his life, but in the meantime he was content to let Martin have his way with him. He kissed Will hard, slow and searching, as if he were trying to memorize the shape of Will's mouth.

"Damn it, Will," Martin said after Will had gone soft and pliant against him. "Feel free to be good and noble in every other aspect of your life, but not this one."

"Where exactly are we?" Will asked, looking over Martin's shoulder. He knew they were a minute's walk from the typical throng of visitors to Hyde Park on a day without rain, but he couldn't see them through the trees.

"The Serpentine is over there," Martin said, gesturing behind Will. "And the barracks are there," he said, gesturing to the side. "After dark, this is a place where men come for assignations. The guards never bother patrolling here." Martin must have caught the incredulous look Will was giving him, because he rolled his eyes. "I wasn't here for the assignations, obviously, but because after I left my aunt's house I didn't know where to go."

Feeling very diplomatic, Will decided that instead of lecturing his friend on the idiocy of sleeping rough while consumptive—or, indeed, ever—he would imagine Martin's reaction to seeing men on their assignations. "Did you enjoy watching?"

"No, you utter pervert," Martin said, laughing. "Think of how much work you had to do to get me to enjoy . . . participating."

"I'm thinking of it now," Will said, leaning in for another kiss. "I'm afraid if I get you hard, you'll rip a seam or injure yourself," he whispered, drawing a finger up the inseam of Martin's pantaloons. He decided that his sad susceptibility to costly clothes would be a secret he took to the grave.

"Idiot," Martin said, and drew him in, a hand fisted in his shirt, for a deeper kiss.

They left the copse of woods and returned to the footpath, walking close enough that they could keep their voices low enough to be private, Will's arm tucked into the crook of Martin's elbow.

Strolling together was a comforting echo of their country walks even though there were people in every direction and horses and carriages jamming up the paths. The ground under their feet was level and neatly packed, so as not to overly soil the shoes of the ladies and gentlemen who promenaded about. The sky wasn't even the same blue as it was in Sussex, dimmed as it was by the smoke and fog of the city. But despite all that, walking and talking with Martin was something Will had known for as long as he could remember.

"I say, is that you, Sedgwick?"

Will stopped short, his arm coming dislodged from Martin's.

"William Sedgwick? Midshipman?"

Will turned toward the familiar voice, and saw a man a few years older than himself, with the upright bearing and slightly sunburned cheeks of a naval officer. "Lieutenant Reese," he said faintly.

"Captain now," Reese said. "You vanished off the face of the earth, man. Staunton and I looked and looked but there wasn't a trace of you. Henries took up a collection." He turned to Martin. "Your friend saved our lives, not to put too fine a point on it. He saved the lives of every officer on that ship and every sailor who would otherwise have mutinied. It was a damned shame that they tossed you out after all that."

Will forced himself to keep his eyes open, to see the curricles and phaetons on the opposite side of the park, to hear the sounds of women laughing and horses neighing. Martin was beside him, safe and sound, wearing shiny top boots and smelling of flowery soap. He slid his hand along the soft wool of Martin's sleeve until his smallest finger touched Martin's. It was 1819, this was London, and they were both alive.

"I really didn't," Will finally managed to say.

"Mark my words," Reese said, ignoring Will and directing his speech directly to Martin, "there would have been a mutiny if Sedgwick here hadn't poured oil on troubled seas, as it were. Where are you living now? Henries especially would want to thank you in person."

"The Fox on Shoe Lane," Will said, his voice sounding like it was coming from far away.

"We'd better be going, Sedgwick," Martin said briskly. "Lady Bermondsey will be waiting for us."

Only vaguely realizing that Martin was lying through his teeth, Will tipped his hat and bade a clumsy farewell to Reese.

"With the traffic what it is," Martin said, Will's arm tight against his side, "it'll be ages before you get to Shoe Lane in a carriage."

"I can walk," Will said. "I'm fine."

After a short pause, Martin cleared his throat. "All right. We'll walk.

"Will," Martin said softly, and Will realized he hadn't moved from the place where he had been standing for the past few minutes, as if rooted in place. "Will." It was all he had to say, that syllable somehow communicating affection and shared sorrows and loyalty and a thousand other things for which even the word *love* was only a rough approximation.

Will looked down and saw that Martin was holding one of his hands, chafing it between his own, in full view of anyone who cared to look that way. It was reckless and stupid and Will's heart was filled with a fondness that was equally reckless and stupid. With his free hand, he wiped away a drop of moisture that had gathered at the corner of his eye, then reached over and straightened Martin's lapels.

Chapter Eighteen

Martin's knowledge of London geography was patchy at best, so he had to rely entirely on Will's guidance to get them to the Fox. As Will seemed to be in something of a daze, Martin feared they would wander the labyrinth of city streets for hours. By the time they reached Shoe Lane, Martin was all but wheezing—not, he thought, from the exertion so much as the bad air. He had taken longer walks in the country without so much as a cough.

"All right there," Martin murmured nonsensically to Will as they turned into yet another dark, narrow passageway. He had been filling Will's ears with soothing foolishness since they left Hyde Park. It was with enormous relief that he finally caught sight of the freshly painted sign hanging above the door of the Fox. He could put Will to bed and trust that Hartley would care for him. Suddenly the prospect of an awkward meeting with Hartley no longer seemed so dire, as long as Will would be looked after and Martin could just sit down.

Martin did not have terribly much experience with public houses beyond the Blue Boar and the inn in the village nearest to Lindley Priory, but he thought the Fox seemed a respectable sort of place, with plenty of clean windows and shiny brass fittings. The air was redolent with the scent of cooking—herbs, rich sauce, and roasting meat—and under that, the smell of ale. Every table was full and the air was thick with the sound of mingled conversations.

"The stairs are through the back," Will said, indicating a door behind the bar. Before they got that far, they were intercepted by Hartley, who, if he were surprised to encounter Martin, did not show it on his face.

"Is anything the matter?" Hartley asked his brother.

"I'm fine. Ran into a shipmate and had a bad moment. Martin's just making a fuss, that's all."

Martin didn't bother denying it. "Thank you for letting me fuss. Would you eat if food were put in front of you?"

"I'll bring supper up," Hartley said, not waiting for Will's answer, and disappeared through one of the back doors.

Will led the way to a stairwell. "I really am all right," he said. "Relatively speaking."

"You're doing wonderfully," Martin said, gasping for air as he climbed the two flights of stairs.

As soon as they had a door shut behind them, Martin pulled Will into his arms and held him as tightly as he could. He didn't say anything, just felt the solid presence of Will's body against his own, the softness of Will's hair against his cheek, the coarseness of his coat beneath Martin's fingertips, all evidence that Will was safe and they

were together. And if he was leaning against Will as much
as Will was leaning against him, that was fine too.

"I can hear you breathe," Will said after a minute, his
voice muffled by Martin's coat.

Martin thought about brushing off Will's concern, but
he didn't think this was the time for dishonesty. "My lungs
hate this city. They hate the smoke and damp. And don't
you dare tell me I ought to have put you in a hackney and
gone home. Don't you dare." He waited, half-braced to see if
Will would protest, but Will only held him tighter.

They were interrupted by three raps sounding at the door,
followed by Hartley entering with a tray. Martin immediately made to step away from Will, but Will kept his arms
looped around Martin's neck. Martin knew what it must
look like, and he felt slightly exposed but also a little proud
that Will would own their relationship like that. And more
than either of those things, he was so glad for Will to have a
brother he didn't have to hide the truth from. He had hardly
gotten used to having his arms around another person; doing
so openly was almost inconceivable.

"I'll put this here," Hartley said, placing the tray on a
small table that was set beneath the room's single window.
"And you'll let me know if you need anything?" He addressed
the question to Will, but flicked a glance at Martin, and
stayed in the room until Martin nodded.

The tray held two plates, a covered dish, and two tan-
kards of ale. Martin lifted the cover and saw that the dish
contained a stew of some kind, aromatic and rich. He put
a large serving onto Will's plate and helped himself as well.

"This is familiar," Will said.

"It ought to be. You spent half the winter putting food under my nose and hoping I'd eat it."

"I meant that it reminds me of those months you looked after me after I got home."

Martin was ready to steer the conversation in any other direction, but maybe after seeing his shipmate, Will wanted to talk about that awful period of time. "A piss-poor job I did of that," Martin said as lightly as possible, paying more attention to keeping the anxiety from his voice than on the words he was actually speaking. "I recall spending a few months dragging you out of damp-ridden opium dens and forcing you to eat solid food. And then my father died and I didn't even have the funds to continue doing that much."

Will furrowed his brow. "What does that mean?"

Martin realized he had said more than he meant, but before he could explain away his words or even decide whether he wanted to, Will pointed an accusatory fork in his direction. "You shook your tenants down to get money for me. I thought you needed to pay off your father's debts."

Martin didn't bother denying it. A part of him was even relieved to have it out in the open. Now Will would know the worst.

"Martin, you had to know I wouldn't want that."

Martin put down his fork. "At the time, what you wanted was to seek oblivion in a cloud of opium, and I was terrified about what would happen when your money ran out. I didn't care one way or another about what you'd think of how I treated my tenants. More to the point, I didn't care about my tenants, or myself, or anybody at all. All I cared about was you. I know that's immoral and I'm trying to do better, but I can't even promise that I wouldn't still do reprehensible things if that were what you needed. I don't care, so you can save your lecture." There. The worst was out, and he was both relieved to have it done with and terrified to find what would come next.

Will let out a slow breath. "Next time consider stealing from the rich and powerful, all right?"

"That's it? You're not cross?"

"Of course I am. But, Martin, I probably would have stolen from a nun if it meant keeping you alive this past winter. I would have stolen from a nun and liked it."

Martin felt himself preening, almost, at Will's admission that he'd do bad things for him, and then caught himself. "Only a rich and powerful nun, though."

"Of course," Will said, with the first hint of a smile since they had left Hyde Park. "Did it ever occur to you that we were together even before we were . . . together? I mean, you're always at the front of my mind, even when we're hundreds of miles away. You're the most important person in my life. Even if we had never gone to bed together, even if neither of us fancied men, we'd still be together. We just wouldn't have a name for it."

"Did it occur to me?" Martin repeated faintly. "Yes, William. It occurred to me. Did it occur to you that even if we had never gone to bed together, you might still be jealous of any wife of mine?" Will looked up at him with a round-eyed surprise, but he didn't deny it.

Martin didn't know which of them stood first, or which of them led the way toward the bedroom. Half an hour earlier he wouldn't have thought it possible that either of them could have wanted this. Will was shaken and anxious; Martin was tired and ill. But there they were, peeling one another's clothes off, kissing with more affection than heat. He had always thought sex was something base and animalistic, and maybe sometimes it was. But it was also this—a comfort after a long day, a reminder that there was someone who wanted to take care of you, a small piece of mercy in an unyielding world. When Will lay back and Martin bent over his lap, he was astonished by the gentleness of the act, the tenderness of his own lips and tongue, the sweetness of Will's hand in his hair. And then, later, his face buried in Will's neck, he found that there could be a sort of surrender in his own release, a slackening of the line between what he needed and what was possible.

Martin woke up warm but still tired, Will's back plastered to his chest. Will was very much asleep, and if Martin knew anything about his friend's morning habits, it would be at least another hour before he even cracked an eye. Carefully, Martin eased himself up to sitting position, extricating an arm from underneath Will's chest and a leg from over Will's hips. Will let out an unsatisfied little huff and tipped over onto his stomach.

This gave Martin a view of Will's dark curls tumbled over the pillow, one wiry arm flung out to the side, and the lattice of scars that covered Will's back. In the morning light, some were faint and fine, mere pale slivers that might have passed unnoticed if not side by side with their raised and ropy mirror images. He knew, from the few things Will had said and the many things he hadn't said, that these marks had been the work of months as the *Fotheringay* made its slow progress from the West Indies to Portsmouth.

Martin had always thought that officers in the navy were spared floggings. It turned out that this was true only insofar as officers were spared *public* floggings. What went on in the cabin was quite a different matter. What went on when the captain was a power-mad despot was a different matter still. Martin bent down, pressing a kiss between Will's shoulder blades, then raised the sheet to Will's neck.

The man they had met in the park yesterday had said Will saved lives. Martin wasn't certain exactly what Will had done—whether he had spoken to the rightfully disgruntled sailors and then been punished for it, or whether it was simply a matter of allowing himself to be used as a scapegoat—but if there was any man in the world who could have done it, Martin believed it would have been Will. And somehow, despite that nightmare, despite the year of oblivion he had sought upon coming home, Will still found joy. He still trusted and loved. Martin wasn't much given to considering the existence of any divine creator let alone going so far as to thank it, but Will's continued existence seemed like nothing less than a miracle and just looking upon him overwhelmed Martin with gratitude.

He might have spent the rest of the morning petting

Will's hair and in general behaving like a daft fool but he needed to cough. His lungs were never at their best in the mornings, mornings in London even less so, mornings after a traipse across town followed by a night in a close and dusty room even less still. He grabbed his clothes and silently shut the door behind him, then coughed as quietly as possible in the tiny sitting room. There was no blood, which was a good sign.

Feeling slightly better, he dressed and sat in the hard-backed chair near the window. The sun was out, at least as far as it was ever out in London, and he could see the room with a clarity he had not the previous night. There was a shelf with a handful of books and a cupboard that held a couple of mugs. When Martin fished his new spectacles out of his pocket, he saw that the books and cups were covered by a layer of dust. Will had distinctly said he was staying with Hartley, but if these were Hartley's rooms he did not live in them. He certainly had not stayed in them last night, nor had Will expected him to return.

On a writing desk was a stack of papers written in Will's familiar scrawl. Martin could tell at a glance that it was a play, and based on the names of the characters listed along the left-hand side of the page, it was a new play, not the one that was to be performed later that week. Martin picked up the sheaf of papers. Will had let him read the last manuscript, so he didn't think this was forbidden. He took his spectacles out of his coat pocket, sat back in the chair, and started to read.

An hour later Will was still asleep, the sun was visible even through the hazy sky, and Martin placed the manuscript on the table where he had found it and walked down the stairs to a small sitting room he remembered passing through the previous day.

He found Hartley deep in conversation with the tall dark-skinned man who had been behind the bar when Martin and Will arrived. Martin vaguely remembered having seen, if not precisely met, this man in Hartley's company last winter at the peak of his illness. He almost certainly owned this public house and—unless Martin had things entirely wrong—was the person Hartley actually lived with, the dusty rooms upstairs existing only to keep up appearances.

"Oh," Hartley said blandly, looking up from a cup of tea. He did not look pleased to see Martin, but then why should he? "So you did stay the night. How's Will?"

"Will's asleep." Martin was horrified to realize he was blushing.

"This is Mr. Fox," Hartley said, gesturing to his companion. "He owns this tavern."

"Sir Martin," Mr. Fox said.

"Mr. Fox." Martin bowed his head in acknowledgment. "I'd like to apologize to you, Hartley."

Mr. Fox got to his feet, kissed Hartley on the top of his head, and left the room, shutting the door behind him.

"You needn't look shocked," Hartley said, his lip curled in a faint sneer, but the tips of his ears bright pink.

"I'm not," Martin said honestly. "I just didn't expect to be let in on the secret."

"It's not like you don't know my . . . proclivities." He stared directly at Martin, a plain challenge.

"Hartley," Martin sighed. "I just spent the night in bed with your brother. I really don't think we need to pretend that either of us are anything but what we are. Besides, if you'll let me, I really do want to apologize to you."

That seemed to catch Hartley off guard. "Nobody's stopping you."

"May I sit?" Hartley shrugged, and Martin sat in the chair Mr. Fox had vacated, his heart racing and his mouth dry. "I'm sorry for blaming you for my father's squandering—" he paused, reflecting that this was not the correct phrasing "—for my father's choices. I thought he looked upon you as a son and I envied you so much I hated you for it, but now I know better." Hartley stared into his teacup and said nothing, so Martin went on. "We were friends once and I know I ruined it." He really looked at the man sitting across from him, saw the traces of the boy he had been friends with, and his eyes got hot. "Oh damn," he said, and took off his spectacles, rubbing his eyes with the heels of his hands. "I didn't mean to do this." He got himself together. "I apologize for not being a friend to you when my father was treating you in an unspeakable manner."

"Apology accepted," Hartley said tightly. "Is that it?"

"No," Martin said, almost laughing. "I'm sure it isn't. I haven't done anything right in years and doubtless there are dozens of other things I ought to be apologizing for, but I don't even know what they are yet."

"My brother seems to disagree."

"Will has always had a blind spot where I'm concerned. I could set fire to a village and he'd make excuses for me. Let's not pretend he's an accurate judge of my character."

For whatever reason, this was what made Hartley soften. "Well, our hearts are all idiots." He glanced at the door through which his companion had exited, and Martin realized that Hartley Sedgwick was arse over teakettle in love with his Mr. Fox.

"I read Will's draft of the new play this morning," Martin said, because this was why he had come downstairs in the first place. "I assume you haven't touched it yet?"

"Not yet."

"It's . . . filled with . . . feelings. Will's feelings. He just . . . puts them in the play, for actors to read and for all the world to see. I don't know how he can be like that."

Hartley gave him an odd look. "That's why I begged him to let me rewrite his first play. I had to. It was—it made me *cry*. I couldn't let other people see it, and also no audience wants to sit there and cry without a little bit of comedy to serve as a shield."

"And you'll do the same with this play?"

"That's the idea. He writes the sentiment, I dress it up in cleverness so it isn't quite so naked, I suppose."

"Oh, thank God." Martin felt wildly grateful. "Obviously, if he wanted to just put his heart out there for all the world to see, that would be his choice. And I suppose it's worth something that even after everything, his heart is so—" He swallowed. "There's no ugliness in there."

"No defenses, either," Hartley murmured.

"I'm glad you're there to protect him," Martin said. He glanced at Hartley, and to his surprise, the man was smiling—a tiny twist on one side of his mouth, but still it counted.

"That was exactly my thought. I said as much to Sam and he thought I had run mad. But he didn't know Will before, so he doesn't understand. There's still a bit of tea left in the pot, if you don't mind it being a bit stewed. You'll find a cup on the dresser."

Martin realized he was being issued an invitation, and he seized it. When he returned to the table, teacup in hand, Hartley was watching him and not bothering to hide it.

"Thank you for bringing him home yesterday."

"I'll always do my best by him. I hope you know that this winter, I didn't ask him to walk away from his life here to look after me."

Hartley looked puzzled, then opened his mouth to speak, but was cut off by the door opening.

"Good morning," Will said, still bleary-eyed and sleep rumpled. "My two favorite people," he said, smiling crookedly. He squeezed Martin's shoulder and reached over to ruffle Hartley's hair.

Hartley swatted his hand away, then got up and pushed Will into the empty seat. "I'll make more tea."

"Where is everybody?" Will asked, yawning.

"It's past nine," Hartley said. "Closer to ten. Sadie and the baby are doing the marketing, Sam's waiting for a delivery from the brewery, Nick and Alf are in the kitchen, haven't seen Kate since yesterday, and Sam's aunts and cousins are everywhere, threatening to feed me if they catch me without food in my mouth. Beware." Hartley flushed slightly at the end of this recitation, and Martin marveled at having lived to see Hartley Sedgwick look so pleased. Hartley murmured something about inventory and left the room, closing the door quietly behind him.

"Do you have anywhere you need to be today?" Will asked, spooning tea leaves into the pot.

"Nothing in particular, but at some point I ought to reassure my aunt that I'm alive."

Will looked up, alarmed. "I didn't even think about that. Will she be frantic that you were gone all night?"

"She was aware that I might not return. She knows how things are between us. She guessed, that day at the cottage," Martin said, recalling how he had felt the previous afternoon when he realized Will could be open around his brother, and understanding that he might have something similar with his aunt.

"Oh," Will said, pouring the now-boiling water into the pot. "She's trustworthy?"

"Yes," Martin said, surprised to feel defensive about his aunt. "And I never actually confirmed her suppositions. I only refrained from denying them." He didn't say that it had been rather nice to be known, and to not be reviled. "I hope you know I'd never be reckless with your safety."

Will nodded. "I do know that. I'm just . . . not exactly overflowing with trust in the aristocracy, present company excluded. While we're on the topic, Hartley knows, of course. And if Hartley knows, then Sam knows."

"Mr. Fox kissed Hartley in front of me, so I'm aware of that situation."

"Did he?" Will poured tea first into Martin's now-empty cup and then into his own. "There are a handful of safe people here, people who know about Hartley and Sam. And quite a few people involved with the theater know about my, um, amatory habits, who would be safe for us to be ourselves around."

Martin turned that thought over in his mind. Will had an entire community of people with whom he could be himself. This city that seemed intent on ruining Martin's health had also provided Will with friends, family, safety, a career. Will's life was in precisely the place where Martin needed not to be.

Chapter Nineteen

Martin knew he had no particular talent for polite conversation, but before his night with Will he had been getting on tolerably well.

"I'm not entirely certain I can invite them back," Aunt Bermondsey said mildly after a disastrous lunch. "You know, you can just ask about the weather. Or the latest fashions in hats. Or whether they prefer cats or dogs. You don't have to sit there sullenly."

"I'm aware I don't *have* to sit there sullenly," Martin snipped. "But I can't think of anything to say. If I remark on the weather, and then they remark on the weather, then I'll just have to say something else, and the very idea makes me want to run screaming out of the house."

"Running screaming out of the house would have been more engaging than sitting there like a lump," his aunt remarked. "My word. I'll concentrate my efforts on balls and musicales and other engagements that don't require much conversation."

"I can't dance."

Aunt Bermondsey shot him a withering glance. "It is a skill that can be learned."

He wrinkled his nose, then decided he had spent enough time acting like a petulant child. "I'm afraid I'm not in an agreeable mood."

"No!" She pressed a hand to her heart. "I never would have guessed. What do you do to amuse yourself in the ordinary course of things? We'll just have to find similar diversions."

That question brought him up short. Left up to his own devices, Martin would live out the rest of his years sitting in a comfortable chair, reading anything he could get his hands on. He might have thought that after getting a taste of freedom, he'd want a go at something different than how he'd spent most of his first twenty years. But maybe he found comfort in the familiar, or maybe he just liked books and indolence. "I'm not entirely certain," he said at length. "I haven't had much of a chance to find out. There was very little opportunity for me to exercise my own preferences when my father was alive." He watched his aunt's face harden. "And after his death, I was preoccupied with caring for a friend who was in difficult circumstances."

"And then with your own illness, I suppose?"

"I wouldn't say that my illness preoccupied me. Perhaps it should have. I think I could have spared myself and my friend a good deal of trouble if I had stayed with you last autumn instead of leaving and making myself more ill."

She regarded him levelly. "I don't think you regret how it turned out, though."

"You are correct, ma'am." He didn't know why he was being so honest with her. Maybe it was because sometimes when he looked at her he caught an occasional glimpse of a mother he knew only from a portrait. Maybe it was because her unconcealed hatred for his father endeared her to him. Or maybe it was just because he didn't have anything to lose. "I can't marry," he said, trying to make his voice as firm and unyielding as he could. "I know it's the logical solution to my predicament, but it's out of the question." He felt almost sick with the knowledge that he was going against her wishes. She had been kind: she bought him clothes and took him to the oculist for spectacles and now she would tell him that he had to do as she said for his own good. There was a part of him that expected his father or a nurse or tutor to materialize and lock him away until he was ready to be compliant.

She looked at him for another long moment and then poured him some tea. "Have it your way. I suppose I can get you a post as a secretary."

Martin blinked. "I beg your pardon?"

"Secretary. You can read and write, can you not? Despite ignoring my letters for years and years?"

"Yes, of course, but—" He didn't know how to say that he had expected her to fight him, to persuade him.

"Don't tell me you look down your nose at work."

"No! I just didn't expect you to listen to me."

Aunt Bermondsey regarded him curiously. "There are other ways you could make a living. Being a secretary is the most obvious, if only because certain men would feel extremely important if they had a titled secretary. But you could also get a post in the Home Office. Nothing too taxing."

He spent a moment imagining this future in which he could earn a living. It was a fantasy—he would be sacked from any post after his first bout of illness, and any work in London or another city was out of the question. But even the theoretical possibility of being able to pay his own way made him feel . . . valuable, maybe, in a way he hadn't conceived of. Then he gritted his teeth and returned to reality.

"I'm afraid, ma'am, that my health won't permit me to hold a regular post, nor to stay in town."

She raised her eyebrows. "I was under the impression that you were doing better."

"I don't think I'll ever recover," he said. It was the first time he had said it aloud to anyone but Will. "But some days are better than others."

She was silent for a moment. "Tell me what I can do for you."

"I would like to be able to pay my own way," Martin said. "I don't want to be a drain on my friend." No, that wasn't quite right. "I don't want to need my friend. I want to be able to pay for whatever care I need the next time I fall ill. I don't want the people who care for me to worry that I'll repeat the events of last autumn." He didn't say that in an ideal world he'd like to be able to care for Will if he needed it; that seemed both unlikely and private, an impossible thought to hide safely away.

"I would not call these ambitions overly optimistic."

"It is when you haven't two farthings to rub together."

She furrowed her brow. "There has to be something you could do. To hear my friends talk, young men seem to be forever getting posts and taking work that their relations consider beneath them—surely not all of them require a man to live in London."

"I expect the young men your friends know all have skills that I do not. My education consisted of reading too many novels and little else. I read and write French, and a little German."

"I'd offer you money—"

"I'd refuse it."

"I'd offer you money," she repeated, "but I haven't any. I have my pin money and Lord Bermondsey pays my bills," she went on, "but I haven't any money of my own. However, if you fall on hard times, understand that I wish to help you. At the risk of trading in maudlin sympathy, it's the very least your mother might have expected of me."

"My mother died when you were in leading strings and you never laid eyes on me until last year, so you needn't pretend it was my mother's dying wish that you look after me."

"You'll permit me to decide what and who I care about, thank you," she said. "And you'll allow for the possibility that I've become fond of you in your own right. My point is that if you fell on hard times, my pin money is not insubstantial. Twenty or thirty pounds would not even make a difference to me. Just assure me that you'll come to me before you get to a desperate state. Meanwhile, what do you plan to do? For money, I mean, if you don't mind my asking so crass a question."

"My solicitor tells me I can likely get fifty pounds a year for Friars' Gate if I let it on a repairing lease. That way I wouldn't be responsible for its upkeep. I can live on fifty pounds."

Lady Bermondsey blanched. Her gown almost certainly cost more than fifty pounds. "Where, darling?"

"Either the dower house at Lindley Priory or the cottage at Friars' Gate. They both belong to me." He had no intention of going back to Lindley Priory unless he absolutely had to, but he mentioned it because he thought the dower house would sound more appealing to his aunt than the tiny cottage she had had seen at Friars' Gate. He was tense with the anticipation of her response. He knew that she couldn't actually control him, couldn't shove him in his bedroom and lock the door. But he still expected her to try to persuade him to do as she told him and he was braced to resist her arguments.

"I can't say that would be what I'd choose myself, but I'll assume you know your own needs, Martin," she said. He waited for the rest, but all she did was take a sip of tea.

"Yes," he said. "And I thank you for that, ma'am."

It might have been the persistent rain, or it might have been the sunless sky, but Will was becoming nervous. For over half an hour he had huddled under his umbrella, waiting at the stage door for Martin's arrival. He had long since concluded that Martin had either forgotten the appointed time, been waylaid by his aunt, or met with some horrible fate. The distance between the Fox and Bermondsey House in Mayfair was less than an hour on foot; the distance between the theater and Mayfair was even shorter. But when Martin was at one end of that span and he was at the other, even a couple of miles felt insurmountable, and Will couldn't know any peace.

In the play, he had written a pair of young lovers who couldn't bear to be apart. But he had modeled them on Romeo and Juliet, on Tristan and Isolde, thinking more of the concept of mutually pining lovers than on any actual experience of his own. He was vaguely appalled to discover that he was acting that way himself. It would have been even more mortifying if he hadn't known that Martin was in the same state. And that, the thrill of knowing that Martin had feelings as soft and stupid as his own, only made Will miss him more.

They had parted the previous morning with lingering kisses and murmured promises to meet the following afternoon, Martin's back against the door to keep it shut, Will's mouth skimming over the invisible, pale stubble on Martin's jaw. Will had wanted to haul Martin back upstairs and lock the door and never let Martin out of his sight.

Finally a carriage pulled up in front of the theater. It was not the same traveling chaise in which Lady Bermondsey arrived at the cottage, but rather a lighter and narrower conveyance, but it bore the same coat of arms on the door. Martin alighted, spotted Will, and made his way across the cobblestones to duck under Will's umbrella.

"A sinkhole opened on Oxford Street," Martin said. "Or, if not a sinkhole, something vast and muddy and very alarming to horses. It took ages to wend our way through the side streets."

They were standing close, close enough that Will could smell Martin's soap. It might have been the dreariness of the weather, but Martin looked paler than he had the previous day, washed out, a bit drawn. "You look tired," Will said.

"Well, you'll have to take me to bed as soon as we finish here," Martin said, arching an eyebrow. "Unless you have other plans." He spoke the words dispassionately, casually, and there was something about the coolness of the delivery that made Will want him even more. This act of putting a public face on their friendship somehow made the private reality that much more precious.

"Come in," Will said. "They started the dress rehearsal, but you're in time for the second act." He folded his umbrella and shook it out, then held the door open for Martin.

As soon as they walked through the door, Will could hear actors repeating the lines he had long since committed to memory. He didn't think he would ever tire of it. There was a chance the play would only last a few nights, that everyone would hate it, that nobody would ever again stage any other play he wrote, but for now he was pleased and proud. That pride was an unexpected sensation, fluttering inside some dusty and forgotten part of his chest.

"Oh," Martin said, a little sound that was hardly more than an exhalation. They had just reached the corner of backstage where they could see the backs of the actors and an expanse of empty seats beyond.

"The woman in the red gown is supposed to be Cecile, the widow," Will whispered. "The man in black is the wicked uncle, and he's—"

"I know who they are," Martin whispered back. "I recognize the lines. I just didn't realize how big this theater is."

"It seats three thousand," Will said, a wave of nausea passing through him as it always did when he contemplated three thousand people watching his play. Hartley had been in agonies for weeks, but Will hadn't quite caught up until opening night was excruciatingly near at hand.

"I've never been to the theater," Martin said.

"What?" Will asked, loudly enough that one of the stagehands shot him a dirty look. Then, softer, "Your father did take you to London a few times. I remember it."

"I was always too ill to accompany him to the theater. Or, at least he told me I was. I'm not certain."

Sometimes Martin would allude so casually to his father's mistreatment of him that Will would momentarily wonder whether Martin knew the gravity of what he was saying. But now he glanced over at his friend and saw the set of his jaw, the tightness around his eyes. He squeezed Martin's arm.

"I know," Martin said, not turning his head. "You'd feed him to wolves." One corner of his mouth quirked up in the beginnings of a smile.

"Wolves are too good for him."

When the manager called for a rest, one of the actresses noticed Will standing there, and the next quarter hour was spent in a flurry of introductions and explanations. Martin was fascinated by the Argand lamps and the hanging transparencies, awed by the enormous chandelier that hung over the stage, but flustered and embarrassed while meeting the members of the cast and crew who came up to Will. Martin was always a bit aloof with strangers, though. In fact, he was aloof with almost everyone. It was easy for Will to forget, because Martin wasn't like that with him. And it was even easier to forget when Martin was dressed fashionably; the price of his clothes somehow transformed his stiltedness into something that passed for snobbery.

"Just say that you're very much looking forward to seeing the play opening night," Will whispered. "And say you're honored to visit backstage and everything is so interesting."

Martin flushed. "Is it so obvious that I'm terrible at this?"

"It would be a miracle if you were otherwise, Martin. Do you want to leave?"

"No. I do find all of this very interesting."

"I'm glad. Oh, here's Madame Bisset. She plays the dowager countess."

"William," said an older woman in full stage makeup and a heavy French accent, kissing Will on both cheeks. She proceeded to speak animatedly to Will, too quickly for Martin to understand. Occasionally she cast a curious glance in Martin's direction, before eventually turning to him and speaking in rapid French.

"She's saying that she very much enjoyed your translation of the play and sent it to her son, who manages a theater in Paris. If he wishes to stage it, she'll take twenty—" he broke off, switching to French to hold a conversation with the lady "—she'll take *ten* percent as a fee."

"I only did it to occupy myself," Martin said when they found seats in the pit to watch the next act.

"If you fancy translating things," Will said, trying to keep his voice casual, "you'd do even better to translate French novels into English. Remember Jonathan York who visited us in Sussex? His father is a publisher, and the lady who used to do translations for him left for Canada. He'd probably pay a few pounds a book." Will had been thinking along those lines since he saw Martin's careful translation of the play. Nobody grew rich as a translator. It probably wouldn't even pay enough to keep Martin fed. But it would be something. "May I mention your name to Jonathan as a possible solution to his problems?"

"Yes," Martin breathed, and when Will looked at him side-long he saw that his friend was almost pink with pleasure.

They found seats in the pit for the remainder of the rehearsal. It turned out that watching the play be performed on stage was more than Will's nerves could take, so instead he watched Martin out of the corner of his eye. Martin was rapt, staring at the stage like a child at the circus.

"That's not how I imagined Esmerelda at all," he whispered. "And I see that they cut most of that scene with the priest. But somehow it's all perfect."

"Do you think so?" Will asked.

Martin must have heard the anxiety in Will's voice because he turned his head. "I'm hardly a capable theater critic, but I think it's lovely. When I read it last, I could tell the lines that were yours from those that were Hartley's but now it's all blended together. Are any of your other brothers coming to see the play?"

"Not this time," he said, and as soon as he said the words his stomach roiled, as if he had cursed himself by anticipating a next time. Perhaps guessing this, Martin squeezed his thigh. "Thank God you're here. I've been putting off watching a rehearsal since I came to town."

Martin was silent for a long moment, and Will thought he had become absorbed in what was happening on stage. "I hope you know how gratified I am to be useful to you."

If it hadn't been for the hand on his thigh or the choked quality to Martin's voice, Will might have thought that a chilly sort of sentiment. Instead he knew it for what it was, and briefly laced his fingers with Martin's.

By the time they passed through the back door of the Fox, Will was all but steering Martin directly toward the stairs. At any other time Martin might have been embarrassed by what amounted to a mad dash from street to bedroom but Will had spent the entire interminable duration of the hackney ride stroking circles on the inside of Martin's thigh. And even before that, in the shadows of the narrow alley behind the theater, sheltered by fog and Will's hand cradled against Martin's face, Will had kissed Martin against the cold stone wall. That moment, the warmth of Will's body, the chill of the wall, the mad thrill of being kissed in near public, of being kissed at all, of loving and being loved—Martin thought he had never been so alive.

There was still some light coming through the window of Will's sitting room, enough to see the flicker of amusement in his eyes when Martin locked the door himself and all but pushed Will into the bedroom.

"In a hurry?" Will asked, falling backward onto the bed.

"You," Martin said menacingly, untying his cravat and flinging it onto the chair. "You know what you did."

"Oh?" Will asked, looking up at him with innocent eyes.

"I truly do not think I could ever have an orgasm in a hackney cab or any other kind of conveyance, but by God I was tempted to try."

Laughing, Will threw his coat and waistcoat onto the floor, then knelt up to help Martin out of his own clothes. Narrowly tailored clothes were not meant for speedy or single-handed undressing, Martin was learning.

"And you," Will said, "with those pantaloons. You could be arrested."

They landed on the bed, their lips finally meeting in a kiss that had Martin digging his fingernails into Will's hips. "At some point," Will said, "I need you in bed for a solid week. Maybe then we can wear one another out and I can hope to spend time with you without wanting to tear your clothes off."

Martin nearly responded that they could do precisely that if they returned to the country. He knew he needed to leave London. He had gotten sick during his past three stays in town and couldn't ignore the pattern anymore. He'd stay for Will's play, but then he needed to go as soon as possible. The news that he planned not to marry, but instead to live off the pittance he could get from leasing Friars' Gate, would also keep until after opening night. If he told Will now, Will would worry instead of enjoying the opening night of his play. Besides, he shouldn't even dream of asking Will to leave London, even briefly. He shouldn't even suggest it. He recalled everything that Will would be giving up. In the country he'd only have Martin. And while Will might think now that it was a fair trade, he'd eventually grow tired of having no company but Martin. Martin knew what it was like to be isolated, and he wouldn't wish it on Will.

"Come here," he said, tugging Will up from where he was kissing a path across Martin's collarbone, and gave him a proper kiss. It didn't have to mean a parting. Will could visit him in the country. That would be better than nothing. It would be enough, more than enough. Martin had never asked for anything like enough, had never expected it.

"Where did you go?" Will asked. "A minute ago you were kissing me, and now you're away with the fairies."

"I was just thinking that I'm grateful for every moment we have together. And also that you should stop making me say these embarrassing things."

That seemed to satisfy Will, who laughed and pulled Martin down to the bed, then rolled them over so Martin was pressed into the mattress by the satisfying weight of Will on top of him. Martin sighed in contentment. It was just kissing, languid, lazy, late afternoon kissing as if they had all the time in the world, until Will whispered, "Do you want to try?" and Martin whispered back, "Yes," and then Will was showing Martin how to touch him, their breaths coming faster, their hands slippery and searching. Martin wasn't sure anything in his life had ever been easy or uncomplicated but this came close, Will rising over him and sinking down, letting him in, whispering praise that devolved into nothing more than Martin's name, repeated and repeated.

"So," Martin said, as they lay together afterward, "that's buggery, is it?" and Will had laughed himself silly while Martin stroked his hair and smiled, unaccountably pleased with himself. They fell asleep to the sound of fiddle music coming from downstairs and the steady rhythm of one another's hearts.

So when Martin woke with a tightness in his chest and the beginnings of a wheeze, his fingertips cold and pale and a trace of blood on his handkerchief, he wasn't surprised. He had been expecting it for a while now, and he supposed he ought to be grateful he had gotten a few more days. For the first time since he had fallen ill, he felt the unfairness of it, as if he were being shoved into a sickroom and kept away from everything that was good in the world.

He slipped into the sitting room, shutting the bedroom door silently behind him, so he wouldn't wake Will with any further coughing. But a moment later Will came out and wrapped his arms around Martin's waist.

"Bad?"

"Not good," Martin answered.

"Too much smoke and damp?" Will asked after a moment.

"As always."

"I'm embarrassed that it took me this long to figure it out," Will said.

"Figure what out?"

"That you first got sick when you were looking after me. The other day you said that smoke and damp don't agree with your lungs, and that describes pretty much every opium den you fetched me from."

"Sweetheart." Martin put his hands over Will's and leaned back against his chest. He was ready to lie—it would have been the easiest thing in the world to say that he had the first signs of illness before Will even returned from sea. But this morning, this closeness, felt too sacred to defile with lies or evasions. "I think it was the city, not the opium dens," he said. "And even if it were, neither of us knew so at the time. The first time I got sick was mild and I didn't pay much attention to it."

"Because you were too busy worrying about me, probably."

"Could be. In case it isn't obvious, I'd do it again."

"You make terrible choices where I'm concerned. Hauling yourself across London after my incident at the park. Refusing to take the paregoric the doctor prescribed. Harrowing your tenants. What's next, Martin?"

Martin remained still, hoping Will would change the topic. He could feel Will's body go rigid when he realized. "Tell me you aren't planning to marry because you want the money to look after me. Tell me that much." When Martin said nothing, Will sucked in a breath. "Martin, how could you?"

"I'd do anything to make sure you were safe," Martin said. He couldn't tell Will that he no longer meant to marry, because that would mean confessing the full precariousness of his future, and that needed to wait until after Will's play. There were tears in his eyes, and he hoped Will couldn't tell in the dark. He didn't know if it was the early hour or the lack of air to his brain or just the fact that Will had rested his chin on Martin's shoulder, but he wanted to fill the quiet with things better left unsaid. "I've loved you since you came home on leave the summer I was seventeen."

Will stayed motionless, then pressed a kiss to Martin's neck. "I didn't know."

"You weren't meant to. Obviously, Will," he said, striving for archness and failing miserably.

"And when did you realize that I loved you?"

Martin raised his eyebrows, not having expected that question, but knowing the answer anyway. "When you woke up early and made tea for me that morning after we first went to bed together. You looked troublingly fond and I thought to myself, well this is going to be a proper disaster."

He turned his head to kiss Will, soft and slow, with one hand cupping his jaw, trying to convince himself that his opinion had changed since that day. But he couldn't lie to himself. Will deserved a full life, a real life, more than what he'd have in an isolated cottage in the country. He turned and pressed an absent kiss to the birds that were inked on Will's shoulder, a reminder that he couldn't keep Will to himself.

CHAPTER TWENTY

"At least let me send for the physician," Aunt Bermondsey whispered as Martin stifled another cough.

"We'll talk during the interval," he answered, and then returned his attention to the stage. He had read the play and seen the dress rehearsal, but still he was riveted by the spectacle of the cast arrayed on stage, the chandelier lit with hundreds of candles, the audience equally glittering in their opening night finery.

"This is going well, yes?" he whispered during a scene break.

"Yes, darling," his aunt answered, patting his knee as she had done the previous fifteen times he asked. "Your friend ought to be proud."

It was odd to be sitting high up in the theater and to know that Will was behind the curtain. He wondered if Will could spot him among the hundreds of almost identically dressed men in the theater's upper levels. Regardless, they were meeting backstage after the play; Will had shown Martin where to go and whom to speak to and told him what to say.

When the curtain dropped for the interval, Martin rose to his feet to greet the theatergoers who stopped by his aunt's box. But after a few minutes upright, he began to feel unsteady. He gripped the back of a chair. "I beg your pardon," he told a matron whose name he had already forgotten. "I'm afraid—my health—a minor complaint." He sat, despite it being gauche for a man to sit while a lady remained standing, because he thought he might faint if he spent another moment on his feet.

When the box cleared and the audience hushed in anticipation of the play resuming, his aunt leaned over. "If I send for the apothecary, he can be waiting at Bermondsey House when we return."

Martin shook his head. "I already have willow bark and camphor. There isn't anything else to do except rest and wait and—" he took a deep breath, or as deep a breath as his lungs would presently allow "—get out of London."

"When will you leave? I could take you myself—"

"No," Martin said, appalled by the idea of his aunt attempting to play nursemaid. "With all due respect, Aunt, I would rather handle this on my own." He wanted to prove to himself that he could. "I'll send you word as soon as I'm home."

"At least take my carriage. It'll be far more comfortable than the stagecoach."

"All right," he conceded. He still couldn't quite believe that his aunt wasn't trying to prevent him from leaving, and he wasn't sure he'd be convinced until he had left London far behind him.

The play resumed, and Martin spent the next hour so entranced that he hardly noticed his mounting discomfort. But as soon as the curtain fell, he became intensely aware of the pounding in his head, the quickness of his pulse. He told himself that this was no worse than that cold he had a few months earlier, and which had disappeared after a few days. His lungs were bad; it stood to reason that minor afflictions would affect him more seriously than they might affect another man, but it didn't mean there was any real danger.

"How bad do I look?" he asked his aunt when the curtain fell for the last time and the audience finished applauding.

"Not well, my dear," she said, frowning. "I badly want to put you to bed with a mustard poultice and I've never had such an urge in my life. If you're asking whether you'll alarm your friend by appearing in such a state backstage, I'm afraid you might."

"I'm afraid I'll also alarm him by not showing up at all." But that was clearly the lesser evil; he wasn't going to appear backstage and distract Will from what ought to be his moment of triumph. If Aunt Bermondsey was moved to tuck Martin into bed, Will would probably act on the impulse, and Martin would be cheating him out of his celebration. God knew Will had been cheated out of enough. Martin could at least make sure he had this.

"I'll write him as soon as we get home," Martin said.

"Quite right," his aunt responded, shepherding Martin down the front of the stairs and toward the line of waiting carriages. He was dimly aware that his aunt was using promises of coin and threats of dire consequence in order to circumvent the line of waiting theatergoers, but Martin was too tired to object.

"But I saw him," Will said for perhaps the tenth time.

"And so did I," Hartley responded. "He was here, in a box with a lady who wore a turban. Perhaps the crush was too great for him to get backstage, or perhaps his aunt had other plans for him. There are a hundred possible explanations for why he isn't here, and you can sort it out with him tomorrow."

Will knew his brother was being perfectly reasonable, but he had a lingering presentiment that something was wrong.

"Drink," said Hartley, handing him a glass of wine. "And then drink more. We earned it. The play went well."

"Better than well," Will said, grinning.

"I thought I was going to faint from nerves. Or have an apoplexy."

"I noticed," Will said, elbowing his brother.

"Now, come and let people congratulate us."

He and Hartley didn't stumble out into the street until well past midnight, neither of them remotely sober. "We're going to get murdered," Will said.

"Pfft. It's twenty minutes if we hurry."

"Do you think either of us are capable of hurrying? Because you look hardly capable of standing upright."

"Come," Hartley said, looping his arm through Will's, "we'll take Portugal Street."

"No, can't go that way," Will said, shaking his head.

"Why not? It's the fastest. Don't tell me you really are afraid of being murdered. A few months of country living have made you soft, Will Sedgwick."

"Can't go past St. Clements. Avoiding temptation."

"Avoiding—oh." Will felt Hartley go stiff beside him. "I'm sorry, it didn't even occur to me. Here, we'll take the Strand instead."

"S'alright," Will said. "Been a long time, and it wasn't you dragging me out of those places anyway, was it? Can't have expected you to memorize the map."

"I suppose I never did give Martin enough credit for that, did I?"

"You never give Martin credit for anything," Will grumbled under his breath. "You know, that's how he got sick."

Hartley fell silent for a few moments. "Even if Martin did ruin his health by following you into filthy places, I daresay he'd do it again."

Will grumbled incoherently.

"You'd do it for him, wouldn't you? I'd do it for Sam, and he for me. When the person you love needs you, you don't refine overmuch on self-preservation."

Will tried to believe this—no, he did believe it. But that didn't mean he wasn't responsible. "It was my fault for being in those places."

"Oh, bugger that. I'd really like to know what a man's supposed to do when His Majesty's Navy does its damnedest to ruin his mind. If the opium helped you escape your thoughts, then so be it. What other options did you have? Gin? Ben would have suggested prayer, but even he used to say that every night you landed in an opium den was at least a night you hadn't walked into the Thames."

"I could have tried harder."

"You tried pretty damned hard and you're still trying, you absolute arsehole."

"You swear a lot when you're drunk."

"I swear a lot about this particular topic, thank you."

They managed to make it back to the Fox and into their respective beds, and all too soon Will woke to the sound of someone knocking on his door. Outside his window was what passed for daylight in London, so he supposed he had to answer.

When Will opened the door, Sam let out a low whistle. "I wouldn't have thought it possible, but you look even worse than Hartley." He handed Will a folded sheet of ivory paper. "A messenger brought this for you," Sam said. "I'd have let you sleep, but figured the letter was from—" He cleared his throat.

"It is," Will said, recognizing the handwriting at once. "Thank you."

Back in his room, he broke the seal.

Dearest Will, your play was every bit as lovely and brilliant as I knew it would be, and I hope you're as proud of yourself as I am of you. I regret not being able to join in your celebrations, but I'm afraid I'm under the weather. Or—why beat around the bush—it's rather worse than that, and there's nothing for it but to go home. It seems that London does not agree with me. It manifestly does agree with you—I've seldom seen you happier. Watching you with your friends at the theater was almost like seeing how things might have been if the events of a few years ago never happened, and I'm glad you have that.

Will put the letter down and paced across the room. That last line sat badly with him. He didn't want to believe that Martin looked at him and saw the ghost of someone long gone, as something that had once been whole but now was broken. He wanted Martin to see him the way he was and love him for it, but it really sounded like Martin was telling him to stay in London in order to resemble someone who was long gone. He needed to talk to Martin, to hear from Martin's own mouth that this was only a misunderstanding. But Martin wasn't there. He was heading home, and Will had a sinking feeling that home meant Lindley Priory—the last time they had talked about it, Martin told Will that he wished they had never left the place.

My solicitor wrote to inform me that he found a tenant for Friars' Gate. In my return letter, I asked him to draw up an agreement that would give you a life interest in the two acres surrounding the gamekeeper's cottage as well as the cottage itself. It seems that this is something I have the right to do despite the entail. I want you to have that; I want you to know that no matter what you have a place to go, that no matter what you'll always have a choice. Before this spring I'm not certain I knew that I did have choices. You helped me remember. Regardless of anything else, the cottage is yours to use.

I'm about to get teary and I'm afraid that doesn't do my lungs the least bit of good, so I'll end this letter now, with the reminder that I remain and will always be,

   Yours,

   Martin

"What the hell," Will muttered, staring at the letter. The man couldn't have let him know his plans ahead of time? Will would have had his bag packed and been ready to leave by the time the play ended last night. He began absently throwing his belongings into his satchel with one hand while rereading the letter.

"Where are you going?" Hartley asked, when Will appeared downstairs with his satchel slung over his shoulder.

"North," Will grit out. "Look at this." He held out Martin's letter.

"Good," Hartley said a moment later. "This is better than last year. He noticed he wasn't well and so he took steps to care for himself. This is good, yes?"

"Yes," Will said, struck by the truth of his brother's observation. "I suppose it's very good. But why the hell does he need to go to Cumberland? Not only can he not stand the place, but he knows my work and my friends are here and he's going to put himself a two days' stagecoach trip away from that?" Will passed a hand over his jaw. "No. That's selfish of me. He said he can use the dower house there. I should be glad."

"Should you?" Hartley looked up from where he was assembling a stack of sandwiches.

"Yes," Will insisted. "Am I going to have to explain friendship to you again?"

"Perhaps, because I'd be far from glad if Sam moved to Cumberland, even if it were for the best reasons in the world." He wrapped the sandwiches in a napkin and stuck them in Will's satchel. "You're allowed to be greedy and grasping. You're allowed to be cross with him. That's sometimes what love is. It's not all sweetness and light."

"Sometimes when he looks at me, I worry that all he sees is what happened on the ship. And I'm afraid that he left me because he's afraid that watching him die will be what finally breaks me. That's why he avoided me last autumn, and that's why he's doing it now."

"Are you certain that isn't what *you're* afraid of? Because I've seen him look at you, and there's no way he's thinking of the *Fotheringay*. He looks at you like you're a miracle, like something precious and maybe a little fragile—fragile in the way that something priceless is, not like some old doorknob that's about to fall off. Not broken," he said firmly. "I think he loves you exactly as you are. You should hear how he talks about you. His face does this thing, where he's all wide eyes and bafflement." Hartley seemed to realize what he was saying. "It's all very disgusting, actually," he sniffed. "In any event, you should get out of my kitchen and go tell him all these absurd things."

"Thank you." Will planted a kiss on the side of his brother's head, and then laughed when Hartley wiped it away with the back of his hand.

CHAPTER TWENTY-ONE

Martin had twenty shillings and a few pounds in bank notes. It was more money than he had carried in years and the clink of coins in his pocket made him feel perversely adult. Here he was, three and twenty, and for the first time he felt fully in charge of his own destiny.

He also had four books from his aunt's library, several sets of clothes that he supposed would do for a rural convalescence, as much camphor and willow bark as his aunt could purchase at eight o'clock in the morning, and a tin of tea. He supposed people had started out on far less.

Foolishly, he had hoped that he would feel better as soon as he stepped out of the carriage, that the first breath of fresh air would restore him to some semblance of health. Instead he coughed, and there was blood on the handkerchief, and this was—well, it was not ideal, but it was what he was working with, and he was going to keep working with it because the alternative was not worth thinking of.

The Tanners' cottage was a five minutes' walk from the

inn. He knew he could walk that distance without coming to any harm, but he was being careful, so he gave tuppence to one of the boys who loitered around the inn and told them they'd have another tuppence if they came back with Miss Daisy and her mum. Then he took his hat off, straightened his shoulders, and took a seat at a table near the door. He felt exceptionally visible, especially without the shabbiness of his old clothes to give him cover. Anyone who had believed him to be plain Mr. Smith would have plenty of time to recognize him as an Easterbrook. But in order for his plan to work, he had to be as honest and upfront as possible, so he gritted his teeth and let people look.

When Mrs. Tanner and Daisy entered, he paid the lad who had fetched them and then gave Daisy another tuppence to bring his satchel to the cottage. That, he figured, would give him enough time to have the conversation he needed to have with her mother.

"Is Mr. Sedgwick with you or is he coming later?" Mrs. Tanner asked. She had immediately taken stock of his fine clothes and probably also noticed his pallor.

"It's only me for now, which is why I wanted to speak to you. My health has taken a turn and I need someone to look after me. I thought Daisy could do it, for whatever wage is customary. It would be light work as long as I don't get much worse. She'd only need to look in on me a few times a day, do the wash, and bring supper. If I need the physician, she'd be the one to fetch him. But if I get worse, I might need nursing, possibly overnight, and that's where things get difficult. She's young and I wouldn't wish for anything untoward to be said. That's why I'm speaking to you first, instead of to her directly."

"That's considerate of you, Mr. Smith," she said cautiously.

"If it's all the same to you, Mrs. Tanner, I think we can dispense with that fiction. I beg your pardon if I'm wrong, but I believe you knew my late father, Sir Humphrey Easterbrook. I'm under no illusions about what kind of man he was, or what kind of misdeeds he must have committed in any place he spent time. I can assure you Daisy would be quite safe in my company—indeed any woman would be quite safe—but my assurance alone will do nothing to stop gossip. However, and I'm afraid there's no delicate way to ask this, but if there is some other family connection between Daisy and myself . . ." He took a deep breath, as deep as he could, which only resulted in a coughing fit. When he steadied himself, he managed to smile at the older woman. He had to handle this well; he needed to make sure she didn't think this was blackmail or extortion or even some kind of high-handed charity. "The fact is that I need to hire someone to look after me, and it would go better for everyone concerned if that person were a family connection. I could be grossly mistaken and it's presumptuous for me even to have this conversation, but my understanding is that it's commonly known that you weren't married to Daisy's father, and I've noticed that—" He stopped himself. He had blathered long enough and now needed to make his point. "Mrs. Tanner, is Daisy my sister?"

She continued to look at him unflinchingly, and he

guessed that she was deciding whether to lie. "Well, yes, Sir Martin, but we thought you knew."

Martin bristled at his title but there was nothing to be done about that. He couldn't renounce it, and even if he could, it would look like he was trying to deny who he was, who he had been. It would feel like cowardice. "And so I did. I wasn't certain whether you did, though."

She shook her head. "As if I wouldn't notice that you're the very spit of him at that age. That morning I walked into your cottage and caught you in bed and you dressed me down, you sounded just like him as well."

"I apologize. It can't have been a pleasant surprise. I wish there were something I could say to assure you that I'm not like him, or at least that I'm trying not to be."

Mrs. Tanner looked at him for a long minute. "If you'll beg my pardon, once I got over the shock, I realized you were only worried about your young man's privacy, which is a sight more than your father would have ever cared about."

Martin opened his mouth to deny that there was anything requiring privacy, to insist that there was nothing untoward about two men sharing a bed. But Mrs. Tanner had seen him and Will together for months; if she had arrived at the truth, then making a show of denying it would do no good. Besides, he was trying to show her that he was trustworthy, and maybe he needed to trust her as well. So all he did was wave over the barmaid and ask for a pair of pints.

"I'm quite poor," he said. "Otherwise I'd try to do something for Daisy, especially given that she constitutes a full half my blood family. As things stand, I realize that instead I'm asking Daisy to do me a favor for a sum of money that might not be worth her while and which might cause her parentage to become the source of a gossip for months to come."

"People have been wondering about Daisy's father for sixteen years, and the only reason I never set anyone straight was that I was afraid her da—your da—would come back and make trouble. But if he's dead, and good riddance to the bastard, then it's no skin off my back." The door swung open, bringing in a gust of fresh air along with Daisy, who flung herself into the chair between her mother and Martin. "Daisy," her mother said, "you'll look after Mr.—Sir Martin—while he's poorly, won't you? Three shillings a week, more if you need to spend the night."

"Right," she said, casting a keen glance at the signet ring Martin wore and then raising her eyebrows at him with the clear message of *It took you long enough.*

"You can start by telling one of the lads in the stables that Sir Martin needs the pony cart to bring him to the cottage."

"I—" Martin had been ready to protest that he could walk the mile to the cottage, but remembered that he was being cautious as well as honest. "Thank you, Daisy."

When, finally, he arrived at the cottage, he felt like he had been gone longer than two weeks. He was surprised to see that the piglets were still small, the house unchanged. Even indoors smelled the same, like candle wax and timber. While Daisy put fresh sheets on the bed and lit a fire, he unpacked his trunk, laying his clothes on the back of a chair and stacking his books on the chimneypiece beside the volumes Will had left behind.

He hoped Will would visit sooner rather than later. He knew he was being selfish: Will had every reason to stay in London. Surely he would at least send a letter once he received Martin's note, and that would be enough. Martin winced when he thought of that note. There wasn't a single word in it that he'd take back, but he feared that he could have been more coherent in his phrasing. And now that he had had time to think about it, it seemed grossly presumptuous of him to insist on giving this cottage to Will and then resume living in it himself. But he had wanted to make sure that Will knew he had a place to live even if Martin died. He probably ought to have said that clearly in the letter. God knew he wasn't any stranger to thinking about his eventual demise, but over the past few months he had stopped thinking about his death as something imminent, as something he could casually allude to in a hastily written note. The threat was still there, but it seemed both more remote, in that he wasn't going to die this time, and more grave, in that he and the people he'd leave behind would have more to lose. It wasn't the sort of thing that could be addressed in a handful of words.

"There you go," Daisy said, wiping her hands on her skirt. "I'll be back tonight with supper." Then, to his surprise and mild consternation, she got to her toes and kissed his cheek.

"Anyone else would sack you for impertinence," he said, his eyes stupidly hot, because it had finally sunk in that this girl was his sister. "You're assuming a lot of my nepotism."

"La, three shillings a week, what'll I ever do without it."

He rolled his eyes heavenward. "This child is my closest living relation. I am to be pitied."

She cackled, kissed him again, and swept out of the cottage. He was beginning to believe that a sharp tongue and terrible manners were a hereditary condition. He changed into a dressing gown and slipped between the sheets, then read until he drifted into a sleep that was only slightly troubled by the fitful dreams of illness.

"I promise we'd have noticed a grown man lurking around the premises," Ben said when Will arrived at Lindley Priory, Martin's family home which was now being run as some kind of charity school for wayward youth. "What exactly did his letter say?" Ben held open the door to a room Will dimly recognized as Lindley Priory's morning room, and which Ben evidently used as an office. Every surface was covered in papers, composition books, and toys in need of mending. It looked like a rag shop crossed with a lending library; Sir Humphrey had to be rolling in his grave.

"Just that he was coming home. I didn't think he'd actually be at the Priory. But I thought he might be staying at the dower house or the inn, but no luck." The dower house had been closed up, and the innkeepers knew Martin well enough to assure Will that they hadn't seen him.

A few children ran careening past the door. Ben stepped into the corridor. "Carrington, Delacourt, and—oh, for heaven's sake—Jamie, go outside if you mean to act feral." Then he turned back to Will. "He hasn't been back in almost a year. I don't think this place holds many happy memories for him."

Will almost laughed at the understatement. "He's been ill, and he needed to go to the country."

Ben frowned at him. "Walk around for a bit and see if anything occurs to you. I'll see that a place is set for you at supper."

Will climbed the steps to the minstrel gallery that surrounded the great hall. Lindley Priory had always been a dark and stuffy place, too far from good roads to be a convenient place for Sir Humphrey to entertain guests and therefore hardly worth the upkeep. Centuries of footsteps had worn depressions on the flagstones of the steps and hall, and everything had the blurry-around-the-edges look of an item that had been handled too much. But on the walls hung portraits of people who looked like Martin. Below, in the great hall, was the hearth around which Martin's ancestors had gathered. He had been raised to lay claim to this place and it would never sit right with Will that the man he loved had been done out of the life he should have had. Will would always, in some small way, grieve the future that Martin never had, even if Martin didn't himself care.

Maybe it was the old familiarity of the setting, maybe it was the fatigue after so long on the road, but Will had the sudden memory of his younger self in this house. He had been fifteen or sixteen, home on leave for the first time, and almost overflowing with happiness. His future felt full of such joy, ripe fruit available for the taking, and all he had to do was reach out. Martin had been so proud of him. Will had long since made his peace with his current state, but maybe it was all right for Martin to regret the future Will didn't have—the loss of that effortless happiness, the narrowing of his prospects. Maybe Martin could be bitterly angry about the harm that had been done to a person he loved, but still love the person Will had become. Will hoped so, because he was fairly certain he was going to die angry with Sir Humphrey for what he had done to his son.

Will wended his way through the maze-like passageways of Lindley Priory. As the home of a single child and his unloving parent, it had been cold and dreary. As a school for boisterous children who were unsuited to typical schools, it was oddly fitting. Nothing in this building of battered stone and ancient oak could be damaged by less than a mortar shell. He heard the sound of a class being dismissed overhead—chairs dragged across floorboards, footsteps just short of a run, barely suppressed laughs, and then a deluge of small bodies pouring out the front door. If anything could chase out the ghosts of Lindley Priory, it was a hundred happy children. If anything was a fair replacement for what Martin had lost, it was this.

He climbed another flight of stairs and made his way to a room on the southerly side of the house, just beneath the attics. The door was ajar, so he pushed it the rest of the way open. Three beds were lined up against the wall, a clothes press overflowed with grass-stained garments, a pair of muddy boots sat on the window sill, and a badly blotted copybook rested on the desk nearest the fire. Any trace of Martin's solitary childhood had been wiped clean by the dirt and chaos of little boys.

Will descended a set of stairs that had always been reliably deserted, but which now contained several children building what looked alarmingly like a siege engine, but they had a teacher with them so he supposed it was all right. From there he slipped into the kitchen and out through the buttery then into the boot room. Every twist and turn of the house was the same, etched into his memory from dozens upon dozens of clandestine entrances and exits. When he finally stepped out into the warm summer air he knew it was for the last time. He'd never come back.

Maybe that was why he let his path continue along a familiar course, out through the gate and through the little wood, then up and across the hills, and finally to the house where he had spent most of the first fourteen years of his life. He hadn't been here in—he stopped to count. Certainly not since leaving the navy. His last leave had been only days, not long enough to get this far north. He had been eighteen, just about to be assigned to the *Fotheringay*, still young enough to think his future held nothing but adventure. Martin had been gloomier than usual, not ill but drawn and tired; a few days ago Martin had said it was that summer he realized he was in love with Will, and Will wondered now whether he had known on some level, if maybe that was part of why Will hadn't wanted to leave him. Of course he had to go, there was no question of anything else, but that leave had been the last moment he was young, the last time he had the luxury of only looking forward, never back.

During that awful visit at Bermondsey House, Will had

meant it when he told Martin he didn't let his mind grapple with what might have been. If he let himself imagine a world in which he had somehow stayed home, he didn't know how he'd claw his way back to the present. But now, when he thought of his eighteen-year-old self standing in that same spot, the boy he had been seemed infinitely fragile, so easily broken, so hard to put back together. He had done it, though, and if he had gotten through the past few years then he could get through anything.

He shoved his hands in his pockets and took a hard look at the house that stood before him. Fellside Grange was smaller than he remembered, a ramshackle pile of slate-roofed chaos, and it was hard to believe it had once housed five children, various parents, and other adults. He'd go in and see his father; he had long since made peace with what it meant to have as careless a parent as Alton Sedgwick, and while he'd never feel warmly toward his father, any bitterness was merely residual, the faint aftertaste of something long gone.

But he knew when he looked at the house that it wasn't his home, and hadn't been for long years. The contours of this house were as much a part of him as the lakes and the hills around him, but any possibility of them being his home was lost to him. This place could join the ranks of things that were lost at sea and in bottles of laudanum and in the clean sweep of time. He had other things instead, things he mightn't have had if he had somehow stayed that boy of eighteen. No, not instead—it wasn't like there had been a fair trade, a bargain. There were things this Will Sedgwick had, and which were as carved into him as this northern geography and that sloppy gray house: a way of earning a living, a life, a love, a home.

And with that he let himself acknowledge the fact that had been just out of sight all day. This wasn't Martin's home either. Of course he hadn't gone to Cumberland, and Will had been badly mistaken to have ever thought so.

He passed a hand across his face and groaned. If he wrote Martin at once, the letter might reach Martin before Will himself did. Three days, maybe four, and he could be at the gamekeeper's cottage beside Martin, home, where he belonged, a future stretching out as bright and sharp as anything his younger self could have dreamed of.

Chapter Twenty-Two

Three days passed without a letter, and if Martin had been slightly less confident of Will's regard—if he had been anything less than dead certain that he possessed the entirety of Will Sedgwick's heart, the idiot—then he might have taken it personally. As it was, he assumed a letter had gotten lost in the post or perhaps that Will had lost track of time what with the excitement surrounding the play.

But when another two days passed without any word from Will, Martin started to worry. He knew that Will loved him, but maybe it was the kind of love that faded with a bit of space. Not the friendship, of course, but the rest of it, the posies and the kissing. Martin had always feared that Will had only been indulging Martin, in the way that he would probably indulge any wish Martin had. That was fine, he told himself. It was better than fine, because this way Will wouldn't have Martin dragging him down.

So he tried not to think about it. He failed miserably, but he didn't go to pieces; he slept and he read and he ate everything Daisy brought him. He took care of himself. He tried to fill his days with things that brought him joy, and when he told himself that he deserved all of them, he almost believed it. He was living his own life, making his own choices, and not doing a terrible job of it. When Daisy told him he felt warm, he took willow bark; in the evening when his lungs insisted on behaving like a bellows with a hole in one end, he even took the paregoric. He read all three volumes of *Frankenstein*, this time without the delirium of fever, and spared a moment of fellow feeling for creatures reared by perverse villains. Then he wrote a letter to his aunt requesting new books. It gave him a strange pang of guilt, as if he were asking for charity or kindness that would be better directed to a more deserving recipient, but he sent the letter anyway; she enjoyed spending money and Martin wasn't going to get in the way of her good time. Besides, chances were she'd send him books she had already read, and then he could write her his own opinions, and that would give them something to write about in their correspondence, which apparently was something he was intent on keeping up.

In fact, when he heard the clop of hoofbeats on the dirt path he thought it might be his aunt come herself to verify that he still lived, and he wasn't even terribly annoyed by it. He got out of bed, pleased to notice that he wasn't shaky or dizzy or anything other than a bit tired. But when he opened the door, it wasn't Aunt Bermondsey but Hartley Sedgwick.

The blood drained from Martin's face as he held on to the door frame for support. "Is he all right—he didn't write but I thought he was busy—"

"What? No, he's fine, as far as I know. He'll be here in a day or two to let you know himself. Your letter said you went home so the idiot ran off to Cumberland. He sent this for you, as he didn't know if you were well enough to pick up your own post at the inn." Hartley held out a letter, which Martin took greedy hold of.

"Cumberland," Martin repeated.

"Well, the next time you write dramatic missives, pay attention to your wording. He assumed—and so did I, until I thought about it—that if you were giving him the cottage, it meant you didn't intend to live in it yourself."

"I meant for him to have use of it if I die before him, but I didn't want to give him a fit by saying so outright. Naturally, if we part ways before that point, he can have the cottage."

"We both know Will, and I wouldn't bet on that happening," Hartley said. He looked at Martin, taking in his slippers and dressing gown, and presumably also his pallor and uncombed hair. "Are you . . . you're clearly not well, so I won't be tedious by asking if you are, but are you in need of anything?" He gazed over Martin's shoulder into the cottage behind him.

"If you come in, I can fix you tea. Daisy brought butter and crumpets when she came to feed the pigs, if you'd care for some. I don't need anything, but I've read every book in the cottage and it'll be days before my aunt sends more, so if you happen to have a book somewhere on your person, I'd be grateful to borrow it."

Hartley's eyebrows were at one with his hairline. Martin didn't know whether it was the mention of the pigs or Martin's daring offer of tea that put them there. "I do, in fact," Hartley said slowly. "One of Will's friends left a French novel at the Fox with instructions to deliver it to you. He said you'd know what to do with it, and that he'd come to collect it in three weeks." He removed three volumes from his traveling bag and handed them to Martin.

"Oh," Martin said, holding the books. "I'm going to translate them. For money," he added, and maybe his voice had done something peculiar on those last words because when he looked back up at Hartley, he saw that the other man was staring at him, but not unkindly. Martin decided to hell with it and returned to the cottage and set about making tea. Hartley could follow or they could keep talking through the open door. Out of the corner of his eye, he saw Hartley looking about, probably searching for something to explain why this was the place his brother was hurrying to, why this was the place Martin referred to as home. Martin poured the tea and set out the basket of crumpets and the dish of butter.

"You can see that it's perfectly comfortable for Will to visit as much as he likes," Martin said. "And I've hired a girl to look in on me so Will doesn't need to feel like the only one responsible for me when I'm ill."

"Visit? He means to stay. If you'll have him."

"If I'll—you must have hit your head. Of course I will. But I never meant to take him away from his life. He has you and his friends and I hate that he's going to walk away from that."

Hartley, who had taken a cup of tea, held it halfway to his mouth and stared at Martin. "He didn't walk away from anything. His friends will still be there. Martin, he's happiest with someone to look after. He always has been. Especially if that someone is you. And Martin, you pillock, you like looking after him when he has the sullens. You know," he said, staring at his mug of tea as if it contained important answers to life's mysteries, "he'll be devastated if you die. So please, for his sake, don't do anything reckless. You didn't see how he was last autumn."

"As much as I'd like to promise that I'll live out my three score and ten with him at my side, that's not a promise I can make." He didn't add that it wasn't a promise anyone could make, because while other couples could indulge in the fantasy that forever would last the same amount of time for both of them, Martin and Will would have to deceive themselves more than most in order to participate in that delusion. "All I can promise is that while I'm alive, your brother will be loved, and that I'll do my best to make sure that after I'm gone he doesn't regret having loved me. I know that he'll grieve me, maybe for a long while. But he's strong and it won't ruin him. He has other things to be happy about, other people who love him."

"I see." Hartley's voice was thick, and he turned to the windows, his back to Martin.

"I believe that's quite enough sincerity for one day," Martin said.

Hartley snorted. But he drank his tea, still standing, both of them eying the chairs as if sitting in them would be admitting some fatal weakness. "I ought to go," he said, long after his cup was empty, "if I want to catch the mail coach up to London." He put his cup on the table, brushed his trousers clean, and made for the door.

"Come back, though," Martin said, after Hartley passed through the door and was a few yards down the lane. "You don't need to only meet him at the inn. If this is his home—" He swallowed. "You're welcome here, regardless."

Hartley looked over his shoulder and gave Martin a quick nod. Martin rinsed the teapot and fed the uneaten crumpets to the pigs, then he swept the floor and took his medicine and did all the needful things that shaped a day.

Thanks to muddy roads and a broken axle, Will didn't reach Sussex until a full week after he had first left London for Cumberland. Just outside Manchester on his trip back south, he gave up trying to sleep in the coach and paid for a private room at an inn, then paid even more for a bath, and by the time he climbed back into the stagecoach he thought it might have been the best money he had ever spent. No use showing up at Martin's door—their door—looking like death warmed over, was there.

By the time he reached the Blue Boar he decided he'd be happy never traveling further than London for the rest of his life. Several minutes after the coach deposited him in the inn yard, his bones still rattled as if in memory of every pothole and rut from Carlisle to East Grinstead.

"There you are," said Daisy, materializing from behind the bar. "We've all been wondering when you'd show up."

"How is he?" Will asked.

"No worse than when he got here. He'll be glad to see you." Will could almost hear the unspoken *finally, you horse's arse*, and could not disagree. "Since you're headed that way, you can bring his supper. There's enough for two." She brought a hamper out from behind the bar. "Sandwiches, a couple of cakes, and a jug of ale. Now be gone with you."

He had been away for less than three weeks, but three weeks in the springtime was the difference between a landscape of lacy delicate green and the heavy verdant abundance that met him on his walk from the inn to the cottage. On impulse, he plucked a fistful of coral bells and a few stalks of foxglove, remembering when Martin had done the same for him. There would be more chances to do this, a rotating calendar of posies to bring one another, from larkspur and apple blossoms to hellebore to sprigs of holly, all laid out before them. They had time. They had time together, and this week apart wouldn't matter, wouldn't cut into their time in any memorable way. Martin was fine, he was fine. Will repeated it to himself like a catechism, like a spell.

When the cottage came in sight, he thought maybe Martin would hear his footsteps and come out to greet him, but the birds were calling raucously to one another and the pigs splashing wildly in their muck and Martin wouldn't have heard his footsteps even if he'd been expected. Will dropped his satchel and the hamper on the bench near the door and pushed open the door, stepping into the single room that was his home, his heart in his throat, his stomach in knots.

Martin was asleep in the bed, his chest rising and fall-

ing, a book open on the pillow next to his head, a pair of
spectacles crooked on his face. Will pulled off his boots and
crawled onto the bed beside him.

"Hey," he whispered, brushing a hair off Martin's forehead and straightening his spectacles. "When did you get
spectacles?"

Martin made a happy, sleepy noise, unguarded and open
the way he only was when on the edges of sleep. Then his eyes
flew open. "When—"

"I just walked in the door."

Something hopelessly fond and relieved flickered across
Martin's face, before being immediately replaced by exas-
peration. "Cumberland. You idiot. When I'm awake we're
having a proper fight about this."

"I can't wait," Will said, and he meant it. He threw an
arm over Martin's chest and pillowed his head on Martin's
shoulder, and the last thing he heard before he fell asleep was
Martin sleepily whispering, "Cumberland. What rot."

When he woke the bed was empty, the spot where
Martin had been already cool. Faint tendrils of light crept
through the windows, but Will couldn't have said whether
it was dawn or dusk. Martin sat at the table, one of Daisy's
sandwiches on a plate before him, writing by the light of a
candle. The flowers, which Will had left outside with the
hamper, were now in a pewter cup at the center of the table.

As Will sat, the mattress creaked beneath him, and
Martin put down his pen.

"There's tea," Martin said, gesturing at the pot.

Will stretched and felt every sinew in his body reject

the idea of getting out of bed, but he crossed the room and collapsed in the empty chair. He picked up Martin's hand—fingertips inky, nails bitten—and kissed his palm. "I missed you. And you don't have to tell me again that I was a fool for having misread your letter. I know it."

"I still can't believe that you could think I'd say home and mean anything else but here. Except," he added, stealing his hand back to bring his teacup to his mouth, "I suppose what I really mean is where you are."

Will was brought up short to hear from Martin's mouth the sentiment he'd repeated to himself so many times, across years and oceans and continents. He swallowed. "I know better now." Will laced their fingers together. "In my defense, you really could have been more clear."

"William. That entire letter was carefully constructed not to get either of us put in the pillory. If I was evasive, it was because I was afraid if I started being honest it'd all come pouring out. A reprehensible degree of sentiment, even if it weren't a confession to criminal behavior."

"I wouldn't mind some reprehensible sentiment one of these days," Will said.

Martin looked at him narrowly. In the shadowy half-light, Will could see the circles under his eyes and that old disconcerting sharpness to his features. "I'll bear that in mind," he said lightly, but he squeezed Will's hand. With the hand that wasn't trapped in Will's he brought his teacup to his mouth. "How long are you here for?"

Will stared. "Well, at least I don't have a monopoly on idiocy."

"What's that supposed to mean?"

"I'm here, full stop, because it's my home, because—as you said two minutes ago—it's where you are, you monumental lackwit."

"Are you certain?" Martin asked, managing to look both pleased and guilty at once.

"I don't know how to make you believe this if you don't already, but I want to be with you every morning and every night and most of the minutes in between. And *not* because I think you need looking after, so don't even start. I can see with my own eyes that you've managed to take care of yourself." He had already noticed the jars of medicines on the chimneypiece, the stack of clean linen, the way Daisy had the hamper of food already prepared. "But I'd like to do it anyway."

"I want it to be a choice for you," Martin said.

Will could have laughed at the idea. A choice, as if walking away were even an option. He couldn't have walked away from Martin any more than he could have walked away from his own arm, nor did he want to. "Loving you is a part of me, probably the best part of me, and even if you want to argue with me about that—and why the hell do you want to, Martin, really—I *want* to be with you, to be near you, to do what I can to make you happy. A choice," he said, shaking his head. "A choice. It's the only choice I want to make."

Maybe that was a satisfactory answer, or maybe Martin had enough sentiment, but either way he let Will pull him into his lap, let himself be held and kissed.

Chapter Twenty-Three

Shadowy twilight had become full moonless dark, and their kisses had devolved into an undisguised and blatant attempt to be pressed close together, a clinging reassurance, more relief than heat. "Let me take you to bed," Will said, speaking the words against Martin's mouth. And then, at a greater distance, "I didn't mean—we don't—"

"I know." Martin got to his feet and coughed more than a few times, then downed the rest of his tea. He climbed into bed and watched Will undress, admiring in a detached and tired sort of way. When Will slid between the covers beside him, the mattress shifted and Martin let himself be tilted into Will's body, his face in the crook of Will's neck, one hand toying with a strand of Will's hair.

"I'm going to say this once and I promise I won't belabor the point," Martin said. He brought his hand to Will's shoulder and traced small circles around the winged birds he knew were inked there. "But if you begin to feel penned in here, you can go where you please and I'll be waiting for you when you get back."

"Can't really imagine why I'd want to go anywhere without you, but—" Will broke off, then brought his hand up to trap Martin's hand against his upper arm. "What are you on about?"

"Ever since we were little children you wanted adventures."

"I've had my fair share," Will said dryly.

"It's just that, even on board the ship, even when things were . . . bad . . ." Martin drew up his courage. He never brought up this topic, never said anything to prompt Will to speak of it. "You still had these done."

"I did," Will said slowly.

"Birds in flight. It's not a subtle metaphor, William. Even then you wanted to explore."

"It's not a subtle—well thank God you aren't a literary critic. Christ, Martin, I've been very stupid this past week but you win the prize." His shoulders were shaking with, Martin was stunned to realize, laughter.

"Care to let me in on the joke?" he asked as sniffily as he could, but the sad fact was that Will's laughter completely robbed him of any acerbity.

"They're swallows, you daft bastard. Swallows always return home to nest. Sailors say that if you get one inked on your body it's a promise that you'll arrive home. Or, if you don't, at least your soul will be carried back. I had these done after I was disrated—officers don't get tattoos, but sailors often do, so . . . when in Rome, I suppose."

"The sailors liked you," Martin said, and it wasn't a question. "Even though they were ready to mutiny and, presumably, do away with all the officers onboard."

"Well, they probably wouldn't have killed the surgeon," Will said mildly. "But yes, they didn't like the officers, but I suppose I had been treated as badly as anybody so we had a common enemy."

"And when they started talking about mutiny . . ." Martin said, hoping Will would keep talking.

"I kept reminding them that all we had do to was get home. The navy has a way of dealing with tyrannical captains. But if we mutinied, a number of the lads would be hanged or be forced to live the rest of their lives as fugitives. There were still incidents," Will said, and Martin suspected he referred to the sailors at whose courts martial Will testified, "but we got home with no life lost."

"So that's what the birds meant? A reminder that your problems would be solved when you got home?"

"Partly. I was in general rather preoccupied with the idea of getting home and seeing you again, idiot." He kissed Martin's forehead.

"Seeing me?"

"Martin," Will said, and Martin could feel the smile against his skin. "Dozens upon dozens of letters. Three indelibly drawn birds with your name on them. And still you act surprised to discover that the thing I want foremost in the world is to be with you."

"With my name—" Oh. *Oh.* He propped himself up on his elbow to examine the birds' roughly drawn black-and-white markings by the faint starlight. They weren't common swallows, but rather house martins. "This is—appallingly sentimental, if I'm honest." But there were tears in his eyes, and Will was already pulling him down for a kiss.

"I knew you needed spectacles," Will said fondly.

"I love you, too, always have, always will," Martin mumbled into the skin of Will's shoulder.

Will tipped Martin's chin up for a kiss and they stayed like that, tangled together, barely kissing. Martin's heart so full it was nearly uncomfortable.

The first visitor came in July. Will had been expecting it, having been warned by Hartley's letter and then by Daisy running up from the inn, but still it was a shock to see Lieutenant Staunton on dry land. They had been midshipmen together, and now Staunton was very smart in his lieutenant's uniform.

"My God," Staunton said by way of greeting. "I've only spent two years looking for you, Sedgwick. I don't mind telling you I expected the worst, and it's damned good to see you looking well. You gave us all a rotten fright by vanishing like that."

Will had always assumed that if anybody from the *Fotheringay* spared him a thought, he would at best be an object of pity and at worst a reminder of tragedy, and that everyone would be glad to forget he had ever existed. Before Will could come up with anything to say, Staunton went on. "And now I hear that you wrote that play. My wife has seen it three times. But here's the other reason I needed to see you." He reached into his coat pocket and removed a parcel wrapped in oilcloth. "I've been carrying this around for years. There were some other things—a shaving kit, a couple of pens—that got lost along the way, I'm afraid. But we all remembered you and your letters and thought you'd want them back."

Will was alone in the cottage, the parcel on the table before him, when Martin came home. "What's this, then?" Martin asked gently.

Will shoved the parcel across the table. "You open it." He watched almost greedily as Martin untied the string and flattened the oilcloth.

"Oh, sweetheart. You thought they were lost."

"That's really them, then?" Will asked.

Delicately, Martin spread the papers before him. "There are dozens from me, but I see a few other hands. Your brothers, probably. Maybe your father." Will knew that Martin could see the worn edges of the letters where Will had handled them again and again, the rips along the folds, the places where the ink smudged under Will's fingertips.

"Sweetheart," Martin repeated. "Mine are in a similar state."

Will tried to say something but the words wouldn't come, and then he let himself be drawn into Martin's lap and fussed over in a way he hadn't quite thought Martin capable of.

The next visitor came the following month. Will remembered him as Able Seaman Davis, a rough-looking northerner several years older than Will, who refused

Will's offers of tea and instead seemed mostly interested in admiring the pigs. "Just wanted to see for myself that you made it," Davis said. "On my way back to Portsmouth." He shook Will's hand roughly, but didn't make any move to leave. "Named my boy William."

"*What?*"

"It's a good name," Davis protested. "And you did good." He didn't elaborate, which was a relief because Will didn't think he could take it.

"Thank you," he said faintly.

"I say, Mr. Davis," Martin said. He had been weeding the vegetable patch. "You don't happen to be skilled at giving tattoos, do you?"

"'Fraid not," Davis said, and if he thought this was an odd question, he didn't let on.

"I wonder if you know anybody who is, and who wouldn't mind calling on us."

After Davis left, Will rounded on Martin. "What on earth was that about?"

"I'm not telling," Martin said.

The next sailor who visited was a stranger to Will. His skin was dark from the sun and leathery from the wind and Will couldn't even make a guess at his age. He introduced himself as Jones. "Davis said you wanted more ink," he told Will.

"That would be me," said Martin. Will watched in confusion as Martin rifled through his papers until he came up with a drawing. "Could you put that on my arm?"

"Have you run mad?" Will asked. "You realize this involves being stabbed with needles."

"Really," Martin drawled, rolling up his sleeve and displaying the scars from years of bloodlettings. "Whenever have I been poked at with sharp objects. At least this time I get to choose. And I'm left with a lovely flower instead of a basin of blood."

Will watched as Martin stripped out of his waistcoat and shirt, and then as Jones traced the flower onto Martin's arm. Will hadn't the faintest idea what was happening, but if Martin wanted—he glanced at the drawing—a couple of pinks inked permanently onto his body, then so be it. He found a bottle of brandy that Hartley had left for them a few weeks back, and poured Martin a generous glass.

"You don't have to hover," Martin griped, so Will went out and pulled a couple of carrots out of the ground and chopped some firewood. He didn't go back toward the house until he saw Jones at the door.

"What do we owe you?" Will asked.

"He paid already," Jones said, gesturing with his chin toward the cottage. "And Davis paid my way here."

Will went back inside and leaned against the doorway. "Care to tell me what that was about?"

Martin blinked in a way he probably thought looked very innocent. "What, I need a particular reason to get three lovely flowers etched—*very* painfully, what the hell, William—into my flesh?"

"Let's have a look." Will sighed and sat on the bed beside Martin. The drawing was of a group of fairly simple looking wildflowers, each bloom consisting of five petals with frilly edges. "I thought they were pinks, but they aren't ruffled enough for that," he mused. He was slightly disappointed to note that they weren't primroses—he still had Martin's primroses pressed in the pages of a book. "Not pinks, not primroses," he murmured, running a careful finger across the new ink.

"You get one more guess." Martin languidly inspected his nails. "I just thought we ought to match."

Will drew in a sharp breath. "You absolutely did not just get sweet Williams tattooed onto your arm. Tell me you didn't."

"All right," Martin said primly. "I didn't." But Will was already kissing him, pushing him down onto the bed and covering his body with his own. "I don't know why you're making such a big deal of this," Martin said. "I chose them because they smell good and because the pigs think they're tasty. That's all." He looked like he was trying to keep a straight face but was making a poor fist of it. "Oh, did you think it had something to do with you? How embarrassing." He was laughing openly now, pressing a pillow over his face to muffle the sound.

"Sometimes I can't believe you," Will said, pulling the pillow away to kiss him, but they were both laughing too hard for the kiss to be anything other than a graceless collision. "I could not love you more."

The summer passed, and with every red or orange leaf that appeared in the woods outside the cottage, Martin half expected the spell to be broken. He kept waiting for the bubble they had been living in to be punctured by the sordid reality of the outside world, because surely something so good couldn't exist except under these precise, protected circumstances.

But the outside world didn't so much encroach as let itself be gently woven into the fabric of their lives. Tenants moved into Friars' Gate, which meant they were no longer quite so isolated, and somehow that did not feel like a bad thing. Every day brought letters—from Aunt Bermondsey (with carefully worded regards to Will), from Hartley (who visited often enough that letters might seem a flagrant waste of paper) and even from Ben (who included little sketches of things that had happened at school, and which Martin suspected were for his benefit, to let him know that Lindley Priory was doing more good than ill). The pigs got fat, Daisy proved herself a brisk but competent nurse when Martin was ill, and Martin earned a few guineas by translating a novel.

When the weather turned, Will dragged the mattress and bedstead into the loft and began to refer to the ground floor as the sitting room, a pretense that Martin might have found absurd if he didn't see how pleased Will was with the secondhand sofa he had procured. On the first night when they could see their breaths clouding before the night sky, Will casually mentioned that if this winter was hard on Martin's health, they could consider going to Italy the following year.

"You want me to become friendly with an entirely new cast of characters?" Martin asked, with a horror that was only partially feigned.

"It's something to think about," Will said, and changed the topic.

Martin thought about their home and everything around it. Shelter, food, books to read, letters from people who cared about them, and a combined income that managed to be neither precarious nor insufficient. This cottage was home, and Martin would dig his heels in as long as it was reasonable, but all those small and precious things that made up their lives together were infinitely portable. And so he knew that if in the coming months his lungs were especially recalcitrant, or if his clothes hung even more loosely than usual, he wouldn't balk if Will mentioned Italy again. He turned his head to where Will sat beside him, huddled against the side of the cottage, and kissed his shoulder.

"Italy, Greece, the moon. It's all the same if you're there." Martin wasn't sentimental often, but when he managed it, he was rewarded by a blinding smile, such as the one he was favored with now.

IT TAKES TWO TO TUMBLE

Some of Ben Sedgwick's favorite things:

* *Helping his poor parishioners*
* *Baby animals*
* *Shamelessly flirting with the handsome
  Captain Phillip Dacre*

After an unconventional upbringing, Ben is perfectly content with the quiet, predictable life of a country vicar, free of strife or turmoil. When he's asked to look after an absent naval captain's three wild children, he reluctantly agrees, but instantly falls for the hellions. And when their stern but gloriously handsome father arrives, Ben is tempted in ways that make him doubt everything.

Some of Phillip Dacre's favorite things:

* *His ship*
* *People doing precisely as they're told*
* *Touching the irresistible vicar at every opportunity*

Phillip can't wait to leave England's shores and be back on his ship, away from the grief that haunts him. But his children have driven off a succession of governesses and tutors and he must set things right. The unexpected presence of the cheerful, adorable vicar sets his world on its head and now he can't seem to live without Ben's winning smiles or devastating kisses.

In the midst of runaway children, a plot to blackmail Ben's family, and torturous nights of pleasure, Ben and Phillip must decide if a safe life is worth losing the one thing that makes them come alive.

A GENTLEMAN NEVER KEEPS SCORE

Once beloved by London's fashionable elite, Hartley Sedgwick has become a recluse after a spate of salacious gossip exposed his most-private secrets. Rarely venturing from the house whose inheritance is a daily reminder of his downfall, he's captivated by the exceedingly handsome man who seeks to rob him.

Since retiring from the boxing ring, Sam Fox has made his pub, The Bell, into a haven for those in his Free Black community. But when his best friend Kate implores him to find and destroy a scandalously revealing painting of her, he agrees. Sam would do anything to protect those he loves, even if it means stealing from a wealthy gentleman. But when he encounters Hartley, he soon finds himself wanting to steal more than just a painting from the lovely, lonely man—he wants to steal his heart.

ABOUT THE AUTHOR

CAT SEBASTIAN lives in a swampy part of the South with her husband, three kids, and two dogs. Before her kids were born, she practiced law and taught high school and college writing. When she isn't reading or writing, she's doing crossword puzzles, bird watching, and wondering where she put her coffee cup.

Discover great authors, exclusive offers, and more at hc.com